"I devoured *The Letters* in one sitting. Suzanne Woods Fisher weaves a cast of authentic characters, real-life problems, and a beautiful setting into a sweet and satisfying story. I can't wait for the second in the series!"

—Leslie Gould, Christy Award–winning
and bestselling author of *Adoring Addie*

Praise for the Stoney Ridge Seasons Series

"Fisher's style is light and engaging. Her setting may be a simple Pennsylvania Amish community, but the struggles of faith, trust, and forgiveness are common to a wide-ranging audience. Moral elements are so deftly woven into the plot that most readers will learn the lesson before realizing there is one."

—*Publishers Weekly*

"Adept at introducing modern themes into stories of the Amish, Fisher has crafted a gentle romance complete with love triangles and unexpected plot twists. As her characters learn from their mistakes, readers will hear the resounding message that relationships can be restored and hearts renewed through forgiveness."

—*Booklist*

"Fisher keeps readers interested without all the bells and whistles."

—*RT BookReviews*

"Suzanne Woods Fisher treats the reader to an interesting inside look at the Amish culture and family."

—*New York Journal of Books*

The Letters

Books by Suzanne Woods Fisher

Amish Peace: Simple Wisdom for a Complicated World

Amish Proverbs: Words of Wisdom from the Simple Life

Amish Values for Your Family:
What We Can Learn from the Simple Life

A Lancaster County Christmas

LANCASTER COUNTY SECRETS

The Choice

The Waiting

The Search

STONEY RIDGE SEASONS

The Keeper

The Haven

The Lesson

THE INN AT EAGLE HILL

The Letters

THE ADVENTURES OF LILY LAPP
(with Mary Ann Kinsinger)

Life with Lily

A New Home for Lily

A Big Year for Lily

The Letters

A Novel

SUZANNE WOODS FISHER

Revell

a division of Baker Publishing Group
Grand Rapids, Michigan

© 2013 by Suzanne Woods Fisher

Published by Revell
a division of Baker Publishing Group
P.O. Box 6287, Grand Rapids, MI 49516-6287
www.revellbooks.com

Printed in the United States of America

Library of Congress Cataloging-in-Publication Data
Fisher, Suzanne Woods.
    The letters : a novel / Suzanne Woods Fisher.
      pages cm — (The Inn at Eagle Hill ; #1)
    Includes bibliographical references.
    ISBN 978-0-8007-2093-3 (pbk.)
    1. Amish—Fiction. 2. Mennonites—Fiction. 3. Bed and breakfast
accommodations—Fiction. I. Title.
PS3606.I78L48 2013
813'.6—dc23   2013012106

Most Scripture used in this book, whether quoted or paraphrased by the characters, is taken from the King James Version of the Bible.

Some Scripture used in this book, whether quoted or paraphrased by the characters, is taken from the Holy Bible, New International Version®. NIV®. Copyright © 1973, 1978, 1984, 2011 by Biblica, Inc.™ Used by permission of Zondervan. All rights reserved worldwide. www.zondervan.com

Published in association with Joyce Hart of the Hartline Literary Agency, LLC.

13 14 15 16 17 18 19   7 6 5 4 3 2 1

Dedicated to my dear dad,
as well as his brothers and sister,
who were raised on the real Inn at Eagle Hill
in Buzzards Bay, Massachusetts

1

The air had the sweet burn of frost. Long out of habit, even in the winter months, Rose Schrock woke before dawn to carve out a little time for herself before the day began. She liked the bitter cold, a cold that seemed to sharpen the stars in the wide Pennsylvania sky. Dawn was her favorite hour, a time when she felt most keenly aware of how fragile life truly was. Between one breath and the next, your whole world could change. Hers had.

On this morning, wrapped in her husband's huge coat, she walked along the creek bordering the farm and climbed the hill. The thin February moon, low in the horizon, lit the sky but not the ground. Her golden retriever, Chase, trotted behind her, saluting trees along the path, baptizing each one as he went. When Rose reached the top of the hill, she sat with her back against a tree. In its awakening hour, the farm below seemed peaceful, lovely, calm. The birdsong symphony had just begun—something that always seemed like a miracle to Rose. How did that saying go? "Faith is the bird that feels the light and sings when the dawn is still dark." And wasn't that the truth?

Rose Schrock had been raised not to complain, so she didn't, but the truth of the matter was, the last seven months had been the hardest stretch of her life: so many things had gone wrong that it was hard to know which trouble to pay attention to at any given time.

Her mother-in-law, Vera, assured her cheerfully that increase in trouble was something she had better get used to. "You can't expect mercy."

"I don't expect it," Rose had told Vera. "I just wish things would go wrong one at a time. That way I could handle them."

Soon, she would need to head back down the hill and wake her boys. Her girls would already be stirring. They were unusually helpful and did whatever chores there were to do without being asked, whereas her two young sons were so sluggish in the morning that it took them half an hour just to get themselves dressed and downstairs. Before Rose left this quiet spot, she had something to do. To say. No, no. She had something to pray.

Lord, I beg your pardon, but I am in a fix. I'm about wrung out from all this, and it's getting so I can barely tell which way is up. I've got four fatherless children—five, if I knew where that oldest boy had run off to—an addle-minded mother-in-law, and barely thirty-six dollars left in my pocket. I'm fresh out of backbone, Lord. And near out of fight. Near out. Lord, if you'd be so kind, look down here and let me know what to do. I need a Plan B.

Rose waited quietly, hoping for a word from above, or maybe just an inkling. Reflecting, she decided it was funny how life could change so fast. She used to have so many plans. Now, her plans for the future were foggy at best. Years ago, money had been the last thing on her mind. Now it was all she thought about. Scarcely seven months ago, she had a husband. Now Dean was gone. A few years earlier, she hadn't minded so much being with her mother-in-law. Not so much. Now she couldn't think of anything worse.

Anything you want to say, Lord? Any advice? A word of wisdom? Rose heard the gentle hoot of a screech owl, once, then twice. A rooster began to crow. That would be Harold, the loudest rooster in the county. The day would soon begin.

A moving bright light in the sky caught her eye. She watched for a moment, intrigued. Then, fascinated. It was a shooting star, darting over little Stoney Ridge in all its glory and majesty. Her jumbled thoughts gave way to a feeling of peace.

What a thing to see at a time when she needed it so badly!

Whenever Miriam had visited her grandmother's farm, it had seemed like an adventure to adapt to the lifestyle of the Old Order Amish. But living someplace was different than visiting and Mim felt she came from a different world. She was raised in a Mennonite church in a large town in Pennsylvania—where her family had used electricity and drove a car. Here, it was quiet. No electricity, no car, not even normal lights. In the kitchen there was the kerosene lantern hanging from the ceiling, which hissed and gave off a flat white light.

It was all different, all new to her. For a girl who didn't like change, it was too much change, all at once. She wished life could just go back to the way it was. She felt sad at all she'd had and what was no longer.

Her eyes blew open. *Just like my grandmother,* she thought, shocked. *I am sounding just like my grandmother.* Whatever Mammi Vera had, it was catching!

Right then, she decided to start a list of things she liked about moving to Stoney Ridge. She scrambled off her bed and took out a clean sheet of paper from her desk drawer.

Number One: Danny Riehl, the boy who sat next to her at school and wore glasses that were hinged together with a paper clip.

Number Two: School.

Mim had mistakenly assumed it would be as easy here as it was back in their old town. After all, here it was a one-room schoolhouse. But this teacher believed in pushing students. It wasn't all bad to be challenged, she had discovered. She loved math. She loved language. The teacher, Mary Kate Lapp, called Teacher M.K., had noticed Mim. She gave her extra math problems. She loaned her a used Latin textbook and told her to study root words. Each week, she assigned Mim new vocabulary words. Words like *modicum*, *interim*, *aplomb*, *insipid*, *pseudo*. She was told to use the words in one sentence. She spent hours constructing descriptive sentences.

Mim looked out her bedroom window and thought about how someone might describe her in one sentence. Where to begin? She was thirteen years old, with dark hair like her father and gray eyes like her mother. She was average height, average weight. Entirely average. Entirely unremarkable. In her mind, she erased those boring descriptions and started all over again.

What else? Mim liked her brothers and her sister and her mother and, some of the time, her grandmother. Mostly, she liked school and loved book learning and was fond of the month of March because no one much liked March. Her favorite color was bright red for the same reason: her new church frowned upon the color red. She didn't understand what made red so offensive, but that was an Amish tradition and so that was that.

But what Mim loved more than anything else was to collect facts. She was excellent at collecting facts. Excellent. She liked to find facts in ordinary things. Her grandmother was always spouting proverbs and Mim would find the fact in them. She shortened her name to Mim from Miriam because she had read that one-syllable names were easier to remember. That was a fact.

Still, so far she hadn't come up with a very scintillating way to describe herself. Scratch all that. So far, her sentence was entirely unremarkable. She wiped down the chalkboard that she had imagined in her mind and started again: "Say what you will about thirteen-year-old Mim Schrock, but don't leave out that she was organized. Very organized. Exceedingly organized." She smiled. Everyone knew that fact about her.

"And she is a champion problem solver," she added to her imaginary description.

That was the main reason she loved to read so much. In books, she learned to find answers to questions. Clean and simple. It was a pity that her grandmother was so against book learning. She only allowed a handful of books in the house. Too much book learning, her grandmother insisted, would make your brain go soft. Mim pointed out that there was no research to support that thinking, and her grandmother shut that conversation down with a Penn Dutch proverb: "De meh gelehrt, de meh verkehrt." *The more learning, the less wisdom.*

Happily, Mim's mother disagreed. With a quiet blessing from her mother, Mim kept her library books hidden in the barn. Most of the barn was crammed with useless junk, especially in the hayloft, but she had found a little corner by a dusty window to claim as her own. Ideal for quiet moments to read, hidden from overly nosy brothers, like the one who was peering in around the doorjamb at her right this very moment.

Eight-year-old Sammy came in and sat on her bed, humming, tossing a softball up a foot or two in the air, then catching it in his mitt. Mostly missing it. She looked over at him and smiled as he scrambled to find the ball under the bed. Sammy was small and stocky and compact like a suitcase. He always told the truth, even when he shouldn't. She would never admit it to anyone, but Sammy was her favorite brother. He was a kind person and enjoyed discussing unusual facts with Mim. And he lent her money from the coffee can he kept beneath his mattress. Her ten-year-old brother Luke had his good points: he was funny and smart and was a bottomless pit of good ideas to do on a Sunday afternoon, but he had a sneaky side to him, like Tobe, the oldest in the family. A person needed to be careful about business transactions with Luke.

Sammy took a very black banana out of his pocket and peeled it.

"That is disgusting," Mim said.

Sammy didn't seem to mind. He finished off that bruised banana in just a few bites. "Did you know that the Great Wall of China can be seen from the moon?"

Now that was a fine fact. Mim scribbled it down in her school notebook, color coded under "Yellow" for Fine Facts. Teacher M.K. would like it. The class would like it. Danny Riehl, he would like it.

Delia Stoltz was running late to her doctor's appointment. Her day had been so busy that she hadn't even stopped for lunch. A boring meeting for the Philadelphia Historic Preservation Society, followed by another tedious fundraising meeting for the Children's Hospital, a mind-numbing Daughters of the American Republic tea, and then a complete waste-of-time board meeting for the local bank, where she listened to a heated debate about whether to provide free coffee for their customers. Delia wasn't sure anyone really wanted her opinion about how to run businesses or charities, but she was in great demand as a benefactress. It was one of the responsibilities of being married to Dr. Charles Stoltz.

Charles Stoltz was the most prominent neurosurgeon on the eastern seaboard. Quite possibly, in the entire country. Delia and Will, their only child—who was now in his last year of vet school at Cornell—wanted for nothing. Charles kept track of all of their investments and financial dealings. She wasn't interested in the actual figures or details of her portfolio, but Charles said she had plenty of money to live well and be a generous benefactor to the community, so she did and she was.

Delia glanced at her watch. She thought about skipping the doctor's appointment altogether, but she was driving right by the office to get home. She would allow fifteen minutes, but if the doctor kept her waiting, she would leave.

She took her Lancome Mulled Wine lipstick from her purse and pulled out a compact mirror. She would be sixty years old next summer. Just this morning, someone had asked her a blunt question: "Delia, have you had a little touch-up surgery? You look *so* good for a woman your age!"

Delia withered that someone with a glance.

She supposed asking such a personal question about whether she ever had cosmetic surgery might seem perfectly normal, but as far as she was concerned, it was perfectly rude.

If that person had a clue about what made Delia Stoltz tick, she would have known that Delia would scoff at the thought of cosmetic surgery. Everyone aged. She never understood why people spent so much time and money trying to avoid it or pretend it wasn't happening. She worked hard at keeping herself up—she had a personal trainer at the gym and swam laps twice a week. When it came to makeup and fashion, she felt simplicity was best. A little mascara, a little blush, a good lipstick. Her closet was filled with classic clothing of excellent quality—well-cut lined wool slacks, silk blouses, an array of cashmere sweaters, and for more formal occasions, an assortment of black cocktail dresses. A good purse was a must. Her preference was Prada. In the purse was a creamy pashmina scarf, at the ready. Add a nice pair of shoes and a few pieces of well-chosen jewelry: pearls, matching earrings, and perhaps, one simply spectacular ring, like the enormous diamond her husband had given to her on their twentieth wedding anniversary.

Now, a woman's hair was a different story. Delia had a standing monthly appointment with Alessandro at the salon for a root touch-up. She accepted most of the signs of aging, but not when it came to hair. Going gray was simply unacceptable.

If that rude someone truly knew Delia, she would know all of that. But while everyone in Philadelphia knew who Delia Stoltz was or knew of her, no one really knew her. She preferred it that way. Utterly private.

When she stepped through the door from the waiting room,

Dr. Zimmerman was there to greet her. "Hello, Delia, how are you today?" he said.

"I'm fine. Shouldn't I be?" she said offhandedly, smiling, but she felt the tiniest little pinch in her stomach. A few days ago, she'd had a needle biopsy of a cyst in her left breast. No big deal, even Dr. Zimmerman had said so. It was so routine that she hadn't even bothered to mention it to Charles. He would have gotten overinvolved, would want to speak to Dr. Zimmerman himself, would order extra tests. Not necessary. She had harmless fibroids in her breasts—lumpy breasts, the doctor had told her—and she was vigilant about yearly mammograms. To the day. Delia was precise about everything.

Every few years, she faced some annoying round of post-mammogram testing. After ultrasounds and biopsies, it never amounted to anything more than a nuisance. This year, Dr. Zimmerman called and said he wanted a tissue biopsy, but because her test results had always come back negative before, she was sure it would be the same this time. Busy as she was, as she always was, it hadn't crossed her mind to be worried. Until now.

Something in Dr. Zimmerman's avuncular tone as he asked about her day, something about the weight of his arm across her shoulders as he escorted her into his private office, made a shiver travel up her spine. But it wasn't until she was sitting in his office and Dr. Zimmerman steepled his fingers together on his desk and said, "I'm so sorry, Delia. The biopsy was positive. You have cancer," that she understood what was happening.

Three little words. *You have cancer.* And for a moment, everything stopped. Her heart. Her mind. Her breath. Everything.

Delia couldn't remember how she got home. She must have been driving on autopilot. She pulled into the garage and noticed the trunk was lifted on Charles's BMW. His suitcases were in the back. She hadn't realized he had business travel planned, but he was often called away for consultations on difficult cases. She hoped he could change his plans after she told him her news. She walked into the kitchen and put her purse on the countertop. Charles was waiting for her at the kitchen table. Strange. Charles never waited for her. She was always waiting for him. She looked at him and knew something terrible was about to happen, like the quiet right before a storm was due to hit. But a storm had already hit at the doctor's office. Surely, there couldn't be two storms in one day. In a moment of clarity, she realized she was in the eye of the hurricane, about to face the dirty side of the storm. The worst part.

Her son.

Her heart missed a beat. "Did something happen to Will?"

"Will is fine. Studying, I hope, with midterms coming up." Charles licked his lips. It was a habit when he was nervous. Why was he nervous? Had Dr. Zimmerman called him? Did he already know? His face was so pale. Charles was never pale, always tan. He was in his early sixties, close to six feet tall; his looks reminded Delia of Gregory Peck playing Atticus Finch in *To Kill a Mockingbird*. She had a tendency to do that—liken people to movie stars. It was something her son Will forever teased her about.

Dee saw a trickle of sweat on Charles's forehead. "Delia, there's something I need to tell you." He took a deep breath and exhaled. "I've fallen in love with someone else. I'm sorry, honey. I'm moving out."

She saw his lips move, but she couldn't understand what he was saying. She just stared at him.

He tried to get her to talk, but she felt nothing, said nothing.

Finally, Charles rose to his feet and said that his attorney's office would be contacting her, and not to worry, he would take care of everything. She would never have to worry about money. And one more thing—he would like to wait to tell Will since he would be going through midterm exams soon.

Then he left.

When Delia heard the garage door close, she took the first breath she had taken in what felt like an hour, since she had left the doctor's office. One deep breath and everything had changed. She had reached her breaking point. It was an indescribable feeling of pain, sheer pain.

How was it possible for a few words to have such power? "I'm in love with someone else." "You have cancer."

Delia felt all the strength leave her body. The body she cared for so thoroughly had betrayed her. There was an enemy within her that, left unchecked, would end her life.

The husband whom she adored and who loved her had failed her. Life as she knew it was over.

Alone and lonely, she covered her face with her hands and gave herself up to despair, weeping until she was dry.

Rose Schrock turned the horse and buggy into the Bent N' Dent's parking lot and tied the reins to the hitching post. The late February sky was filling with lead-colored clouds, threatening to snow. Grabbing a basket by the door, she hurried down the aisle with her list in hand. She had run out of ground cinnamon and needed it for a cake for Sunday church, so she stopped by the spices. She felt distracted, preoccupied with the ongoing worry of trying to find a way to support her family. She'd been on the lookout for Plan B for days now, but nothing had happened; not even the tiniest glimmer of an idea or opportunity had appeared on the horizon.

An English lady with Sharpie pen eyebrows, a tuft of wood-pecker red hair, and frosty orange lipstick ringing her big white teeth stood planted in front of the spices, oohing and aahing over the low prices. "Look at this, Tony," the lady called out. "Only fifty cents for a half pint of freshly ground pepper."

Rose watched the lady load up her cart with spices and felt a spike of panic. *Please don't take all the cinnamon. Please, please, please . . .*

An English man came down the aisle to join the lady. "I asked the clerk at the counter about places to stay in Stoney Ridge," he told her. "She said there was nothing around here. No inn. No bed-and-breakfast. Said we'd need to head closer to Lancaster." He was every bit as flamboyant looking as his wife, with a white walrus mustache under his substantial nose and pointed cowboy boots on his feet.

"That's a shame," the lady said, standing on her tiptoes to reach the top shelf of spices. "I wouldn't mind spending more time in this town and mosey through the shops. It doesn't feel as tourist-y as the other towns."

Something started ticking in Rose's head, a sound as real as a clock.

The man watched his wife fill up the cart with spices. "Do we really need all those spices? You don't bake."

"I can give them as gifts," the lady answered. She pushed the cart up the aisle and the husband trotted behind.

Rose looked through what spices remained on the shelves:

cardamom, cloves, curry. No cinnamon. Cleaned out. She sighed.

The man and the lady stood in line to pay for their groceries. Rose wheeled her cart behind them, debating if she should ask the lady if she would mind giving up one of the containers of cinnamon. Just one. "The weather's turning real sour, Lois," the man said, peering out the storefront window. "We should get on the road. Might take us awhile to find a place to stay and it's getting late."

Tick, tick, tick. The sound in Rose's head got louder.

"What are we going to do, Tony?" The lady's voice took an anxious tone. "You know you can't drive at night. And I've got a dreadful headache."

Rose's head jerked up. The ticking sound stopped in her head and a bell went off.

There *was* no place for visitors to stay in Stoney Ridge. Her mind started to spin. What if she started an inn at the farm? The basement of the farmhouse was finished off with drywall and had an exterior entrance. It was filled with her mother-in-law's junk-that-Vera-called-heirlooms but it could be emptied out. And she could cook breakfast for the guests. Rose was a good cook. Even Vera had said so, and she wasn't a woman given to handing out compliments.

But would the bishop let tourists stay at the farm? Maybe there was a rule about this kind of thing. Maybe that's why there weren't any bed-and-breakfasts in Stoney Ridge. But then, she thought, maybe it's better not to ask. It was always easier to apologize later. Besides, Bishop Elmo seemed like a kind man. Surely, he would understand a mother's plight. The church had been good to them, generous and gracious, but she needed to find a way to take care of her family.

Would an inn bring in enough cash to solve her ongoing cash shortfall? She doubted it. But it would certainly help.

She paid for the groceries with the wad of bills wrapped in a rubber band that she kept in her dress pocket. As she picked up the bags, her heart felt lighter than it had in months. The best cure for sadness was doing something. Her eyes searched the skies, finding a small opening where the clouds parted and blue sky showed through. "Thank you," she said, grinning ear to ear. "Thank you for Plan B."

She ran over to the car where the man and the lady were loading groceries and invited them to stay at the farm.

2

The kitchen smelled as sweet and spicy as Christmas Day. Bethany Schrock took the cake out of the hot oven and set it on the counter to cool. She saw her younger brothers, Luke and Sammy, cut eyes at each other, sniffing the air like foxes. Those boys could eat any time of the day, any day of the week. They crowed with happiness as she mixed butter and powdered sugar to make icing for the cake. Then they hollered when Bethany told them they had to wait until after supper to sample it. Finally, fed up with them underfoot, she shooed them upstairs to clean their room.

Bethany was still reeling over her stepmother's big news. Rose had met her at the door as she walked in from work. She told her that there were English strangers staying for the night. In Bethany's very room! Rose had a new business idea: to turn the farm's basement into an inn. Bethany knew Rose was under pressure, but now it appeared she had gone raving mad. Yes, clearly too much pressure.

Rose had seemed so excited about this idea that Bethany didn't have the heart to tell her all the reasons it wouldn't work—how awful it would be to have strangers poke around their property, how easily influenced her little brothers could be by English visitors, how impossible English folks were to please. She knew that from personal experience, but that information was best to keep private.

Most importantly, having Rose so excited about this venture would delay the inevitable—they needed to return to York County, where they belonged. Where Bethany belonged. Where her sweetheart, Jake Hertzler, lived.

A sound of pounding footsteps came from far above her. Those brothers were either just coming or just going. It was hard for them to ever settle.

Then Luke came tearing down the stairs like a scalded cat, with Sammy following on his heels, threatening to hang him out of a window. About halfway down, Luke tripped and went nose over like a barrel down the rest of the stairs. He landed at the bottom with a thud and sprawled, unmoving.

Bethany watched in horror and flew to his side. "Luke?" Sammy galloped down the stairs and stood over his brother.

Luke opened one eye. "Sammy wants to throw me out the window."

Sammy stamped his foot. "I knew you were just playing possum! You rat!"

"No name-calling," Bethany said, helping Luke to his feet. She was sure she'd be worried into an early grave for trying to keep these little brothers out of *theirs*. "What's gotten into you two?"

Sammy pointed at Luke. "He said there's a ghost on the third floor. He said he saw a lady with bright red hair and lips. And she called him 'honey.' He said that, Bethany. He's a liar."

This was such a typical scenario. Sammy and Luke were

barely two years apart, but Luke was taller, faster, smarter, more clever. He was constantly tricking or baiting Sammy and it drove Sammy crazy. But Bethany wasn't worried about Sammy. He may not be quick or fast, but he had his own talents. "He's no liar, but he's only half right. There is a couple up there, staying in my room. Rose invited some people she met at the Bent N' Dent to stay here."

"Why'd she do that?" Sammy said.

In walked Rose through the kitchen door, carrying a basket of eggs from the henhouse, with Mim trailing behind her. "I met them at the store," Rose said after she hurried to close the door to Mammi Vera's room. "They needed a place to stay and we are people who try to help others in need." She set the basket on the table.

Mim looked shocked. Bethany realized that Rose hadn't told her the news about the inn. Mim's eyebrows knit together in a frown. It was a look Bethany knew well. Mim was the logical, practical one in the family. Rose often said that if an idea could get past Mim, it was probably a pretty good idea.

"Boys, go bring the sheep into the pen for the night," Rose said. "The goat too. And lock those latches! We don't want them wandering over to the neighbor's again. The girls and I are going to get dinner ready." Luke and Sammy went outside, whooping and hollering about how fast they could run. She watched them through the window. "Everything's a contest with those two."

Mim set the table and Bethany mixed up some biscuit dough, while Rose topped the casserole with some cheese and melted it under the broiler. Bethany remained silent, spooning biscuit dough onto an oven tray and putting it in the oven, as Rose explained the inn idea to Mim. Bethany chanced a look at Mim out of the corner of her eyes, watching her absorb the news. Mim's eyes had widened behind her large round glasses, and she was blinking rapidly, a sign that she was listening hard. Bethany had repeatedly told her to stop blinking like that—she looked like a newborn owl. But Mim could be the one to set Rose straight. She could be the leader of the campaign to pop the balloon of this harebrained scheme. Yes, she was the one.

Rose took the casserole out of the oven. "Bethany, would you please take this tray up to Lois and Tony? I invited them to join us for dinner, but Lois has a headache." She began heaping two plates with spoonfuls of casserole.

They're strangers! Bethany wanted to say but thought twice before saying it. She felt confident that the idea would fizzle out of its own accord. Still, if Bethany *were* to say something, this was what she would say:

Rose, you don't know anything about them. Folks are always saying that the Amish are too naïve, too trusting, and you've just proved them right. You met these people at the Bent N' Dent. All we know about them is that the lady uses very strong perfume and she's stinking up my room with it. That's probably the very reason she's not feeling well. Her perfume is making her sick. You just watch and see—I'll be sick too, all because of that heavy perfume poisoning the air in my room.

Rose topped each plate with a warm biscuit, added two slices of cake on the side, and handed her the tray. Bethany sighed a grievous sigh.

"Bethany, they're very nice people," Rose said, reading her mind. "Go!"

Bethany stole a look at her sister. Mim's glasses had misted over; that was always a sign that she was thinking deeply. *Come on, Mim, say it. Don't hold back,* Bethany thought. *List all the flaws with new ideas the way you usually do.* She could count on Mim. Her little half-sister did not like change.

Mim opened her gray eyes wide and took a deep breath. "I think it might just work."

Bethany squeezed her eyes tight. As usual, she was going to have to be the one who righted the ship for this family. With Tobe gone missing, she was the eldest, and so the worries reached her first.

She looked at her stepmother, so hopeful and eager. She even looked young again. Her sparkle was coming back. It was a sad and sorrowful state of affairs that Bethany had to be the one to do this, to say this. But someone had to. "Rose, have you spoken to Mammi Vera about this? After all, it is her house."

The next morning, Rose could hear her sons' high-pitched voices carry from the barn all the way up to the porch. She hoped Vera couldn't hear them. It had taken some finagling to make sure Vera didn't catch on that there were English people staying in the house last night. It worked out surprisingly well. No lies were told and none were needed—may God forgive her for even thinking such a thing. Last night Lois had a headache and stayed upstairs. Vera had stayed in her room all evening and slept late this morning.

Luke and Sammy were giving Tony and Lois a tour of the farm and were finishing up by the horse pasture. "All I have to do is catch sight of Silver Girl and whistle, and she'll come running," Sammy was telling them. "That's how good a horse she is." The way he said it, the way he looked at the horse with such admiration in his small face, gave Rose a deep, swift rush of love for her youngest. He was growing up so fast.

Silver Girl was a maiden mare, soon to deliver. Rose had bought her for a song from Galen King, her closest neighbor, a younger fellow who was known for his horse smarts. Two for the price of one, Galen had said. He was being kind. Flash, Vera's buggy horse, was getting along in years, and he told Rose he would train the foal to take Flash's place in a few years.

At first, just the name *Flash* raised a red flag to Rose. Her buggy skills were rusty. She needed a horse that wouldn't break out and bolt. Galen told her the flash was for the streak of white down his forehead. Rose's confidence in Flash and her driving skills was improving, but she still didn't drive at night, though Galen assured her that Flash could drive the buggy himself. She hadn't forgotten that she had once heard Galen tell her boys, "Es is em beschde Gaul net zu draue." *Even the best horse is not to be trusted.*

Tony lifted the suitcases into the trunk of the car as Lois continued the conversation with the boys. Rose wiped her hands on her apron and hurried out to relieve Lois of the ever-increasing complications of any conversation with Luke and Sammy.

"Now, who again is the oldest of you two?" Lois asked the boys.

"I am," Luke answered quickly. "By almost two whole years. Taller, too."

"Nuh-uh," Sammy said, standing on his toes. "Look how them pants are short."

"Those pants," Rose corrected. He was right, though. His

skinny ankles showed clear. Something else to add to her to-do list—let down the hem in Sammy's pants.

When Lois and Tony asked Rose how much she charged for a night's lodging and two meals, she gave them a blank look. She hadn't given any thought about what to charge guests. Tony handed her a one-hundred-dollar bill and called her an angel. She was glad to have it, sorry to take it, relieved to know she could pay some bills, and mortified to need it, all at the same time.

Tony said that after news of Rose's fine, buttery blueberry cornbread leaked out, she had better batten down the hatches. "Folks will be beating a path to your door."

Rose doubted that, but it was a nice thought. Lois gave Rose a hug and handed her a container of ground cinnamon. "A pretty little bird named Bethany told me you needed this."

She waved goodbye to Lois and Tony as the car drove out of the driveway. It had turned out well, inviting those two to stay over. Rose had gone to bed feeling more right and quiet on the inside than she had in many, many a night.

She inhaled the scent of cinnamon. A little bird named Bethany? From the look on Bethany's face as she headed upstairs to deliver the tray of food to Tony and Lois—like she was heading to the gallows—Rose would have thought she would be back downstairs in the blink of an eye. Not so. Bethany stayed upstairs talking to them until dinner was on the table.

Rose smiled. Mim was easier for her—what you saw, you got. She was still a little girl. The boys? They were easy to read. But with Bethany, Rose felt as if there were two trains of thinking going on and she wasn't sure which track she was on. She could never predict what Bethany would think or do.

Take last night. Rose wasn't sure why Bethany had objected so strongly to the idea of starting an inn at the farm. She would have thought Mim would list out objections, in her frank way. Mim was the pessimist of the family—so like Vera in that way. Every picnic was going to get rained on, every cup half empty. Vera was only sixty-four, but she'd been dying of old age since she was thirty-five. Mim and Vera should be closely aligned, good friends, because they saw things in the same way, but they weren't. There was often a tension between them. Too much alike, perhaps? Bethany was a polar opposite to Vera—and yet she was the one who had a sweet way with Vera.

Bethany was clever and headstrong. She acted first, thought about things later. Being full of vinegar and spunk wasn't a bad trait, but that combined with being prettier than a girl had any business being . . . mix in her poor judgment and—oh my!—she was a continual worry to Rose.

She was well aware that Bethany kept holding out hope that they would return to their old town, back to Jake Hertzler. He was a good enough fellow, charming and amusing, but Rose was never quite convinced that Jake was as besotted with Bethany as she was with him. She had hoped that Bethany's enthrallment with Jake would fade away, that she wouldn't hold out hope to return to their former town. Besides, they had no home to return to. Vera's farm was their only refuge. Bethany, nineteen now, should have an understanding of their circumstances, but maybe she was expecting too much from her. For all of Bethany's charm and beauty, she gripped tightly to cockeyed optimism. She was like Dean that way.

She remembered when Dean had hired Jake, almost two years ago. Was it that long ago? Jake had an accounting background and was a whiz with numbers. Rose had questioned the wisdom of hiring someone—even an hourly employee—when the business's profit margins were so thin. Schrock Investments had been paying over 6 percent dividends a year until the recession hit. Then, those same investments were barely paying out 1 percent and Dean was scrambling to keep up the same rate of dividends. He assured her that with Jake handling the paperwork details, he and Tobe were freed up to find more investors. "It's the answer to our cash flow problem," he had told her. "An inflow of more investors will keep us afloat. We'll weather this downturn in the economy and be back on our feet." He snapped his fingers, to indicate how quickly things could turn around.

Rose had been curious, bordering on suspicious. It struck her as slightly off—as if they were using money from the new investors to keep the old investors from fleeing. It didn't seem like it was addressing the basic problem—the investments were no longer bringing in high returns. But what did she know? She didn't ask Dean anything more. Now she wished she had.

Harold, their big Barred Rock rooster, strutted along the gable of the henhouse, all puffed up and sassy. Rose led Silver Girl out to the far pasture to graze in the morning sun. She ran a hand along the horse's big belly. As she unclipped the lead off of the horse's harness, she saw her neighbor, Galen King, try to corral their straying goat through an opening between their yards. She hurried to meet him.

"I'm sorry, Galen!" The boys had forgotten to bring the goat in for the night. To their way of thinking, he was never hard to catch, so they didn't bother tying him. The goat wasn't given to wandering far from anything green he could nibble. Usually, that meant Galen's yard.

Galen shooed the goat into the pasture. His manner was slow, befitting a man who worked with animals and knew not to frighten them. He lifted his chin toward the pregnant mare. "How's she doing?"

She turned back to look at Silver Girl. "Just fine. She's not due for another month or so." Nearby, Harold let out a piercing crow.

"Every day, that rooster thinks he's king of the world and has to tell everyone all about it." Galen glanced up at him and cupped his hands around his mouth. "Graeh net zu gschwind, Harold." *Don't crow too soon.*

Rose grinned. Dark and wiry, Galen had a quiet, watchful look about him—until he gave up one of his rare smiles. He had been Vera's neighbor for years, yet up until the last year, Rose hadn't spoken to him of anything more than weather or horses. He wasn't overly blessed with the gift of conversation, but she had found his words always held something good in them—like a satisfying drink of cold lemonade on a hot summer day. Rose shielded her eyes and looked at the crowing rooster, strutting along the roofline of the henhouse. "Sometimes I wonder if we're all a little like Harold. Real life carries on around us while we strut in our own yards, thinking we're the ones in charge of things."

As she spoke, she turned to look at Galen. She saw his eyes lift quickly to the hills behind the farmhouse, as if he didn't want to be caught looking at her.

"Rose, I just bought some new Thoroughbreds off the racetrack. Turning them into buggy horses. They're green, very green, and they're skittish. They'll bolt at anything."

Oh. Rose latched the pasture gate behind her, wanting Galen to see that they did, occasionally, latch gates around here. "We'll take care to make sure the goat doesn't wander off."

Galen gave her a quick nod. That was what he had come over to hear.

"Did the goat cause you any trouble?"

Galen lifted a shoulder in a half shrug. "Just the usual. It likes the compost pile."

"I'll send the boys over to clean it up."

He shook his head. "Don't worry yourself. Naomi was raking it up as I brought the goat over." He folded his arms. "Sure you need a goat, Rose?"

No, she didn't need a goat. Or twelve cranky hens. Or five sheep. Certainly not a bossy rooster. But especially, she didn't need a goat. A goat was nothing but a nuisance. She wished she could sell it, or just give it away, but Dean had brought it home for the boys on a whim. Rose didn't have the heart to get rid of it. She couldn't take that away from Luke and Sammy. Too hard to explain all that to Galen, though. "I haven't seen Naomi lately. Is she well?"

Naomi was Galen's seventeen-year-old sister, the baby of the family, the only sibling still at home. She suffered from fierce headaches that forced her to stay in bed for days. Galen was very protective of her. It was a quiet joke around the church that if Naomi sneezed, Galen dropped everything to be at her side with a tissue. "She's had a headache the last few days but seems to be feeling better today."

He started to leave, so she quickly said, "Would you like a cup of coffee? I just brewed a fresh pot for Vera."

"Can't." He was in a hurry, usually was.

Rose knew Galen wouldn't slow down for a cup of coffee. But she needed to talk to him and hurried to catch him before he slipped through the privet. "Galen, could I ask your advice on a matter? A business matter?"

He stopped, turned to face her, didn't say anything, but he was listening.

"I'm thinking of converting the basement into an inn," she went on. "As a business."

Galen was quiet for a moment, thinking. "Why would you want that kind of an undertaking? You've got a lot on your shoulders as it is."

With the Securities and Exchange Commission lawyer hounding her, he meant. With children at home, especially two young boys, who needed constant surveillance. With a mother-in-law who was ailing.

"The thing is . . . it seemed like a way to support my family." She bit her lip, waiting for his reaction.

Tipping his head, he studied her, his lips a speculative twist. "I see." His expression said he didn't see at all.

Rose's heart sunk. She shouldn't have told him. She braced herself, expecting him to point out that she had no real idea what she was doing. And wasn't that the truth?

What if Galen said something to Bishop Elmo? To others? She wasn't ready to discuss this. The last thing she needed was another reason to have folks eyeballing her. She couldn't afford to make mistakes in this new church. Why had she said anything to Galen? They were neighbors, that's all. He'd always been kind to them in his quiet way, especially after what happened to Dean, but she shouldn't expect him to be an advisor to her. Gracious sakes, the man had enough troubles of his own with his frail sister.

"Why?"

Hadn't she just told him? "To make a living."

"No," Galen said firmly, almost impatiently. "No, that must not be all there is to it."

The past seven months had been difficult as she adjusted to widowhood and being a single mother. She knew it was time to pick up the threads of her life and move forward.

"You're here in Stoney Ridge for a reason. Is this the reason?"

Rose spotted her mother-in-law on the front porch steps to the house. The easy answer to Galen's question would be to say they were here for Vera. For the longest time, the older woman just stood there, looking out at the yard and pastures, a slightly confused expression on her face. Rose watched her turn and head back into the house, feeling a spike of concern. Vera was getting more and more forgetful.

Galen cleared his throat. "There must be one hundred easier ways to make a living than operating an inn. Think. Why do you really want to do this?" His voice was urgent. "What was it that gave you the idea in the first place?"

Rose closed her eyes, conjuring the image in her mind. "I've always wanted to have people come to my home, to be restored and refreshed. I love the feeling I get when people are eating at my kitchen table. It makes me feel so good inside, deep down."

An awkward feeling slid over her. She looked down, watching her own fingers make a pleat in her apron. Galen's eyes were on her, waiting for her to continue. She could practically feel them boring in her soul.

"I like the idea of it," she continued. "Of creating a place where folks can catch their breath and feel welcomed. And I do need to find some ways to bring in money. I don't want to have to work in town and have the boys come home to an empty house." Not entirely empty. Vera would be home. Nearly empty.

She chanced a glance at him.

He gave her a soft, slow smile. "Well, let's check out the basement and see what it would take."

For a moment, all she could do was stare at him, stunned. Galen King was *nothing* like she'd thought he'd be. He was a helpful neighbor to Vera but preoccupied with the task of raising his younger siblings. Ten years ago, his father had broken his neck after being thrown from a horse and Galen became the man of the house, overnight, without warning. People tended to think that Galen was surly, recalcitrant, a real grump. He had a tough exterior that made him seem older than he was. It was an image he liked to cultivate, but he was never able to pull it off for long. Underneath his curmudgeon exterior, he had a heart as soft as butter left on a sunny windowsill.

Over the last seven months, Galen had gone out of his way to look after the Schrocks—fixing fences, finding the right horse for Rose, returning straying animals and straying little boys. He made himself quietly useful. Soon, Rose began to see that was what he did, the kind of man he was—and that everyone, including the Schrocks, depended upon him to do it.

Rose took the basement key from her pocket as she walked to the basement door. Even that was a plus—the basement had its own exterior opening. That topped the list of Bethany's many objections—that guests would be interfering with the family. Meals and all. Rose didn't see it that way—as soon as she got the basement fixed up, guests wouldn't need to go to the house. She would deliver breakfast to them. As for dinner, she didn't plan to offer dinner at all. She only did so last night because Lois and Tony were in a fix on a stormy night. She reached into her pocket and felt the one-hundred-dollar bill. Imagine that! God's blessing.

Galen and Rose walked toward the musty, dusty basement. She hadn't been in it since they'd moved to the farmhouse last year. That realization triggered memories of their move. Her mother-in-law was the one who had insisted that Dean and Rose bring the children and live with her after their home was taken over by the bank. Dean had put it up as collateral to the bank for loans, and lost that bet. "I'll have someone in the church help me set up that small room beyond the kitchen for a bedroom for me and we're right as rain," Vera had told them.

"But it's putting you out of your own house—" Rose had said.

"No, it's not. I'm not really able to climb those stairs anyway. Bad knees. This way I have company and a little place to myself. What could be better? I've been waiting for the day when Dean and his children would come back where they belonged."

Vera kept insisting, Dean acquiesced, so Rose knew she had no choice. They moved the family and all their belongings into the large farmhouse in Stoney Ridge—about an hour's drive from Dean's office in York County. Rose had hoped that moving to Stoney Ridge might be a turning point. Instead, it became a point of bracing oneself for the storm.

Rose worked the key in the lock. The door was warped, so Galen had to use his shoulder to push it open. As they stepped inside, something scurried by their feet—a gray mouse. Then another. When Rose's heartbeat returned to normal, she followed Galen the rest of the way inside. She could see just enough to make her cringe. She waited for Galen to say something, the way she waited for her children to talk. People would talk when they got their mind around the subject.

When Galen had looked all through the basement, he folded his arms across his chest. "It's worth a try." It wasn't entirely below ground, another plus. The house was built into a hillside, so the front window of the basement was large and the room was filled with sunlight. It was a big enough space that Galen thought it could be divided into two bedrooms and a sitting area. Maybe a small kitchen could go against one wall—cabinets and a refrigerator and an oven. And a bathroom. Definitely a bathroom. He took the pad and paper from her hands, his fingers brushing hers.

He scribbled down a list of things Rose would need to do to make the basement ready for company. He started a new page with a list of people he thought she should talk to, including his sister in Indiana who had started a bed-and-breakfast. When he was finished, he handed Rose back the paper. There was something fundamentally reassuring about how he took her idea seriously, and she was touched. Rose felt an excitement for the future she hadn't felt in months. Years, maybe.

"You're doing a lot for a neighbor," she said.

He held her gaze. "A friend, you mean." He walked to the door, then turned to her. "Of course, you'll need to run this all past Bishop Elmo."

Rose noticed how smudged and dirty the windows were. She could get the boys working on that this very afternoon.

"Rose? Did you hear me? I think you should talk to Bishop Elmo."

She glanced up at him. "Dean used to say that it was easier to apologize later than to ask for permission first."

Galen's dark eyebrows lifted in surprise. "Wammer eppes oft dutt, waert mer's gewehnt." *Do a thing often and it becomes a habit.*

She gave him a sharp look. Was that Galen's way of commenting on Dean's character? Or lack of. He had known Dean for many years, but Rose didn't realize that he understood his nature too. One more thing she had underestimated about Galen.

He kept his eyes fixed on her. "I find it hard to believe that Vera would go along with this idea."

"I haven't quite . . . told her yet." Galen opened his mouth to say something, but Rose beat him to the punch. "I know. I know. I will tell her. I just wanted to sort a few things out first."

Galen let out a puff of air. "Good luck with that."

3

Bethany rolled up her spare clothes and stuffed them in her cubby, pinned her prayer cap into place, then slipped out the kitchen door of the Stoney Ridge Bar & Grill. She had to hurry. She needed to get to the post office before the mail went out at three. She had received a letter from Jake Hertzler yesterday and wrote one back, immediately.

Jake wrote, regularly at first, then with less frequency. Sometimes, when weeks had gone by with no word from him, Bethany would get angry and tell herself that she was going to end it and move on with her life. After all, they were only about an hour apart and he had never come to visit her, not once, despite her many invitations. But about the time she told herself it was over, a letter from Jake would arrive full of apologies, explanations, and the endearments she longed to hear, and she would forgive him yet again. She let out a sigh. Jake was lucky to have her. Not many girls would be as patient and understanding as she was.

She needed to drop by the farmers' market and pick up a bag of Brussels sprouts from the Salad Stall to take home later today. She paid the young man, Chris Yoder—whom she happened to know was courting her friend, M.K. Lapp—for the Brussels sprouts and retrieved the scooter she hid behind the market dumpster each morning. Her sister, Mim, didn't like any green vegetables, but lately she was willing to try Brussels sprouts, if smothered in fried bacon. Two weeks ago, it was broccoli. Mim's finicky eating habits were beneficial to Bethany. Bringing things home from the farmers' market served as a beneficial decoy.

Rose was under the impression that Bethany worked at the farmers' market five days a week, and Bethany didn't feel any compulsion to correct that impression. She couldn't remember how that impression got started—maybe, when she told Rose that she had *applied* for a job at the farmers' market. But the only job Bethany was *offered* came from the Stoney Ridge Bar & Grill. So she took it. And on a dare one day from another waitress, Ivy, she wore English clothing. Her tips doubled that day. Tripled the next. Since then, Bethany kept spare English clothing in her cubby and changed into them each day. The good thing was that no Amish ever came into the Stoney Ridge Bar & Grill.

Too expensive. Too worldly. In that order.

The bad thing was, she was living a whopper of a lie. But that was a worry for another day. A person shouldn't worry about too much at one time. Women were prone to worry and men didn't like women who worried too much. She had read that very thing in *A Young Woman's Guide to Virtue*, published in 1948, one of the few books allowed in her grandmother's house besides the Holy Bible and the *Ausbund* and the *Martyrs Mirror*. All very serious stuff for a nineteen-year-old girl.

She had retrieved her hidden scooter from behind the dumpster when she heard someone call out her name—a young

Amish fellow from her church. She had never noticed him. Maybe once or twice. His name was Jimmy Fisher, he was dangerously good-looking, and anyone could see that he thought he was something special. All the girls at church talked about him as if he could charm the daylight out of the sky.

She had to walk the scooter through the farmers' market to reach the road, but she kept up a quick pace, ignoring Jimmy Fisher.

"Hey! Hey, Bethany! Bethany Schrock!"

Too late.

Bethany didn't slow down but turned her chin slightly, just to acknowledge his existence. Just to be polite. Not so that he would think she had any idea who he was.

Jimmy jogged to catch up to her. "I don't think we've formally been introduced. Aren't you a friend of M.K. Lapp's?"

She slowed to a stop. Just to be polite. "Maybe," she said coolly. So, she was face-to-face with the famous Mr. Irresistible. *A Young Woman's Guide to Virtue* warned of forward and bold young men. They were to be avoided. She started walking on her way.

Jimmy followed behind. "Couldn't you slow down for a moment. Be sociable?"

Bethany turned to face him. It occurred to her that he might just be friendly.

Jimmy took off his hat, held it to his chest, and grinned. "I'm James Fisher, proprietor of Fisher Hatchery. Friends call me Jimmy." He thumped his heart. *Thump, thump, thump.* "My heart leaps to make your acquaintance."

She tried not to roll her eyes. "Well, James, I am in a hurry."

"You're always in a hurry. I see you zooming in and out of here each day. But I can't quite figure out what the big hurry is." Jimmy stroked his chin, deep in thought. "That scooter gets stashed behind the dumpster and you seem to disappear. Makes a fellow wonder where a girl spends her day." His blue eyes sparkled with mischief.

M.K. Lapp had warned her to stay clear of Jimmy Fisher—that he was crazier than a loon. Right now, he didn't strike her as unhinged—more like a fellow who was too clever for his own good. His was a charming scalawag's smile, and she trusted it for about as long as it took to blink.

Jimmy took a step closer to her. "Maybe if you let me take you home in my buggy, we could get to know each other." He took another step toward her. "I can keep secrets."

In such situations, *A Young Woman's Guide to Virtue* recommended that a young woman hold up her head, ignore such ungentlemanly behavior, and quietly remove herself. Remain pious and ladylike at all times, the book said. Unflappable. Imperturbable.

He wiggled his eyebrows in an outrageously flirtatious manner. "What do you say, good-looking?"

Shootfire! The arrogance of this fellow really ground Bethany's grits. She narrowed her eyes and planted her fists on her hips. "You, Mr. Irresistible, can just take your buggy and—"

"Bethany! Mom's looking for you!" Luke and Sammy ran up to her, red-faced and panting. "Mammi Vera's having a sinking spell!"

Rose had waited for just the right moment to speak to Vera about turning the basement into an inn. The right moment had yet to come, but she couldn't wait any longer. She had stopped by the phone shanty to pick up her messages and discovered a paying guest wanted to arrive tomorrow. He said his cousin Tony had recommended the place to him after learning he had a business trip in Lancaster County. Rose's first reaction was sheer panic. This was all happening too fast! She wasn't in a position to have people stay at the farm yet—the basement would take time and work to get into shape. That meant a guest would have to stay in the house . . . and this particular guest happened to be a *man*. A stranger. This was a bad idea. A very bad idea.

But on the heels of that thought came another one. Maybe this turn of events was from God. After all, the entire idea came about because she had opened the conversation with God. At Galen's urging, she had gathered her courage one afternoon and driven over to Bishop Elmo's. He met her out by her buggy and listened, without any hint of expression, as she explained about the inn. A thoughtful, kindly man, he stroked his scraggly white beard for a moment, then his face brightened and he clapped his hands together in delight—as if he had only wished he'd thought of it himself. She left with his blessing and a lightness in her heart.

Maybe God was encouraging her to step out in faith and trust that it would all work out. This man wasn't entirely a stranger—he was a cousin of Tony's, who seemed like a good man. She remembered that one-hundred-dollar bill Tony had slipped into her palm. Think how nice it would be to have some steady income right now.

Rose picked up the phone and called Tony's cousin. She tried to sound as if she did this every day of her life—took reservations and gave directions to find the farm. As she hung up the phone, she blew out a puff of air. She had to face Dean's mother about this . . . new venture. She couldn't keep hiding guests in the house.

She rubbed her face. How often must Vera rue the fact that she was the one who encouraged Dean to move his family to Stoney Ridge?

While Rose had been grateful for her mother-in-law's provision of a home, especially after Dean had passed, she knew Vera well enough to know she had an ulterior motive to such a generous offer. Not long after Dean's funeral, Vera spelled out her expectations: return to the Old Order Amish church and all that went with it—school, clothing, no car, no electricity.

"Those are my rules," Vera told Rose firmly. To Vera's way of thinking, this was the chance to bring her grandchildren back to their roots, back to where she felt they belonged.

"Fine," Rose said without any objection, which shocked Vera. Rose had never minded standing up to Vera, but she was prepared for this. She had been raised Old Order but left the church, long ago, before she had been baptized. She sensed that she needed to keep the family intact and united, so she went through the instruction classes, confessed her sins, renounced the world, and joined the church. That vow wasn't made to a group of people, but to God. She felt joined, like a limb to a tree, to the church and to her family and to God.

The children went along with it—switching schools, adjusting their clothing, selling the old minivan. Even Bethany was accommodating, though she said she wasn't ready to attend instruction classes with Rose.

Aside from missing the convenience of her minivan, Rose and the children adapted surprisingly well to the lifestyle change. They had always spoken the Penn Dutch language in their home, and they were familiar with Old Order ways from visits to Vera's home. In so many areas, they were making adjustments and weathering the storm.

But another storm started to brew. Vera had become forgetful. She misplaced objects, forgot dates right after she looked at the calendar, couldn't remember little words like "hat" or "horse," or she would say another word in its place. She had weakness in her right side. The doctor diagnosed it as a series of mini-strokes, brought on by stress. This doctor put her on a blood thinner and gave her daily exercises.

Even if Rose wanted to leave (and to be entirely truthful, she often did), how could she ever justify it? Dean had been Vera's only son.

Rose pulled open the curtains to let the natural light into the room. "It's a beautiful day today. Spring will be here soon."

Vera blinked her eyes. "Where's Bethany? I only want Bethany."

Rose sighed. "Bethany works each day at the farmers' market. She'll be home after three. I have time now to help you with your exercises."

"I'll do them later. With Bethany."

"We need to do these every morning and every afternoon. The doctor explained that to you."

"Women shouldn't be doctors."

And thus began the morning routine with her mother-in-law. Rose slowly coaxed Vera's right hand open, rubbed lotion into each little nook and cranny. "The doctor said that hands often curl up tight when someone suffers apoplexy."

"She was a quack."

"She wasn't a quack. She said your strokes are causing this weakness, but in time you'll regain some of these skills. She said these exercises will help keep your fingers limber."

"That's enough for now."

"Each one needs to be bent and straightened half a dozen times, and your wrist needs to be rotated." A routine of exercises needed to be done twice a day, morning and night, and Rose or Bethany did them faithfully. While Rose patiently started working Vera's fingers in her lifeless right arm, Vera kept a steady stream of rebukes, complaints, and criticism flowing. No amount of soothing calmed her.

Rose knew embarrassment over having to be tended to in such a way was what fueled Vera's sharp tongue. She always forgave her. She knew God was calling her to meet this situation with grace. "Do you see how much stronger you're getting? Dean would have been proud of you."

"Don't think I don't know why Dean did what he did." Vera pushed Rose's arm away. "I know you pushed him to the brink. I heard that argument. Everyone did. The whole county could've stayed home and heard every word."

Patience. Patience. We are living in her house. "So you've told me." Rose was accustomed to Vera's vinegar and beans, but those sharp words still stung. The thing was—Vera spoke the truth. She had a hard time forgiving herself for that argument, for what happened the next day. Maybe she did push Dean to the brink.

She took Vera's hand in hers and started bending the elbow, straightening and bending, straightening and bending. Five more, four more, three more. "I have something to tell you. Some good news." Rose tried to keep her voice as calm as a summer day.

Vera looked away.

"I've come up with an idea about how to support my family."

"It's about time. I might be land rich but I'm money poor.

And this land is going to Tobe, when he comes home. It's rightfully his. You can't expect me—"

Rose lifted a hand to stop another onslaught. "I've been praying on this and I think I've found a solution. I'll be able to be home for the children and to take care of you." She tried to keep the statement flat, to mask the swells of uncertainty inside her.

Vera peered at her with her one droopy side of the face, curious.

"I'm going to start a bed-and-breakfast. An inn. Here at the farm. Convert the basement. You won't even know guests are here." In the awkward silence that followed, Rose's already-shaky confidence plummeted. "I spoke to Bishop Elmo and he gave me his blessing. Of course, I'd like your blessing on it." She chanced a glance at Vera, who was blinking in surprise, her mouth hung wide open. Rose carefully straightened Vera's blanket. She was taking this news better than she thought she might. What a pleasant surprise.

"Absolutely not!" Vera shouted.

Naturally, Vera Schrock did not brood upon things of the past, the way some people dwelled on such things, but the old ways of her people still came to mind from time to time, often at unexpected moments. Such as this morning.

Her daughter-in-law Rose did not follow the old ways. The old ways would never have approved of turning a home into a . . . stopping station for strangers. The old ways respected that the Plain people were set apart, that they were not to mingle with the English. The old ways . . . She could go on. And what was the point? No one listened to her. She was always the last to know anything, anyway.

Vera tried to lift a coffee mug and couldn't raise it an inch off the table. Her chest tightened with sudden despair. Something terrible was happening to her, something she couldn't fight and simply could not stop. Her right side kept getting weaker and weaker—not stronger like the quack lady doctor promised, after tossing all kinds of pills at her and charging her an arm and a leg. Vera couldn't get words out the way she used to, but she had them in her head. Lately, her thoughts felt like a tangled ball of yarn. They flitted through her mind like a robin hopping from tree to tree, never staying in one place long. The confused state she often found herself in was occurring more and more often, and she didn't like the idea of Bethany and those other children—what were their names? the dark-haired girl and those two wild boys?—well, whatever their names were, she didn't like them seeing her this way.

She was frightened.

Terrified.

At least she was when she remembered.

And then those horrid hiccups would return.

Rose had tried a number of fail-safe cures to stop hiccups that she got from the healer, Sadie something-or-other. She used to be Sadie Lapp, Vera did remember that, but she couldn't remember her married name. Anyway, last week, she had Vera pinching her nose shut with her two thumbs, and plugged up both ears with her fingers, while Rose or Bethany would pour a glass of water down her throat. Vera stomped her foot when she was close to drowning, and then the glass was taken away. It had worked.

Just thinking of that horrid cure made her even more anxious, and sure enough, those awful hiccups started up.

4

If it was going to happen, Bethany just wished it would go ahead and happen. The basement had been cleared out, remodeled, freshly painted. She couldn't wait to get the furniture moved in and a shingle hung so that Rose's ridiculous bed-and-breakfast was officially under way. She was sick and tired of giving up her bedroom for strangers. Twice now, she'd had to sleep with Mim in a scrunched-up bed and listen to her whiffling snores all night long. Mim should know that any little thing would wake Bethany. She hardly slept. Too much responsibility weighed on her mind. She was the oldest now, since Tobe had vanished, and she had to take care of everybody.

The man who stayed in Bethany's room had the gall to come downstairs for breakfast and complain about the loud sound of mooing cows! "Well, we *are* close to a dairy farm," Rose said. "And this *is* the countryside."

But the man was not happy. And his "donation" was a mere twenty-five dollars.

To top it off, Mammi Vera heard the man's complaints about the mooing cows and pitched a fit. No wonder her grandmother kept having these mini-strokes. She was constantly pitching fits.

And here was another thing: Bethany was growing weary of getting yanked away from whatever she was doing to settle her grandmother down. It took a fair bit of work to calm Mammi Vera. Being her grandmother's favorite wore her out. She knew the only reason was because she looked so much like a Schrock. The younger ones took after Rose, her father's second wife.

Bethany didn't think of Rose as a stepmother but as a real mother. Part of the reason, she supposed, was because Rose didn't believe in labels that fractured a family and divided them up. She insisted that Bethany and Tobe think of Mim and the boys as siblings, not steps or half. Rose referred to herself as Bethany and Tobe's mother. She did all she could to keep the family together. Including Mammi Vera.

But mostly, Bethany thought of Rose as her mother because she was always there for her. She was a rock. She was safe.

Unlike her real mother.

Bethany could hardly remember her real mother. It was sad that there were no pictures of her. If Bethany were a bishop, she would change that rule, first thing. She grinned. Imagine that—a woman becoming a bishop. It would never happen! But she would love to have a picture of her mother. She had deserted their family when Bethany was just a toddler.

A few years later, her father married Rose, and Rose became her stepmother. That was the happiest day of Bethany's childhood. Bethany admired her more than anybody she had ever met. Rose was always thinking of others and she took the brunt of everything, especially her grandmother's sour tongue, yet she wasn't beaten down by it. When Mim complained about the work required to get the basement into shape as an inn, Bethany replied, "But isn't the point to give Rose a chance? Isn't that the whole point?"

As close as Bethany felt to Rose, she couldn't call her "Mom." In her heart, she had a real mother and, one day, she hoped to find her. To ask her why she left.

Luke and Sammy came galloping through the back door. "Bethany, come see! Galen's brought over some furniture for the basement." They galloped back out again.

Hallelujah! If Rose was determined to see this crazy notion through, at least get those strangers out of their house and into the basement.

"You boys quiet down out there!" came a cry from the depths of Mammi Vera's gloomy bedroom.

"They're already back outside, Mammi Vera," Bethany called back. She looked out the window and saw Naomi alongside her brother, Galen, coming up the driveway, in an open wagon filled to the brim with furniture. She wiped her hands on a dishrag and hurried outside.

Naomi waved eagerly when she saw her. It always surprised Bethany that Naomi was so fond of her. There couldn't be two more opposite girls in all the world over. Naomi was frail and thin and often took to her bed. Bethany was strong, curvy, and had never been sick a day in her life. Naomi was pious and pure and reserved, while Bethany was blunt and outspoken, with a hot temper. Why, hadn't she nearly spouted off a curse word or two at Jimmy Fisher just yesterday?

And all the while, Jimmy Fisher just watched her with those mischievous eyes, enjoying her outburst. Not at all offended, he had made good on his offer to give her a ride home in his buggy so she could hurry back to Mammi Vera's side. It was her job to settle Mammi Vera down after pitching one of her fits that ended in relentless hiccups.

Nonetheless, the buggy ride home did not change Bethany's opinion of Jimmy Fisher: he was arrogant and cocky just because he was so handsome and charming and likable.

She wondered if he might drop by sometime. She didn't want him to, but she wondered if he might.

Naomi hopped off the wagon and hurried to Bethany. "My brother emptied out the attic! He brought over extra beds and rugs and tables for the new bed-and-breakfast."

"Not a minute too soon," Bethany said. "I can't handle having strangers in the house. Asking questions and poking around the house. One of them walked right into Mammi Vera's room yesterday and she screamed bloody murder."

"She's always lathered up about one thing or another," Luke piped up.

Bethany pointed a finger at him. "You respect your elders." Then she shooed him away. "Get Sammy and make yourself useful. Go help Galen unload the wagon." She turned back to Naomi. "Come and see how the basement's starting to take shape. You won't believe it."

Naomi followed Bethany to the basement door. It had been divided into two bedrooms, a bathroom, and a living room with a small kitchen. A week ago, after Rose and the boys had emptied everything out and put it in the hayloft, Galen brought a few young fellows from church and they built the interior walls, added drywall, and installed a bathroom and a kitchen, tapping into plumbing that was already there. All in two days. Then Rose and Bethany and Mim painted the entire interior a fresh creamy butter color with white on the woodwork. The place was transformed.

Naomi clapped her hands in delight. "I think this is going to be wonderful, Bethany! And best of all—it means you won't be moving back to your old town."

"Well, I don't know about that," Bethany started. "I'll help Rose get some debts cleared, then I'll be heading back, for sure." No doubt.

"I hope not." Naomi leaned forward to whisper in her ear. "Did I happen to see Jimmy Fisher drop you off in his buggy yesterday?"

"That was purely an accident," Bethany said. She hoped her reputation wasn't sullied because she had been seen with the likes of Jimmy Fisher. "And it won't be happening again, I can guarantee you of that."

"He is awfully good-looking," Naomi said, blushing a deeper shade of red. "But just so you're warned, he goes through girls faster than a bag of potato chips."

What? What was Naomi implying? Did she think Bethany was sweet on Jimmy Fisher? She wanted to scotch that suspicion. She was just about to say so when the boys burst through the door, carrying a big rug under their arms.

"I'll go help Galen," Naomi said.

Bethany instructed the boys to lay the rug straight in the big room—the only room it would fit in. The boys ran outside to bring in some more furniture. Bethany looked around the room. She had to hand it to Rose. It was starting to look less like an afterthought and more like a place someone would want to come to stay. Galen deserved a lot of the credit too. Encouraging Rose, organizing the work to get done. Rose kept insisting that she could manage herself, but Galen ignored her objections and kept at it. She wondered why he was being so kind. She looked out the window, watching

Galen hand something to Rose and tell her something. Rose laughed in response.

Oh. Of course! He must think of her as an older sister.

Rose tried not to let it show, as she helped unload Galen's wagon full of spare furniture, but her stomach was still churning from this morning's phone call. Allen Turner, a lawyer for the Security Exchange Commission Legal Affairs, called to inform her that Tobe was under suspicion for altering the company books.

She put a box of towels in the bedroom and sorted through them to see which could be used and which should be cut up into rags. As each pile grew, her thoughts drifted to Tobe, to Dean, to that awful time when everything imploded.

Someone had sent a letter to the Security Exchange Commission asking for an inquiry about Schrock Investments. How could they keep up such high returns, the letter had asked, when the rest of the economy was doing so poorly? It didn't add up, the mysterious letter writer accused. That was the first portent—when Dean received a phone call from Allen Turner requesting a meeting after receiving that letter. A tipoff, Allen Turner called it.

Not much later, checks from Schrock Investments started to bounce. Dean made the appalling discovery that there was no money in the bank, though statements said otherwise.

Investors caught wind that Schrock Investments was in trouble and demanded their money. Trapped between a rock and a hard place, Dean declared bankruptcy. Then the claims began from investors, which heightened the concern of the Securities and Exchange Commission. Allen Turner was waiting at the office one morning for Dean to arrive. He had a subpoena for the company books, which Dean handed over. He had nothing to hide, Dean insisted. Allen Turner was stunned to realize that the books were actually physical books, ledgers—no electronic transfer of funds. But Dean didn't use computers. "I'm a Plain man," he explained to Allen Turner, "and I run my company in a Plain way."

"With the added benefit of no paper trail," Allen Turner pointed out, unkindly and with suspicion. He left, shaking his head, those black ledgers tucked under his arm.

It made her sick to think Allen Turner would doubt Dean's integrity. To her knowledge, Dean had never once broken the law. He was a straight-as-an-arrow type. She couldn't even remember that he had ever gotten a parking ticket. But something had happened and no one seemed to understand what. Rose couldn't sleep nights, knowing how many folks had lost so much money. It wasn't like Dean had just spilled punch at a Sunday picnic. For a moment, she closed her eyes as she thought of all the people, scattered across the country, who had invested in Dean's company, Schrock Investments, trusting him with their savings.

That was the day that Tobe ran away. He left a note on his pillow that said,

> *Dad and Rose, Don't worry about me. Don't try to find me. I'll be fine.*

Tobe had worked for Dean's company since he turned sixteen. Dean didn't know where Tobe had run off to, or why.

Throughout their marriage, Rose and Dean had had their share of quarrels and misunderstandings like any married couple, but they argued that night in a way they had never argued before. Finally, Dean grew silent, sullen. Then he said to her, "I'm going to fix it. I'm going to fix everything." He went to the door, snagged his hat off the bench, and jammed it onto his head. At the threshold, he turned back and gave her a long look, then shoved the door open and headed down the driveway. She watched him disappear into the darkness. The next morning, his body was found, drowned, in a pond. Even now, months later, she shuddered as she thought of that day. The worst day of her life.

She dropped the towel and rubbed her face with her hands. This entire situation was so complicated and—almost eight months later—only seemed to get more complicated. When would it end? Would Tobe ever show up again? A part of her didn't want him to. What might happen to him if he showed up? She couldn't bear thinking of him, indicted, faced with jail time. If . . . *if* he was guilty.

It seemed Allen Turner thought he was. This morning Allen Turner had told her that Jake Hertzler had been called in for questioning and reluctantly admitted that he suspected Tobe might have been involved in keeping a second set of books. Jake said if that were true, then it was possible Dean had handed over cooked books to the SEC—ones that had been altered to appear as if they complied with accounting regulations.

"Tell me everything you know about Jake Hertzler," was how Allen Turner had started the telephone conversation this morning.

"He's a nice young man. Very polite, very likable. He was new to our church and looking for work. When Dean learned he had some experience with accounting, he hired him on an hourly basis to help with some paperwork."

"What kind of paperwork?"

"Preparing statements to the investors. He never handled money, other than to make bank deposits. Never withdrawals. I know that for a fact."

"But your husband trusted him?"

"Of course. Of course he did. There was never a reason not to."

"Mrs. Schrock, was it possible that your husband had stopped paying attention to details?"

Maybe. *Probably.* "I find it hard to believe that Jake would accuse Tobe of keeping a set of altered books. Jake was a good employee. He worked hard to help Dean and Tobe. Everything changed when he came on board." At least for a while.

"How did everything change?"

"Dean was able to spend more time finding investors. He was very grateful for Jake's help. And don't forget that the problems had started long before Jake had been hired. Dean had been struggling to pay dividends for over a year."

"I see." He paused and Rose knew that he didn't see at all. "But you didn't answer my question. Could your husband have stopped paying attention to details?"

"Is that what Jake said?"

Silence.

"Why would you believe Jake?" she asked.

"He gave us information in a deposition," Allen Turner explained. "He was under oath."

Well, that's the problem right there. Plain people don't take oaths. They shouldn't need them. Telling the truth isn't optional. She was afraid it would sound like a deflection, a distraction from what he was after, and that wasn't how she wanted to seem to Allen Turner. She wanted to convey an image of strength, of confidence, that she was sure Dean and Tobe would not have done something illegal—not intentionally.

"When did your husband realize that there was a cash problem?"

"When checks started bouncing and he discovered there was no money in the bank. Soon after that, he filed for bankruptcy. He needed protection from investors and he needed help from the bank to try to figure out what was going on. But he was always planning to make good on the principal investments. He didn't declare bankruptcy to avoid anything. I have no doubt of that." Dean had been adamant that declaring bankruptcy was the only choice—no one could go after them personally, they could only go after the assets of the company—the office, the land it was on, the office equipment. Still, she hated living with those debts over her head. Allen Turner said he was optimistic that up to fifty cents on the dollar could be returned to investors who made claims.

But those claims, only about one fourth of the investors, came from non-Amish, non-Mennonite investors. The rest were all Plain folks who had put their trust in one of their own. What about them? she had asked Allen Turner. "If they aren't willing to pursue the claim in court," he said, "there's nothing that can be done for them, legally."

And *that* was a burden, among others, that weighed on Rose. She was determined to pay every single person back the principle they had invested in Schrock Investments, even if it took her years and years. She felt responsible for these people.

"Mrs. Schrock, it's imperative that we find your stepson. Do you know where he could be? Any idea at all?"

When he asked her that question, her heart started to race.

Tobe was in danger, as surely as he was when he was a reckless young boy, doing foolish things like Luke did now—climbing to the tops of trees, teasing the goat. He thought he was invincible. "You've caught me unprepared," she said. "I can't think of anything. But I'll try. I'll . . . make a list."

Allen Turner said he would call again soon to see if she had any idea where he could be. "If you hear from him, you need to let me know."

As if she would need a reminder.

When would it ever end? She threw the last towel into the rag pile and grabbed the empty box, startling Chase, the dog, into action. He sprang from sleeping by her feet and began to bark, then chased his tail. Watching that silly old dog act like a puppy made her lips tug in a smile. *Maybe that is one of the reasons God gave us dogs*, Rose thought, watching Chase spin in a circle. A gentle nudge from above to "hangeth thou in there," even on days when you just feel like you're only chasing your tail.

Bethany lifted a large tray filled with dishes to take out to the dining area to a group of Rotary businessmen. Her friend Ivy had started their orders but needed to leave early today for a dentist appointment, so Bethany agreed to stay and finish up her section. She set up the tray and looked at Ivy's orders to see how the meals should be served around the table: left to right was how they were taught. When she finished serving, she refilled coffee cups and water glasses, made sure everyone had serving utensils. Hopefully, this big table would guarantee generous tips. Not always, but usually.

As she spun around to check the other tables in Ivy's section, she noticed the unmistakable black felt hat of an Amish man who had been seated at a table against the window. Her heart caught for a moment. The man's head was tilted down to look at the menu. It didn't matter—she wouldn't be recognized, not with her English outfit and hair pulled in a ponytail. And lots of makeup too. Ivy had treated her to a makeover a few weeks ago and given Bethany her old mascara, eyeliner, and blush. Lipstick too.

Bethany turned to a fresh page on her pad and went to the table. "Do you know what you'd like to order for lunch?"

When he didn't answer, Bethany looked up from the pad. Her heart dropped. The Amish man was Jimmy Fisher, grinning at her like a cat that cornered a mouse.

"That feisty girl was late bringing me supper again!" Vera said, sitting by the kitchen window.

Rose knew whom she meant: Mim. Whether Vera truly forgot her grandchildren's names or she was just being ornery, Rose didn't know.

"I told you that I'd help you with supper, Vera."

"Last time you tried to cut my food, I nearly choked to death."

"Now that's not true, Vera. It was just broth."

"Because you think I'm fat."

Rose swallowed another sigh. Vera constantly raked conversations, looking for slights or insults. She had always been sharp tongued, never been a picnic to be around, but Dean's passing brought out her mean nature on a full-time basis. It caused Rose endless distress. The children deserved a home filled with laughter and love, not sadness and strife.

I'm not going to think like that. I'm not.

She went outside to get a fresh breath of air. A breeze soon made the sheets on the clothesline lift and luff. Rose reached out to touch one. Cold but dry. She unclipped the pins and folded the sheet. The sun felt good on her face. *Lord, Sir, I know I keep petitioning you for a string of miracles, but could you please give me patience to endure that woman? Not just patience, but sincere gratitude. She's put a roof over our heads. Help me be truly grateful.*

She saw Bethany come hurrying toward the house with the boys trotting close behind, spilling with news about the bald eagle pair they had been watching for a few days.

Vera knocked on the window and hollered to them to hush up. "Er is en re Saegmiehl gebore." *He was born in a sawmill.* It was what she said to the boys whenever they were too loud, which was often, or didn't close doors, which happened regularly.

"Sorry, Mammi Vera," Bethany called out, but there was fire in her eyes. Something must have happened at work, but Rose didn't know what. There were times when Bethany seemed to get in a frame of mind that was prickly as a stinging nettle. Bethany went right into the kitchen. Rose saw her crouch beside her grandmother to talk to her. It was Vera's only bright spot of the day—when Bethany came home from work.

"Mom, we think them eagles is going to build a nest in the dead tree on the top of the hill. Near the creek," Luke said.

"*Those* eagles are going to build a nest," Rose corrected.

"Exactly," Sammy piped up. "Wouldn't that be something?"

Grammar was forgotten when the boys were excited. Rose couldn't help smiling at the look of wonder on the boys' faces. "It would be something special to watch." Before the boys could start in on more details about the eagles, Rose sent them to the barn to fill the wheelbarrow with hay to feed the goat and sheep. "Don't forget to latch the gates, Luke and Sammy. That goat's been getting out on a regular basis. We want to be good neighbors to Galen."

"We *are* good neighbors," Luke said. "He just doesn't like goats."

No one liked goats, Rose thought, but didn't say. She had already soundly scolded Luke today for trouble at school. Sometimes, she thought that boy learned everything at school but his lessons. Mim said she was mortified to own up to having him for a brother. Today, it appeared Luke drew a very exaggerated picture of Sammy's ears on his arithmetic workbook. Sammy was sensitive about his rather sizable ears. He took it upon himself to correct Luke with a sound punch as soon as they were out to recess and away from the teacher's eyes. Mim said that the boys were rolling together across the playground, each trying to get in a good punch.

Teacher M.K. had little patience with such boy nonsense. They were kept after school and sent home with a note, explaining their crimes. Rose knew she was a fine teacher and needed to keep discipline in the schoolhouse, but she had to smile when she pictured them tumbling around the playground. Rascals to the end.

As she finished folding the last sheet, Rose felt her heart set to right. She was ready to face the evening. *Thank you, Lord, for bringing a little sunshine into a winter day.*

5

Lately, Miriam Schrock had set her mind to finding so-lutions. A few nights ago, she had gone down to the kitchen, late at night, and had seen her mother at the kitchen table, answering letters from investors. She had sneaked a peek at the letters one time and found a similar theme in all of them: "Greetings in the Name of Jesus! I had $2,452.95 (or $3,497.34 or $1,496.75) . . ."—mostly amounts under $5,000. It was impressive to Mim that each letter-writer knew the fig-ure down to the penny—"in Schrock Investments with Dean Schrock and I would like you to know I need that money very badly." The writer would describe his or her current ailment or financial need and conclude with: "I hope and pray you can send me my money back. Thank you kindly."

That night, Mim could see the anxiety in her mother's face as she tucked a $10 or $20 bill in the letters. She knew what her mother was doing. Rose Schrock would pay back every cent, no matter how long it would take her. She was advised by the SEC man to not do anything until the claims had been settled. But her mother didn't pay any attention to the advice of that SEC man. So Mim insisted that her mother keep track of what she was paying people and created a color-coded accounting book for her. It included pages for income from the new inn, pages for outgo, pages to pay bills, and pages to keep track of payments to former investors.

Her mother was pleased and said Mim was a first-rate problem solver. That made Mim feel very happy, because she knew her mother was facing a mountain of problems. Frankly, Mim didn't know how some of the problems created by her father's investment company would ever get solved, but it made her feel good to help where she could.

Bethany's suggestion was to ask the letter writers to forgive the loans. Her mother refused. She said it was a matter of honor. Those people offered the money in good faith, and in good faith, her mother would return it to them.

"Dad was the one who lost those people's money, not you," Bethany would respond. Her sister was angry with their father, for many reasons, mostly because of his puzzling and untimely passing. "Are you going to spend the rest of your life paying for his sins?"

Her mother always had the same answer to give. "Bethany, your father didn't set out to hurt people. He got in way over his head and didn't know how to find a way out of it. He got desperate. That's why he made the decisions he made."

That answer didn't make any sense to Mim. Instead, she refused to think about her father. At least not about his passing. Everything about his death was complicated and illogical, and Mim liked logical and uncomplicated problems.

Besides, she had another pressing problem on her mind.

Mim had fallen in love. She did not fall in love quickly. She had been in love only 1.5 times. One time with an Irish boy named Patrick who had carrot red hair and worked at the library near Mim's old house. She thought that any boy who would work at a library must be a wonderful boy, even though Patrick had never noticed her. The .5 time was when she first laid eyes on Jimmy Fisher, whom Bethany called Mr. Irresistible in a sneering voice. He had made Mim breathless with his winks at church. When she discovered that he winked at all the girls, including the ancient ladies who lived in the Sisters' House, she reversed her feelings. That was the only logical thing to do.

But then she was seated next to Danny Riehl in school last August, and she knew her heart was in trouble. Danny Riehl was the smartest, nicest boy she had ever met. He knew more facts than anyone she had ever met. She watched Danny Riehl's long fingers curl around his book, one leg stretched out, one bent under the chair. She liked to hear him read aloud. He was at that age when a boy's voice was especially squeaky.

Today, Teacher M.K. had asked Mim and Danny to stay late and help her take old pictures off the wall and put up new ones. When they were done, Mim and Danny were in the coatroom, gathering their overcoats, hat and bonnet, and lunch containers. Mim felt she must say something. "My mother saw a shooting star streak across the sky."

Danny looked up in interest. Great interest. To her knowledge, he had never noticed or acknowledged Mim before that moment. "A few weeks ago? When there was a new moon?"

She nodded.

"It was a meteor."

Dumb, she thought with a sinking feeling in her stomach. Of course it was a meteor. She should know that. It was as obvious as saying that he had a black hat on. Or both his legs ended nicely below his trousers. She searched her mind for something better. "Astronauts can see the Great Wall of China from outer space."

He nodded. "It's the only man-made object that can be seen from the moon." Danny put on his jacket, then opened up his lunch cooler. Inside was a small mouse, quiet and friendly looking. "I found it in the schoolhouse. If Teacher M.K. had seen it, she would have whacked it senseless with her broom. I'm going to set it free in a field behind the schoolhouse." He looked at Mim. "Want to come?"

"Yes," Mim said before he could change his mind.

They walked to a farmer's field and Danny carefully set the mouse free near the base of a corn shock. It stayed in one place for a moment, whiskers quivering, before scurrying off. When it disappeared, he turned toward Mim. "What would you be, if you could be anything?"

Mim frowned. Was this a test? She saw an eagle circling over the pond and wondered if it was one of the eagles that had been buzzing around her farm, and if so, if it was the mister or the missus. "I suppose I might like to be an eagle." She shielded her eyes to watch the eagle soar in the sky. "They live for thirty years and like to eat fish best of all and their nests can weigh up to two tons. And they mate for life, which I think is terribly romantic." She cringed. *Oh no!* Why had she added that part about mating for life? Why couldn't she have just stopped at the nest part? It's actually true, she thought, that you could feel your own flush crawl up your neck.

But Danny didn't seem at all embarrassed. He nodded solemnly. "Do Luke and Sammy know those facts?"

"I have told them but I don't know if they listen."

"Sammy, probably."

"Yes. Sammy might be listening. Not Luke."

"Come on," Danny finally said, as if he had been deciding something. "I'll show you what I want to be."

Danny led Mim on a trail up a hill that framed one side of the lake. There was a telescope in a case, wrapped inside a big plastic trash bag, hidden in the branches of a tree. "This is a reflector telescope that my dad bought for me at a yard sale. We had to fix it up, but it's better to use a reflector than a refractor because it uses mirrors to reflect the light, instead of lenses."

Reflectors? Refractors? Mim had no idea what he was talking about.

Carefully, he unwrapped the telescope, set it on the ground, aimed the scope at the sky, and slipped in an eyepiece from a little velvet-lined box. "This is the best spot I've found for studying the planets. Usually I come at night, but lately I've been coming early in the morning. Looking for Saturn. It's just starting to be visible in the east. Since I keep my scope outside but covered, it remains the same temperature as the air. Otherwise the lens can get fuzzy."

He stepped away so she could look through the eyepiece. He had it centered on the thin moon, rising in the east. It was amazing to see it through a telescope—even in the daylight, she could see the faint tracing of the dark side of the moon.

"That's called earthshine," Danny said. "A few days after a new moon, when there's just a very slim crescent, you can sometimes see earthshine on the unilluminated portion of the moon. Earthshine is caused by sunlight reflected off the earth and onto the moon."

Fascinating facts! "I've never noticed earthshine before, but I've never looked through a telescope before, either."

"You can use binoculars. Beginning astronomers don't

realize they don't need an expensive telescope. Really, just a dark night and sharp eyes. You don't need much else."

She straightened. "Danny, do you want to be an astronomer?"

He pushed his glasses up the ridge of his nose. He hesitated, as if he was weighing whether he should admit something of such great importance. "No. I want to be an astronaut." He took off his hat. "Almost. I want to be almost-an-astronaut."

The sun had already begun to set by the time Mim parted ways with Danny and walked up the driveway. There had been a spurt of snow the day before, and a little of it lingered in shady places. It crunched under her feet as she approached the house.

Her mind was filled with the moon and school and facts. Mostly she thought about Danny, stargazer and mouse rescuer. Danny with the lovely blue eyes and the glasses that were held together at the hinges with a paper clip.

Mim stood outside her mother's room, watching her fold a mountain of laundry that was on top of her bed. Her sleeves were pushed up past her elbows, her curly brown hair wild around her face. By her mother's feet there were laundry baskets, one piled on top of another, clothes pouring out, one basket filled to the brim with socks.

"Ah! I see you there." Her mother smiled at her.

Ask me. Ask me about being in love. "Hello."

"You look as happy as Christmas morning," her mother said, turning her attention back to the laundry basket. "You must have had a good day at school."

Just as Mim opened her mouth to tell her about why it was a good day, about Danny Riehl and his telescope, a ringing bell sound floated up the stairs. Her grandmother needed something.

Her mother's shoulders slumped. "Mim, would you finish folding this laundry while I tend to Mammi Vera?" She tossed a crunchy sun-dried towel to Mim and hurried down the stairs.

Delia Stoltz didn't know which was worse: the discomfort and soreness from yesterday's lumpectomy, waiting to hear from the doctor if the margins were clear, or waking up fresh to the knowledge that her husband was gone and he would never come back. Her life would never be all right again.

Her bed felt huge and empty now, and when she slept, she did so with her arm around a pillow. She dreamed of Charles almost every night, sometimes good dreams of happy and joyful times; mostly, terrible dreams of abandonment, loss, and sorrow.

The phone rang and rang. All Delia Stoltz wanted was to be alone. She was sore from the lumpectomy. The only call she wanted was from Dr. Zimmerman's with the pathology report about the sentinel node biopsy—and don't expect that for a week or ten days, they had said. Why did it have to take so long? She tried to focus on the good news, that the cancer seemed to have been caught in early stages, and that the initial tests in the hospital looked like the lymph node was clear of cancer cells. But she knew enough to wait for results from the extensive testing before she could allow herself to feel relieved.

Each time the phone rang, she jumped. And each time it turned out to be someone other than the doctor, she became more and more irritable. Like now. Caller ID showed it to be Charles's office. She hadn't seen Charles since the day he left. He had called a few times, but she had never picked up her phone. The messages he left infuriated her—patronizing, with avuncular concern.

Slowly, she got up from the wing chair she'd been sitting in. The pain from the incision made her wince a little as she rose to her feet. In the kitchen, she filled the teakettle and put it on to boil. The phone rang again. Maybe Charles was finally feeling remorse and regret over his impulsive behavior. Maybe he wanted to come home. She hurried to the phone and picked it up without looking at Caller I.D. "Hello?"

"Hello, Mrs. Stoltz, I'm calling for Robyn Dixon." Robyn Dixon, Charles's attorney, daughter of Henry Dixon, who handled their living trust. Henry was semi-retired and had passed many of his clients on to Robyn. She was representing Charles in a malpractice suit, the first he had encountered in twenty-five years of neurosurgery. "Ms. Dixon would like you and Dr. Stoltz to meet her at the office tomorrow afternoon to go over some initial paperwork for the—"

"For the what?" *What did Charles want? A divorce?*

"Legal separation," she said. "Two o'clock, tomorrow afternoon. Do you know where the office is? Shall I send a car?"

To make sure I get there? "No. I can manage just fine."

Softer now, the assistant added, "Mrs. Stoltz, would you like to have your attorney present? I could call your attorney and set it up."

Delia swallowed. She thought Robyn Dixon *was* her attorney. "Yes. Please call Henry Dixon and tell him I will require his presence at tomorrow's meeting."

She could practically hear the whirl of confusion in the assistant's mind. "I'm not sure that would be appropriate—"

"My teakettle is whistling." Delia put the phone down on its cradle and stared at it for a long while.

The next day, just two days after the lumpectomy, it took Delia most of the morning to get ready for the two o'clock meeting. She wanted to look her best, her absolute best, and she was determined to keep Charles from learning of her surgery. She had warned Dr. Zimmerman's office to keep this private, and even had the surgery done using her maiden name, just to avoid any chance that someone might recognize her name and inform Charles. She had all kinds of feelings about Charles—deep anger, betrayal, even hatred. And love, yes, love. How could you shut that off after twenty-seven years? They had raised a wonderful child together. She didn't know what she wanted from Charles today, but not pity. Never pity.

She allowed herself an hour to get to Robyn Dixon's office and was grateful for the extra time when she noticed the fuel warning light for her gas tank. She sighed. She pulled into the gas station and stared at the pumps for a while, trying to figure out which buttons to push. As busy as Charles was, he had always taken care of these little things for her. He didn't want her to ever pump her own gas.

Suddenly it all seemed too much. Too much to deal with, too much to figure out on her own. She was trying her best to put up a brave front, but it was too hard. Everything was too painful. A tear rolled down her cheek.

Now she knew what she wanted out of this meeting today: she wanted Charles to stop this nonsense and come home. She didn't want a legal separation or a divorce. Tears came faster now, streaming down her cheeks, one after another after another. Her face would look red and puffy for this meeting. And she had worked so hard to look good today.

"Darlin', can I help you with something? Are you having trouble with that pump?" A woman fit the gas nozzle into

Delia's car and pushed the right button to start the fuel. Delia stared at her. She had sprigs of bright red hair jutting up from her head like a firecracker in mid-explosion. "My name's Lois."

Embarrassed, Delia swallowed back her tears. "I'm sorry. I've just had too much on my plate lately."

"Oh, I know how that can be. I surely do. About once a month, my Tony and me have to get out of the city and clear the cobwebs. We like to head over to Amish country and breathe some fresh air." She picked up the squeegee and started to wash down Delia's window, then squeegee the excess water off of it. Delia wondered if she might work here and if so, should she tip her? How much would be appropriate?

"Just last month," Lois continued, "we went to a wonderful new place in Stoney Ridge and met this darling Amish family and we just feel so renewed and refreshed. My Tony can't stop talking about that Amish gal's blueberry cornbread. We came home feeling like we'd gone to Hawaii. Good as new." She finished cleaning the window as the gas nozzle clicked. "I'm telling you, sugar. A trip to Lancaster County cures what ails you." She patted Delia's arm and turned to go.

Oh! So Lois was a customer. Delia stared at the gas nozzle as Lois's words sunk in.

Cured what ailed you? Renewed? Refreshed? Good as new? "Wait. Wait! Lois! Where did you say that Amish hotel was?"

Lois was getting into her car but popped her head back up, over the roof of the car. "Town is called Stoney Ridge, east of Lancaster. Off Route 30. Head to Main Street, turn right at the Sweet Tooth Bakery, drive a mile or so, and you can't miss it. Big white farmhouse with an even bigger red barn. A goat is in the front pasture and sticks his head over the fence.

Tell that little innkeeper—Rose Schrock is her name—that Tony and Lois sent you. She'll treat you right." Lois climbed in the car, then popped her head back up again. "If you get lost, stop at the Sweet Tooth Bakery and ask where Rose lives. Be sure to get a cinnamon roll. Don't miss that!" She waved goodbye and drove out of the gas station.

Delia got back in her car and glanced at the clock. One thirty. She drove to the attorney's office, parked under a shade tree, and took a moment to reapply her lipstick in the rearview mirror. Across the parking lot, she saw Charles's BMW pull in. She decided to wait until he went inside so she wouldn't appear slow moving as she got out of the car. If she moved too fast, she felt dizzy, or pinched by pain, or both. Delia saw Charles reach over and kiss someone, a passenger in the car, then he jumped out of the car and hurried to the passenger side to open the door for the woman. He was practically skipping, with a lilt in his step that she hadn't seen in years. When had he last opened her car door? She couldn't remember.

Out of the car stepped Robyn Dixon. The other woman.

Delia's heart felt like a jackhammer. She watched the two of them head into the office building, laughing together over something. Delia leaned her forehead against the steering wheel, trying to gather her thoughts, to pull herself together. She couldn't do it. She couldn't go to that meeting. She felt as if she might hyperventilate or have a coronary episode or have a seizure. Or all three. She started the car, drove out of the parking lot, stopped by the bank and withdrew as much cash as the ATM would permit, then headed west on I-76 to Lancaster County.

6

For a few days, Rose and the children were all a-flurry, setting things right in the basement, turning it into a cozy place. With everyone helping, the basement began to look like a real home. Sammy and Luke tumbled in and out, underfoot, but every time they got near, Rose gave them a chore.

Rose could hardly believe the transformation. It smelled different, looked different. She went around all the windowsills with a wet rag and then . . . it was ready for the first guest. Whenever, whoever, that might be. No one had stayed with them since the fellow who didn't like the sounds of cows mooing in the morning. Rose felt a spike of worry, that all of this effort to create an inn would be for naught, but then she dismissed those doubts. Already, this venture was bringing the family together. Why, for that matter, the neighborhood too. Galen and Naomi had gone the extra mile for them. Good was coming out of it. God always had a plan, she reminded herself.

After she finished dusting, Rose walked through the rooms. She needed to get sheets on the beds, towels in the bathroom, maybe a few calendars to hang on the walls. She turned in a circle and felt an inside-out excitement. She said a prayer over each room, asking God to fill it with his chosen guests—those who needed rest and refreshment. In his time.

Rose heard the boys shrieking outside, chasing each other. She was just about to tell them to stop acting like wild Indians when they disappeared. She closed the door to the basement, thinking about how she needed a different name than the basement. What was it Galen called it? A flat? Yes, that was it. She liked that idea, because it was flat. A guest flat.

A car pulled into the driveway and came to a stop. Ever so slowly, a woman opened the door and eased out. Rose stood at the window a minute studying her, wondering if she was lost and needed directions. She was tall and elegant, with pale hair pulled back in a bun. She wore dark sunglasses, but Rose could see that her features were fine, delicate. Suddenly the boys were back, whooping and hollering like they were being chased by a swarm of yellow jackets. Rose went out and shooed the boys away before she turned her attention to the driver of the car.

"By any chance are you Rose Schrock?" the woman asked, pulling her sunglasses off her face.

"Yes. Yes, that's me." Rose took a step closer. Something about the abject relief in the woman's face spiked concern in Rose. "Are you all right?"

"I'd like to book a room at your hotel."

Oh. *Oh!* A guest. A guest! "Well, I need to get fresh sheets on the bed, but then you would have the entire base—flat—to yourself. How long did you want to stay?"

The woman looked at the setting sun. "I have absolutely no idea."

As Delia Stoltz got out of the car, she suddenly heard shrieks of laughter, and a little boy flew around the corner of the house, another slightly taller boy in hot pursuit. The boy in the lead ran to one of the sheds between the house and the barn and tried to hide in it, but his brother caught him before he could get inside, and they tusseled and shrieked. The older boy was trying to put something down the younger boy's shirt and finally succeeded, at which point the smaller boy began to hop up and down while the older one ran off, laughing.

The mother, Rose Schrock, appeared out of the basement to the house. She wore a plum-colored dress and a matching apron and had a stack of sheets in her hands. Clearly out of temper, she yelled something in another language at the two boys, who immediately stopped their shrieking, looked at one another, and slowly approached her. Rose addressed herself to the older boy, who made some excuse, and the younger boy, in his own defense, pointed back toward the shed. She listened a minute and began to talk rapidly in a low voice, too low for Delia to hear. She was giving her sons the what for, Delia supposed.

At first Delia hesitated. If the woman were the quick-tempered type, perhaps she should get back in the car and leave. The last thing she needed right now was a woman out of temper. But as Delia watched her, she found she couldn't stop looking at her. Her eyes flashed as she lectured her sons, neither of whom was taking the lecture silently—both were trying to talk back, but Rose Schrock didn't pause to listen. She had abundant brown hair tucked into a bun, covered with a thin organza cap, though the bun had partly come loose in little ringlets around the nape of her neck. Her eyes were gray and warm, fringed by dark lashes and framed by dark eyebrows. She was quite pretty, without a stitch of makeup.

The boys looked around and became aware for the first time that a stranger had come. They instantly stopped fidgeting and stood like statues.

"Pardon the commotion," Rose Schrock said with a smile. "We're a noisy crowd. So you aren't sure how long you'll be staying?"

"If that's all right," Delia said. "I don't want to trouble you."

Rose only laughed. "You don't look like the type to trouble anybody. We grow our own troubles—it would be a novelty to have some we aren't already used to. These are my sons, Luke and Sammy." She reached for Delia's hand. "Why don't you come inside?"

A moment or two later, Delia watched Rose put fresh sheets on the bed and plump the pillows. Delia thought it was strange that she didn't ask for any money or registration information. She showed Delia how to turn the lanterns on and off, and the pilot light on the stove.

When Rose went up to the house and Delia was alone in this sparsely furnished . . . basement! . . . panic rose. She hadn't thought this through. She had a toothbrush in her purse, of course, who didn't? She had a change of clothing in her gym bag, kept in the trunk of the car. But that was all. No nightgown. No face cream. Not even a book to read.

Maybe she should go back to Philadelphia. She could leave some cash on the nightstand and leave. She heard a knock on the door and Rose popped her head in again. "I noticed that you didn't have much luggage, and thought that maybe something had happened to your things. So, I brought a few items for you." In her arms was a nightgown, a *Farmer's Journal* magazine, a spare toothbrush and toothpaste, and a hairbrush. She lowered her voice. "I included some ladies' unmentionables." Color filled her cheeks, and her voice dropped. "Just in case you might have forgotten to pack some."

Mouthwatering aromas wafted down from the house. Delia's stomach rumbled. She hadn't eaten much today.

A big yellow dog came bursting through the door and hurried over to sniff Delia.

"That's Chase," Rose said. "He's a good friend and companion."

Delia looked at the dog. "Is he named Chase because he chases squirrels?"

"No. Because he chases his tail."

The big dog watched Delia. It took a few steps forward, sat on its haunches, and lifted a paw as if it was saying hello to Delia. She tentatively reached out to shake its paw. It was the oddest thing—there was a look in this dog's soulful eyes as if he knew Delia was hurting and felt empathy for her. What an absurd thought!

"Oh, you've passed the test. He likes you. You must have a knack for pets."

Delia had never had a pet. Why did it suddenly seem as if she had missed something? "I'm afraid not." Her son had always wanted a dog but Charles refused. He said that he'd had enough animal rearing in his childhood to last a lifetime. A slight smile tugged at Delia's lips. It was ironic that Will was going to be a vet—not a neurosurgeon like Charles had planned for him to be. She had never told Will, but she had been a little disappointed by his decision too. She had hoped he would follow in Charles's footsteps. After shaking this big dog's paw, she felt a glimmer of understanding of something Will talked about—that when an animal knew you, you felt some kind of special connection to it.

Already, Delia's life was changing. She was changing. Her stomach tightened. She had never liked change, and here she was faced with overwhelming change.

A knock at the door startled Delia.

Rose looked over at the door. "That's my daughter, Mim, bringing some dinner down to you. Just in case you haven't eaten."

Tears pricked Delia's eyes. How long had it been since someone had fussed over her? Maybe she would stay one night. Just one. She put down her purse. "Thank you, Rose. For everything."

After Rose and Mim set dinner up, they left. Delia sank down in a chair at the table. It was after six and she was hungry, exhausted, and sore. She ate like she hadn't eaten in days. Afterward, she took a long hot bath, climbed into bed with the *Farmer's Journal*, and listened to the peculiar sound of buggy horses as they clip-clopped along the asphalt road. It was so quiet here, so strangely quiet. Tomorrow, or maybe the next day, she would decide what she needed to do next. For now, she was right where she needed to be. She had no doubt of that. In the middle of an article about raising feeder pigs, she fell into a dreamless sleep.

Bethany didn't know what to make of the newest guest in the farmhouse basement. The lady drove up in a fancy car and went straight to bed. Three days had passed and she still lay there. Mim said she spoke in the manner of a British queen.

"Am I to presume you are Miriam?" the lady had asked her when they first met, shaking her hand. She said everything about the lady was stylish and expensive.

Rose brought meals to her and tried to keep the boys away from playing near the basement windows. She said that it was obvious the woman needed a good rest and that was the least they could give her.

Well, that lady could sleep all she wanted, but Bethany did suggest to Rose that she ask for room payment up front, just in case the lady expired in her sleep. "It happens, you know," she whispered to Rose. "I heard about it at work. A maid walked into a hotel room to clean it and there was a dead body. Just lying there. Decomposing."

Rose laughed. "Delia Stoltz isn't dying. She's just . . . I don't know what. She's worn out. And she's here for a reason. The Lord brought her to us. He has a plan."

That was just like Rose—always attributing unexplained events to God's sovereignty. Bethany believed in God, how could she not? But there were a lot of things that happened in life that were just . . . bad. She didn't think it was fair to blame God for a person's bad choices, bad decisions. Take her father's final choice, for example. That certainly wasn't God's fault.

Then whose fault was it? Bethany didn't know. Mammi Vera blamed Rose for his death, but that wasn't right and it wasn't fair. Bethany didn't know what would have become of them without her stepmother. Rose was taking care of her father's cranky mother, she was looking after his children, and she was determined to pay back all of her father's debts, one by one.

Bethany was doing all she could to help. It was the least she could do for Rose. Before she and Jake got married.

She heard a horse and buggy come up the drive. Curious, she wiped her hands on a rag and peeked out the window. Why, it was that audacious, flirtatious Jimmy Fisher. Bethany quickly looked in the washstand mirror Rose had left on the kitchen counter. She pinched her cheeks and bit on her lips to give them a little blush, smoothed back her hair, and hurried outside.

Jimmy jumped out of the buggy when he saw her. "Well, well, hello there."

"I don't know why you act so surprised," Bethany said. "You know I live here."

"I haven't seen you at the market in a while and thought I'd stop by. I was passing through."

"Passing from where to where?"

"From there to here." He grinned. "I have a little side job for Amos Lapp, down the road. Snow geese are causing damage to his winter wheat field. If they're left alone, they'll leave a bare spot of wheat several acres in size."

Bethany had heard about them. Thousands of snow geese had been wintering in a wildlife area of Stoney Ridge.

Luke and Sammy appeared out of nowhere, wide-eyed. "You gonna shoot all them birds?"

"Nope," Jimmy said. "There's a limit to the amount a fellow can shoot." He bent down to the boys' height. "I'm gonna set some firecrackers and flush them out."

The boys let out a whoop. "Think it'll work?"

"Will a frog hop?" Jimmy stood and wiggled his eyebrows at Bethany. "I'm known far and wide for my pyrotechnical skills."

How could he say something so ridiculous? Why was she even listening to him?

"Speaking of work," Jimmy said, "I came by to let you know I've heard of a job opening. A good one." He lowered his voice. "One that does not require the art of deception." His eyebrows hopped up and down.

"Where?" she asked.

"The Sisters' House." He took in Bethany's confused look and explained. "Not too far from here. You would know them from church. They're a bunch of elderly sisters, living together. They need a little extra help and I thought of you."

She knew those old sisters at church. Everybody did. They sat in the front row, looking like a chain of cutout dolls in their starched white prayer caps and matching dresses, all of them nodding off during the second sermon.

Still, Bethany hesitated. "What kind of help?"

"Get their house organized. It's a little cluttered up."

Organizing a bunch of little old ladies? She saw herself carrying out chamber pots and hanging wet sheets to dry. And what if they were all cranky like Mammi Vera could be? Older people often got cranky.

He winked. "Gotta strike while the iron's hot, if you know what I mean."

She didn't. This fellow's winking and eyebrow wiggling was scandalous. She had never met anyone as bold and coarse and outrageous as Jimmy Fisher.

Luke pulled on Jimmy's sleeve. "Are you gonna blow up them birds?"

"I'm not blowing up anything. I'm just trying to scare those birds out of Amos Lapp's wheat field. He wouldn't even let me take a single shot at them. Said they're too beautiful to eat. I might disagree, but I always respect my employer's wishes."

"Can we come with you to watch the firecrackers?" Luke asked. Sammy nodded.

Jimmy looked at Bethany. "Sure, if it's okay with your big sister. It's quite a sight to see all those geese take to the sky at one time."

"I suppose they can go." She glared at the two boys. "As long as they promise to stay out of your way."

"Maybe you'd like to come too. It won't take too long. We could talk about your new employment at the Sisters' House." There was more eyebrow wiggling.

Bethany wondered if Jimmy Fisher suffered from facial tics. Or Tourette's syndrome? She had seen someone with Tourette's once, over at the Stoney Ridge Bar & Grill. But that particular fellow swore like a sailor and he didn't wiggle his eyebrows.

She decided she should go along, just to keep the boys in check.

Rose didn't know where the boys had gone, or Bethany either. She was moving the goat and the sheep from the far pasture toward the pen attached to the barn. She waved to Galen, who was exercising a horse in a fenced paddock. A strange sound, like the steady rat-a-tat of a drumbeat, filled the air. The goat and the sheep started to bolt, splitting off into different directions. Galen's horse reacted nervously, rearing and running in the paddock. Chase barked frantically, trying to get the animals into the pen. Then the air was filled with honking geese.

Galen ran over to help Rose gather the goat and sheep. "Are you all right?" He scooped up one of the stray ewes in his arms like it was a bag of potatoes and carried it into the pen.

"Yes," she said, shielding her eyes against the setting sun, watching the geese overhead. "Just surprised. What was that noise?"

"Sounded like gunshots." Galen closed the pen latch and turned to face her. "I'll help you get those sheep to market this spring."

Rose cringed. "I just can't do it. They've become pets for the boys."

Galen looked at her with that slightly amused look he often gave her, as if he wondered if she might be a little dotty.

"I'm thinking about shearing them, though, and selling the wool."

"To whom?"

"I haven't planned that far," Rose said honestly. "Seems like every time I make a plan, something happens to change it."

"Well, life's a twisting stream."

Most wouldn't think to hear such quiet philosophizing out of Galen, but she had come to expect it. Luke and Sammy galloped down the driveway. "You wouldn't believe it, Mom!" Sammy said. "Hundreds and dozens of snow geese flew in the air! A couple fell to the ground. Jimmy Fisher said it was easier than shooting fish in a barrel."

"What type of gun did Jimmy use to shoot the geese?" Galen asked.

"He didn't!" Luke said. "He used firecrackers! He thought the ones that fell to the ground died of sheer fright. My eagles came flying around to see what was going on." Luke spread out his arms and soared around the barnyard.

Galen frowned. "Doesn't that boy realize how dangerous it is to set off firecrackers at this time of day? Livestock is feeding. Why, your mother was practically trampled by the sheep."

Trampled? There were only five sheep. But Rose thought it was kind of Galen to remind the boys to show concern. Those two little boys needed constant reminding.

Galen looked at Sammy. "Where is Jimmy Fisher now?"

"He's on his way home with Bethany," Sammy said.

"With two geese!" Luke added. "Mom, he's bringing them to you to cook for dinner."

Rose's spirits lifted. "A goose delivery? It's too late to start for tonight, but maybe I'll cook it for Sunday supper."

"Jimmy said he'd dress them for you," Sammy said. "And guess what else? We saw the eagles carrying branches in their talons. We think they're building a nest in the big tree up there." He pointed to the very tree, high on the hillside, that Rose liked to sit under some mornings to greet the dawn.

Rose shielded her eyes and looked up. There, in the dead branches of the oak tree, was the start of a big mess of sticks. "Well, I'll be." She turned to Galen. "An aerie. Right here. Wouldn't that be something? To have a bald eagle pair choose this very farm for their home?"

Galen's gaze turned to one of the eagles, bringing in sticks to the tree. "It'd be a pity for us all."

"You may call it a pity, but I'll call it a blessing," Rose said. "Think of all the publicity the inn might get. Why, this could be very good for business."

Galen frowned. "You might be changing your mind when folks set up telescopes to gawk at the eagles after the game commissioner tapes off your property."

"I would still feel blessed that an eagle couple had sensed that this farm would be a good place to raise their young."

Galen lifted his eyebrows, as if he didn't know what to make of that. "Tell Jimmy Fisher I want to talk to him before he heads home," he said before he slipped back through the hole in the privet.

Luke and Sammy exchanged a look. "Jimmy's in trouble," Luke whispered.

For three days, Delia had stayed in her nightgown, mostly in bed. Rose's daughters, with anxious faces, brought meals on a tray down the stairs. Delia tried to appear calm and reassuring to them, but inside she felt that she had lost the will to live.

Last evening Rose asked her if she needed a doctor, because there was a very nice doctor in town who made house calls, but Delia assured her that she just needed some rest. So Rose refilled her mug of tea and promised to do a better job of keeping the boys shouting distance away from the basement.

Rose must be a restful person to live with, Delia thought. The farm was a restful place. She had been lucky to meet red-haired Lois at the gas station and find this place.

It felt so strange, so troubling, that she could not sleep well. She lay down, slept and woke, slept and woke, disturbed each time by foolish dreams. She dozed for a few minutes now and then, because when she opened her eyes, she remembered shreds and pieces of disjointed, implausible dreams. Then she would be wide awake. These senseless dreams came from being overtired. She had heard on *Oprah* once that dreams are never really senseless, that if you take the disjointed sections apart and rearrange them properly, they will make sense. She decided that was foolish fodder.

This afternoon, Delia stood at the window and watched ordinary people do ordinary things. Rose's eldest daughter had come back from work, a handsome fellow had stopped by in a buggy to pay a call on her, those two little boys with small black hats ran back and forth from barn to house and back to barn. Those two looked like they were always up to something. Every once in a while, Rose would call to the boys from the house, but it seemed to Delia like trying to herd cats.

She watched Amish men and women drive past the lane in buggies or zoom on the road in those odd-looking scooters. These were people with families—men, women, and children who lived normal lives. Their hearts were not heavy with anxiety as hers was. They knew what each new day was going to bring, while she had no idea what was going to happen. She envied them, their sense of security. She didn't think she would ever feel secure again. How could life change so quickly?

One morning, you woke up on a sunny winter day, happy, your mind filled with nothing weightier than the thought of where to have lunch with your friend or what to cook for dinner. And then a conversation began, or the telephone rang, or the lab report arrived, and everything you thought you knew for certain was suddenly called into question.

Tomorrow would be Sunday. Rose had brought her a handwritten list of churches in the area, gently suggesting that Delia might want to consider going. She looked over the list and saw one for the denomination she belonged to in Philadelphia.

After Will was born, Delia and Charles used to go to church each week. Delia had insisted that they provide Will with some kind of spiritual foundation. Charles didn't object, nor did he ever get involved. Over the years, Charles accompanied them less and less. At first, there was always a reason—an emergency at the hospital, an out-of-town conference. Then the excuses stopped and he just admitted he was tired and needed a morning to relax. Delia kept going until Will became a teen and started to object too. He said the youth group kids were weird. Charles insisted that Delia not force Will to attend church if he didn't want to. So she didn't. Naturally, Will slept in on Sunday mornings. And then Delia stopped going too.

She heard the faint buzz of a saw from a neighboring farm and remembered when she and Charles were first married, how the two of them would work together, fixing up their first house. They had loved each other back then, passionately and thoroughly. They enjoyed each other's company. She wondered what had happened to make it end. Life, she supposed. A child, busyness, schedules. And there was Charles's success. She knew she was the envy of her friends, of everyone in town. She wanted for nothing. But success had a price too. Loneliness. Charles was hardly home, and when he was, he was very distracted and distant.

A few months ago, just as they had sat down to Thanksgiving dinner, Charles was called away on an emergency. That wasn't unusual, but Delia felt so let down, more than she typically did. Will had told her not to be disappointed—it was easier without Charles. He was right. She and Will had a wonderful evening together—watching old movies and eating so much until they couldn't move from the couch.

Still, it saddened her that Charles missed so much. Will wasn't home very often and who knew where he would land after he graduated from vet school? His concentration on ornithology was very rare. He had offers from the states of Florida and Alaska. An organization in Europe had showed interest too. Who knew where he might land? All she knew for certain was that their days together as a family were coming to an end.

When Will decided to go to Cornell for vet school after college, Delia's loneliness became more acute. She'd been hoping he'd attend graduate school closer to home, someplace where he could come home for holidays or drop by on weekends. Now she was almost relieved that he lived so far away, too far to get caught in the complications of dismantling a marriage.

She wondered what would happen to her friendships if Charles divorced her. She remembered a woman named Carla whose husband had left her for a younger woman. Everyone dropped Carla like a hot potato, as if she suddenly carried a contagion that threatened to infect their own marriages. Delia, included. How stupid of her. How uncaring.

She also felt betrayed, bereft, heartbroken, abandoned, all those emotions she'd imagined women must feel when their husbands walked out on them. She was so sure she would never, ever be one of those women—but here she was, in Carla's shoes. And just like Carla, she had never seen it coming.

A wave of exhaustion hit Delia. As she eased back onto the bed, she considered calling Charles, but she was afraid if she phoned, he would be angry that she hadn't come to the lawyer's meeting and then she would cry. She refused to cry one more tear over this failed marriage.

Soon, she should call the doctor's office for a follow-up visit, to see if her pathology report was in. But what if it was bad news? What if the cancer had spread? That news could wait. She didn't think she could handle anything more right now.

She told herself she didn't care, anyway.

7

Bethany was horrified when Rose invited Jimmy Fisher to come over for a big goose dinner on Sunday. Never mind that he had provided the geese, dressed them too. Yesterday afternoon, after Jimmy had returned from his talk with Galen, he was cheerful as ever and set to work butchering the geese. Bethany couldn't get her head around that—everyone was sure Galen would chew him out for setting off those fire-crackers, but Jimmy came back acting like he was having the best day a man could have. When the boys asked what Galen wanted with him, Jimmy only said that Galen preferred to volunteer what he wanted you to know.

As Jimmy butchered the geese, he found the stomachs full of wheat, even their throats, almost to their beaks. The boys couldn't stop talking about it. The whole topic turned Bethany's stomach, which only amused Jimmy Fisher.

She did *not* trust that boy with the blue, blue eyes. She was just waiting for Jimmy to spill the beans that she worked at the Stoney Ridge Bar & Grill and wore English clothes. She knew he was holding it over her head, acting smug, like he'd got the best of her.

Rose had invited Naomi and Galen for the goose dinner. The strange lady in the basement too. Somehow Rose had convinced that lady to try going to church in the morning—which she did—and to come for the goose dinner when she returned. Bethany figured Rose wanted to try to get that lady out of bed.

Around one in the afternoon, the guests arrived at the house, acting quiet and uncomfortable. Except for Jimmy, who didn't have enough sense to know how awkward the situation was; Galen, who didn't speak much and kept to himself; a depressed English lady; a grandmother who got the hiccups if she had a fit; a little sister who spouted off facts; and two brothers who couldn't sit still. At least Bethany had sweet Naomi to talk to.

Rose didn't seem to realize it was an awkward collection of people, either. She welcomed everyone in as if they were family. She gave them jobs to do to help get dinner on the table—Jimmy and Galen brought chairs in from the other room, Delia cut carrots for the salad, Mim set the table, Bethany and Naomi made biscuits while Rose made gravy.

All this bustle made Mammi Vera, seated at the kitchen table, frown with disapproval. She complained that Rose was always telling people what to do, but the truth was, everyone relaxed when they had tasks. Soon, there was cheerful conversation and banter going on. Rose was able to do that—to create that kind of atmosphere. Why couldn't Mammi Vera see that?

When Rose pulled the roasting geese out of the oven, Naomi breathed in the scent and thanked Jimmy Fisher for providing such a good dinner. It hadn't occurred to Bethany to thank him. Sometimes, she wished the Lord would just knock her over with sweetness and goodness, because she didn't seem to be getting the knack of it on her own.

"You wash up good, boys," Rose said to Luke and Sammy as they burst through the door. "I'm going to civilize you if it's the last thing I do."

"Civilize them?" Mammi Vera said. "They need so much more than civilizing."

Rose ignored that remark and steered Delia to a chair at the table. As everyone found their seats, Galen moved to the head of the table.

"That's Dean's place!" Mammi Vera said, her voice as shrill as a penny whistle. Galen froze, midair. He was the last to sit down; there were no other available chairs.

"Galen, you just sit right down and don't give it another thought," Rose said, frowning at Mammi Vera.

"She's getting more and more like a dictator," Mammi Vera muttered to no one in particular.

"Yes, but a benevolent dictator," Rose answered, tying napkins around the boys' necks, for all the good it would do. After the silent prayer ended, a flurry of activity began. Rose began to carve the geese.

Luke sniffed appreciatively. "Do I get a leg?"

"Here you go. But save the wing for your brother." Rose served him and passed the platter of goose meat as Bethany passed the gravy.

"The gravy would be better if it had more substance," Mammi Vera said, peering into the gravy bowl. "Next time, add a little more flour."

"The goose is cooked just right," Jimmy Fisher said cheerfully.

Mammi Vera sniffed. "It's passable."

Bethany's discomfort had taken a new turn. What must Jimmy Fisher think of them? The boys' stomachs were grumbling unpleasantly as they tore into their meal. They were practically inhaling their food; their stomachs were bottomless pits. Their plates began to look like graveyards of bones. Mammi Vera made caustic comments every chance she could, and Mim used a finger to capture the absolute last drop of honey that dripped off her biscuit. She reached out to kick Mim in the shin.

"Ooph!" Galen, sitting next to Mim, grimaced in pain. Bethany had kicked the wrong person. She kept her eyes lowered, suddenly fascinated by what was on her plate.

Mim, oblivious, looked up. "Does everyone know that honey is the world's purest food?"

Her sister was always spouting off odd facts. Bethany had heard enough details on the subject to have already forgotten more than most people ever know about the properties of honey. "Yes, we all know that, Mim," she said, to cut short the talk of honey.

"I didn't," Jimmy Fisher piped up.

"Mammi, you have some food on your chin." Bethany reached over to wipe her grandmother's chin with her napkin.

Luke reached out and grabbed a biscuit, then another.

"Do not bolt your food, Luke," Bethany whispered. "Teeth are quite useful for chewing." He was half wild, was Luke. Boys were.

Luke stuffed a biscuit in his mouth and talked around it. "Sammy and I are starting a business. Renting sheep. To make money."

Galen tried, unsuccessfully, to swallow a grin. "Now, tell me what exactly can a sheep be taught to do?"

"Mow grass, for one," Sammy said. "Warn you about snakes and coyotes and wolves."

"And they can add fertilizer while they're working," Jimmy said. "No extra charge."

Vera let out a cackle of a laugh, like the sound a hen might make if the hen were mad about something.

Luke turned to Galen. "A good sheep can be trained. I could train one to bring your mail up to your house."

"Why not just train the goat?" Galen said. "He spends more time at my place than yours anyhow."

Luke and Sammy looked at each other. "We could rent the goat!" Luke said. He turned to Galen. "Want to be our first customer?"

"I'll give it some thought. I'm pretty busy now, though, with buggy training a green batch of Thoroughbreds. Jimmy is going to start working for me. Starting Monday." Galen glanced at Jimmy. "Early."

Sammy's face lit up. "Jimmy, you'll be able to come by here every day!"

Jimmy Fisher did that crazy up-down eyebrow wiggling at Bethany and she felt a flush creep up her neck.

"Rose, have you thought of giving a handle to your bed-and-breakfast?" Galen said.

"Like what?" Mim said.

"What about Eagle Hill?"

Everyone stilled. It was Delia Stoltz who volunteered that suggestion. She had been so quiet during dinner, they had practically forgotten she was there.

"Why, Eagle Hill is a fine name, Delia," Rose said. "A wonderful choice."

"It is *my* farm," Vera added, her feathers ruffled. "Everyone seems to forget that."

"Every farm needs a name," Rose said.

Vera turned to Rose and narrowed her eyes.

"Now you're taking over my farm. I can't imagine what's next. Maybe you'll be the first woman bishop of Stoney Ridge."

And a silence like cold, still air filled the kitchen.

Bethany could see Rose look at Vera for a moment, holding her peace.

Then Rose laughed and the tension was broken. "No, I don't have aspirations to be a bishop, Vera. I'm having enough trouble with this tribe of wild Indians, right here."

Bethany exhaled. Rose had a way of defusing a difficult situation; she never failed.

Vera sat there, sulky.

Bethany knew that look on her grandmother's face. It was time to take action, before something worse happened. "Come, Mammi Vera," Bethany said as she jumped up to help her grandmother rise to her feet. "You've been sitting all day. It's bad for your circulation. You have to get up and walk around." She caught Jimmy looking at her, then quickly away, as if she had caught him at something. She glanced around the table. "We'll be out on the porch if you need us. Mammi needs fresh air."

It was no great surprise to Rose to hear those kinds of remarks come out of her mother-in-law. Rose knew Vera wasn't in favor of creating an inn in the basement, but she also knew Vera wasn't in a position to make decisions about the farm's future. She had no understanding of the dire financial situation they were in. She had always turned a deaf ear and blind eye to any talk or news about Schrock Investments and acted as if it was all too complicated for her.

Rose felt a flash of annoyance, most of it with herself. When Vera insinuated she was taking over the farm, she couldn't disagree. Somebody had to steer this ship before it sank. Sometimes, she felt as if she had turned into another person, as if someone else walked around in her shoes. But the hardness Vera referred to was a result of dealing with the mess Dean had left behind.

As she dried the last dinner dishes and put them away, she hung the wet rag over the faucet and went to the window to see what was going on in the yard. Galen and Jimmy had the boys and Mim engaged in a game of horseshoes. Bethany and Naomi's capped heads were together, talking earnestly. Vera was resting in her room. Delia sat on the porch step in the sunshine, head bent back, watching the sky. What was she looking at? Soon, Rose figured it out. Some kind of noisy drama in a tree. She watched one of the eagles descend like an arrow into the tree, and a flock of birds blasted into the air, filling it with strident, high-pitched squawking.

Eagle Hill was a fine name for the farm. No matter what Galen had said about the game commissioner and people nosing around, she considered it a blessing that an eagle couple had chosen it for their nest. She walked out to join Delia on the porch step. On the western horizon, the sun was a crimson orb, sinking into the treetops.

"The big one is Mrs. Eagle," she said to Delia. "The smaller one is the mister."

Delia had smiled at that and Rose felt pleased. Just as pleased that Delia had agreed to come for dinner, though she didn't say much and she didn't eat much—she just nibbled at her food.

"What kind of eagles are they?"

"See their white heads? That's how you know they're bald eagles. They're a threatened species in Pennsylvania. Thankfully, they're no longer an endangered species. It's a wonderful comeback story. Things can get good again."

Rose smiled and Delia gave her a curious look.

"Someday, I hope to get a porch swing out here," Rose said. "Seems like porch swings are just as good for grown-ups as they are for children."

Rose and Delia watched the eagles dip and dart above the row of pines that lined one edge of the driveway. A whole dancing flock of birds disappeared, dark little dots against the sky.

"I hope you don't mind me saying that your mother-in-law is a ball of fire," Delia said.

Rose burst out laughing. "I don't mind at all. You're right. And she hasn't been well lately. It's made her an even hotter ball of fire."

"Your eldest daughter is very patient with her. Goodness, she reminds me of an Egyptian servant girl, all but fanning your mother-in-law with palm fronds."

Rose smiled. This, to Rose, was Bethany's greatest gift— her patience and kindheartedness to Vera. Bethany was always showing care to Vera in special ways: giving her shampoos, rubbing lotion into her crepe-papery arms and legs, asking her questions about her life as a little girl. No wonder Vera adored her.

Delia brushed off her trousers. "Didn't you go to church today?"

"It was an off Sunday," Rose said. "We have church every two weeks. A good day for a big goose dinner." She looked over at Delia. "I saw your car leave this morning. Did you go to church in town?"

"I did."

That was all she had to say and Rose didn't want to push her.

Delia stood up to leave. "Thank you for including me today."

"I'm glad you came. We can be a noisy crowd."

"Yes, but you're a noisy crowd of love," Delia answered.

To Rose's surprise, she suddenly felt Galen listening to their conversation. Not just watching, but listening. When she turned her head and saw his eyes, she thought she caught a glint of something—amusement? Pity? She couldn't tell.

It had to be admitted that Rose Schrock set a fine table. Naomi had been the one to accept the supper invitation of those two little rapscallions who came flying through the hedge to rap on the door. Galen wouldn't ordinarily have done it, but then his life was no longer ordinary.

He barely walked in from feeding the stock when Naomi met him at the door with a fresh shirt and told him to clean up, because the neighbors were expecting them. He knew she was enamored by the Schrock girls, especially the eldest one, Bethany. Galen didn't see the need for friends, but he understood that Naomi had a different point of view. "Hurry, hurry, hurry," she said, bossing him around like he was a child and she was the parent.

Next thing he knew, they were on their way to the Schrocks'. No sooner had they arrived, and Naomi and Bethany had put their heads together and twittered like little chickens.

Galen was relieved to see Jimmy Fisher, his new apprentice, at the house. Jimmy talked such a blue streak that Galen hoped he wouldn't be expected to say much.

A month or so ago, Deacon Abraham had dropped by to ask Galen if he might consider taking Jimmy under his wing.

"And why would I do that?" Galen had asked him. He knew Jimmy Fisher, had known him for years. He was known as a fellow with a fondness for the ladies.

"I'm worried about the boy," Abraham had explained. "He's at a crossroads and I'm not sure he knows it." Jimmy's mother, Edith, had gone to visit her cousin in Gap while she happened to be in an off period in her on-again, off-again courtship with Hank Lapp. She met a widower in Gap and up and married him. Jimmy's brother, Paul, was finally engaged and would be taking over the family chicken and egg business. "Jimmy Fisher is a boy with a lot of potential, none of it realized."

"Why me?" Galen had asked.

"Haven't you seen that boy's love of horses? If you could give the boy some training, shape him, give him discipline, why, Jimmy Fisher might just amount to something."

It took Galen quite a long time to get his head around the thought of taking on an apprentice. Especially Jimmy Fisher. But you didn't say no to the deacon.

Galen had plenty of misgivings. Then he found out Jimmy had used firecrackers to flush out the snow geese from a wheat field and felt the first hint of interest in the boy. Most of Galen's work with horses was to train hot-blooded, just-off-the-track Thoroughbreds to buggy work, and that included desensitizing them to the unexpected. An apprentice who knew about firecrackers might be useful—assuming Jimmy Fisher had enough sense to know when and when not to use them. That was his main worry about Jimmy Fisher. Did the boy have *any* sense? Until Galen had confidence in him, Jimmy would be carefully supervised.

When he was seated at the Schrock table, Galen was faced with more choices to eat than he had seen on a table for quite some time. His gaze swept down the table and stopped at Rose.

"This is my vermin stew, Galen," Rose said, dishing a spoonful of vegetables for him.

"Oh?" he said politely. "What kind of vermin?"

Rose didn't miss a beat. "Whatever the boys caught today in their traps."

"It was a polecat," one of the little boys said. He seemed as full of mischief as his mother.

"Now, Luke, don't be giving away my recipes," she said.

"I happen to love polecat," Galen said, trying hard to be sociable. It was an unfamiliar labor, since he mostly worked at avoiding it. But he knew Naomi would be giving him the what for if he didn't at least try to be friendly. Besides, she had promised they could leave as soon as dinner ended.

He thought it might have ended abruptly at that awkward moment when Vera snapped at Rose and called her a future bishop. Vera Schrock was known to salt her speech rather freely with criticism. There was nothing hard about Rose—in fact, it was obvious to him that she was far too soft for what she had to cope with. She had tender expressions when she looked at her children, or at the stable of animals she kept. She could never quite get a lock of hair to stay fixed, and was always touching it nervously with one hand. "It won't behave," she would say, as if her hair were a child.

After dinner ended, Galen didn't get to his feet right away. The sense that he needed to hurry, which had been with him most of his life, had disappeared for a space.

8

The next day, Monday, responsibility descended upon Jimmy Fisher with a weight far beyond anything he had ever felt. He wondered what had possessed him to agree to work for Galen King, of all people, though he knew the answer to that. The work ethic of the Plain people was legendary, but Galen took it to another level. He never stopped working. He was a single-track man, all business. Jimmy held to a more leisurely philosophy about work.

Most people in the church were intimidated by Galen, but not Jimmy. Galen was perceived as a little unusual. He didn't say much, didn't socialize much, had a skill for avoiding various single women who did their best to lay a trap for him. The funny thing about Galen King was how hard he was to keep in scale. He wasn't a big man—in fact, was barely middle-sized—but when you walked up and looked him in the eye, it didn't seem that way. Jimmy was a few inches taller, but there was no way you could have convinced him that Galen was the shorter man. Galen had that effect on everyone. Jimmy had seen men straighten up when Galen walked past. He'd seen women tuck their hair in their cap.

Even children quieted around him. Not that Galen had ever noticed he had such an effect on others. It would have meant losing five minutes off whatever job he had decided he wanted to get done that day.

By the time the sun was overhead, Jimmy had sweated through his shirt. The first breather of the day came when Naomi brought some gingered lemonade out to the barn. Early that morning, a new lot of horses had been delivered to Galen from Saturday's auction in Leola. Galen wanted to start buggy training them straightaway. Jimmy thought Galen should let them settle into their new surroundings. These two- and three-year-old colts came right off the racetrack in Kentucky and were skittish as foals. He said as much to Galen, but his helpful suggestion was ignored. It didn't bother Jimmy. He kept on making helpful suggestions and Galen kept on ignoring him. Jimmy would rattle off five or six different questions and opinions, running them all together.

After lunch, Galen led a chestnut mare, the one with white stockings and a blaze down her forehead, out of the stall and into the yard. Jimmy walked over to the fence to watch Galen work the mare. Galen considered her to be the prime of the lot he had just purchased.

Jimmy couldn't see why. "She's not the best-looking horse I've ever seen," he said.

"I'm not interested in her looks," Galen said.

She had her ears pinned and her eyes turned so she could watch him in case he got careless. "You ought to blindfold her."

"I want her gentled, not broke." Galen got her to accept the weight of the buggy shaft, but the minute the shafts touched the sides of her belly, the mare kicked as high as she could get. Jimmy got a big laugh out of that.

"There's plenty of fine horses to buy in this world, Galen. Why would a man like you want to waste time with a filly that ought to be hobbled and blindfolded?"

Again, Galen ignored him. The mare tentatively lifted the near hind foot with the thought of kicking whatever might be in range. When she did, he caught the foot with the rope and hitched it around a post. It left the mare standing on three legs, so she could not kick again without throwing herself.

"Look at her watch us," Galen said. The mare *was* watching them—even had her ears pointed at them. She was trembling with indignation.

"I wouldn't take it as much of a compliment," Jimmy said. "She's not watching you because she loves you." He didn't know why anyone would bother with such an ill-tempered horse.

"Say what you will," Galen said. "I've never seen a more intelligent filly."

"Maybe a little too smart for her own good."

"Like my apprentice."

Ouch. That stung. Jimmy had a love for horses that went bone-deep. Most folks assumed he was nothing but a flirt— but he took horsemanship seriously. There was a time when he toyed with racing and that ended badly. He learned his lesson. But he had never stopped loving Thoroughbreds. That's why he accepted Galen's out-of-the-blue offer to work for him. No one in Stoney Ridge knew Thoroughbreds like Galen King. It was part of his blood, his heritage. His great-grandfather had raised Percherons. The Kings were known far and wide for their horse-savvy, and Jimmy wanted to soak up everything he could from Galen.

Late in the afternoon, Sammy Schrock slipped through

the privet to watch the horse training in action. Unlike Luke, Sammy was a silent, small boy. He stood apart shyly and stared at the mare. After a while he couldn't stand it any longer and his words wrestled their way through his shyness. "If you'll let me help, why, I'll do anything. I'll muck stalls, saddle soap harnesses, sweep the barn." He sounded hopeful, a boy who loved to be useful.

As Galen hesitated, Jimmy could see the boy's disappointment. "Give him a try, Galen. After all, the boy's only chance for learning how to gentle a horse is by watching me work."

Galen let that float off. "Sammy, you need to ask your mother if it's all right."

The boy ran home at once.

"Now, Galen, that was downright charitable of you. I wonder if you're getting soft."

Galen snorted. "His mother will say no so I won't have to."

Jimmy thought about that for a while, not at all sure Galen had called that right. Rose Stoltz didn't strike him as a smother-mother type. He watched her the other night and she almost seemed too good-natured to be true. It was clear she was older—she had fine wrinkles around her mouth—but her skin was still soft and her face, as she bustled around feeding people, was quite lovely.

If he were only a decade or so older, Jimmy thought, grinning, then shook that thought off. Besides, Jimmy was finding himself besotted—yes, besotted—with Rose's stepdaughter, Bethany. As usual, love fell out of a clear blue sky—as fine a day as one could want, with the creek sparkling and sun shining and hints of spring in the air.

But even Jimmy had to admit to himself that he found himself besotted with girls on a regular basis. He reminded himself that he was turning over a new leaf and becoming a horse trainer. Getting besotted with ladies on a regular basis would have to be reckoned with. It was time to get serious about life.

No sooner had Jimmy taken one team in and brought another team of horses out to the yard, and Sammy was back, puffed up and proud. "She said yes! She said Luke could come too, if it's all right with you. Not today, though. He's in trouble and can't leave the house."

Galen was shaking his head, but he didn't look nearly as upset as Jimmy might have thought. "What's Luke got himself in trouble for?"

"Teacher M.K. told everyone it was 'No Complaining Day' and Luke complained about it."

Jimmy laughed, then he noticed that Sammy was bareheaded. Jimmy had brought his old black felt hat with him and put it in the barn. It was hanging on a peg, and he went back in and got it for the boy.

"Here, you take this," Jimmy said, surprised at his own generosity.

When Sammy put it on, his head disappeared nearly down to his mouth, which was grinning.

—⁀◇⁀—

It was almost time to make supper and Rose was already a day behind in her tasks. She had linens to change in the guest flat, two pies to bake, and a pile of clothing to iron for Sunday church. Seated by the kitchen window, Vera watched Bethany walk back slowly from the mailbox, absorbed in a letter she was reading. "Bethany is spending too much time mooning over that boy."

The iron hissed as it slid over a dampened prayer cap that Rose was ironing, leaving behind a knife-sharp pleat and the smell of hot starch. "Jake Hertzler?"

"Yes. She fancies him far too much. He's Car Amish," Vera said, as if that explained everything. "What if she falls in love with him?"

Vera didn't seem to realize that Bethany already thought she was in love with him. At least, as in love as an impulsive, shortsighted nineteen-year-old girl could be. Rose set the iron upright on the ironing board to give herself time to think. She could only imagine what Vera would have to say if she heard that Jake Hertzler had pinned blame for Schrock Investments' downfall on Tobe, her precious grandson. Fur would fly! She still couldn't believe it herself. She didn't want to believe it—she preferred to think that Allen Turner's job was to be suspicious about everybody.

Vera coughed and Rose's thoughts returned to her ironing. She carefully lifted the freshly pressed cap off the ironing board and set it on the counter, then plucked a white shirt of Sammy's out of the laundry basket. "I don't deny that it's troubled me how devoted Bethany has been to Jake. Far more devoted to him than he is to her. I worry she'll end up with a broken heart."

"Then you should do something about this," Vera said. "Soon. Before that boy realizes what he might be missing and comes calling. Dean would have nipped this. Nipped it in the bud. You don't want grandchildren who aren't truly Amish."

Grandchildren who would never know Dean. That familiar sadness about Dean swept over Rose. It surprised her to realize that the sadness was only a visitor now. Not a permanent guest.

"A fish and a bird can't fall in love."

Rose sighed. It always, always circled back to this. Vera blamed Rose for the path Dean chose: leaving the Old Order Amish church to marry Rose, raising the children with the use of electricity and cars, pursuing higher education and getting his broker's license.

What Vera refused to believe was that Dean had quietly passed his GED and was taking accounting classes at the junior college—that was where Rose met him. At heart, he was not a farmer nor a craftsman. He was a man who liked to use his mind, not his hands. It was just a matter of time, he had told Rose, before he planned to leave the Old Order Amish church, especially after his first wife had abandoned the family. He couldn't remarry if he stayed in the Old Order Amish church, even though he hadn't initiated or wanted the divorce.

To be fair to Vera, Rose acknowledged that Dean let his mother believe what she wanted to believe. It didn't bother him that Vera blamed Rose for everything. Or his first wife for everything else. One thing she had quickly learned about Dean—he wanted everyone to think well of him, especially his mother.

As she picked up the iron and started on Sammy's white shirt, she remembered a time, soon after they had bought their first home and didn't have much money to spare, when Dean volunteered to pay for a new roof for the church they had just started to attend.

Rose had been raised in an Old Order Amish home but had left, disillusioned, after an acrimonious split occurred in her church. Soon after—maybe too soon, she later wondered—she met Dean, was dazzled by him—he *was* dazzling!—and married him. As she navigated her new role of stepmothering, she knew it was time to return to church. Since Dean had been divorced and remarried, they couldn't return to the Old Order Amish church. They found a Mennonite church that welcomed them in.

One Sunday morning, Dean had stood up in church and said he would take care of the entire amount of the roof.

"Why did you do that?" she had asked him on the way home from church. "They were asking everyone to make donations. They never expected one person to pay for it all."

He shrugged. "I wanted to."

"But we don't have the money to make the next mortgage payment. We don't have enough to buy food for the week!"

He gave her a hangdog expression. "I know."

How irresponsible! she thought. *He did it to impress the minister. To deflect the unhappy fact of his first marriage.*

Then, softening, because there was something about Dean that always made her excuse him, she decided that he did it because he couldn't help it. He was a generous man and enjoyed making others happy.

She did not think at the time, though she did think it now: *He wanted the entire congregation to admire him. He wanted to be a hero.*

Through the kitchen window, she saw Bethany walking slowly, head tucked, engrossed in reading a letter. Was it from Jake? Oh, she hoped not.

"Our neighbor Galen King is sweet on Bethany," Vera said.

"What?"

"I've suspected for some time now that his feelings for Bethany went beyond neighborly interest." Vera smiled her crooked smile, delighted to upstage Rose with news. "The signs are all there—think how often he's been coming by. He shows up looking Sunday-scrubbed with a lilt in his step. He's happier than I've ever seen him."

Rose finished ironing Sammy's shirt for Sunday church and hung it over the back of a chair. "I think you're confusing him with Jimmy Fisher."

"Who?"

"Jimmy. He was here for dinner the other night." *And if you'd been paying attention,* Rose thought, *you would have noticed a change in Bethany.* She was glowing, awash in some internal light, wonderstruck, glancing in Jimmy's direction whenever she thought he wasn't looking—which was seldom.

"Oh! The one who kept waggling his brows. Well, handsome is as handsome does." As Vera mulled that over for a while, her eyes grew droopy and soon she nodded off.

Rose spread Mim's Sunday dress, a deep blue, over the ironing board to spray starch all over it. She didn't know what to make of the crazy notions that flitted through Vera's mind. The thought of Bethany and Galen was ridiculous. Bethany was a beautiful young woman, but in so many ways, she was still a child. Galen was a man who had never been young.

Vera might be talking about other people, but at its heart was always a concern for herself.

9

Spring had appeared violently, rain and sun and rain again. The earth was muddy and Bethany's feet sank into the front lawn as she walked back from the mailbox with Jake's brief letter in her hands. Her last letter to Jake had been returned with a red stamp on the envelope: OCCUPANT MOVED. NO FORWARDING ADDRESS. It upset her to no end because he didn't have a telephone or cell phone. Letters were their only means of staying connected—what would happen to them? To their future? So when she saw his handwriting on an envelope in today's mail, she was thrilled and relieved, delighted to discover that he had to move to another apartment and had forgotten to tell her. That was all. Perfectly understandable! Then her smile faded. There was no return address on the envelope.

"Is that true?" A voice spoke close to her ear. Startled, Bethany slid the letter into her dress pocket and turned around to see Jimmy Fisher.

"What? Is what true?" she asked.

"That," he whispered, pointing to the porch. "What your

sister there said. Is it a fact? Pinching your nose makes you intelligent?"

Bethany looked at Mim sitting on the porch in the sunshine. She sat, holding her nose, reading. Beside her sat the little brothers, both holding their noses.

"My little sister knows nearly everything," Bethany told Jimmy. "And what she doesn't know she makes up."

For a moment they looked at each other in silence. Then each began to laugh. When she stopped, Jimmy kept smiling. He took a step closer to her and didn't disguise his frank examination of her face. "Where've you been all day? I've been looking everywhere for you."

She lifted her chin. "I don't know what you can be thinking, Jimmy Fisher."

"Are you going to quit your double life soon?"

Her smile faded. "Why do you always want to talk about that?"

"Normally, I have many other thoughts running through my fine brain. But when I get around you, I can't stop thinking about the first time I saw you working at the Stoney Ridge Bar & Grill in your fancy clothes. It's all I've got left in my head to work with."

Her mouth dropped open. It was just like Jimmy Fisher to say something she didn't expect to hear. "Why can't you just act like a normal fellow?"

"Normal is relative."

"So you consider yourself normal, do you?"

"Certainly," Jimmy said. "I never met a soul in this world as normal as me." He leaned toward her and whispered in her ear. "Maybe if you agreed to go on a picnic with me to Blue Lake Pond some fine spring day, I'd have more to talk about."

"I'll have you know that I have a boyfriend. Jake Hertzler."

Jimmy grinned. "Your imaginary boyfriend, you mean."

By the time she got her wits about her and tried to come up with a snappy retort, Rose was clanging the dinner bell and Jimmy had disappeared through the privet to Galen's. As she made her way into the house, she could hardly keep the grin off her face. *But no,* she thought as she opened the door, *why should I feel happier? There's no reason for it. It's ridiculous. What is Jimmy Fisher to me? He comes and he goes. You already have a fine young man waiting for you, Bethany Schrock.* She frowned. *Someplace.*

Jimmy Fisher had worked farms all his life and knew how hard the labor was, but it was different here at Galen King's. He had never worked like this before. He quickly established the habit of arriving in time so that he could start the day with a good breakfast, cooked by Naomi. Both for his sake and for hers.

He felt a little sorry for Naomi—her brother wasn't known for being much of a talker and all her siblings had married and moved away. Jimmy wasn't sure what the future held for a girl as shy and delicate as Naomi King, though she was a first-rate cook. He supposed she might be able to attract another shy fellow, but who would ever start the conversation? Jimmy decided he would give the subject of Naomi's empty love life some consideration. He liked to help people. He was just that kind of a fellow.

Jimmy Fisher put three heaping teaspoons of sugar from the bowl on the Kings' kitchen table into the cup and stirred it and drank carefully. It was very hot and very sweet—the way he liked it. "Why did you put eggshells into the coffee?" he asked Naomi.

"It takes the bitterness away," Naomi said. "Doesn't it seem like the bite is gone?"

"With that much sugar in it, there wouldn't ever be a bite." Galen sat at the table and drank his coffee so quickly that Jimmy thought he must have a throat made of iron. He seemed to be swallowing steam. He gulped it down and bowed his head, signaling a silent prayer. Then he bolted out of his chair, nodded to Naomi, and headed down to the barn to take hay out to the horses. Jimmy swallowed the last of his sweet coffee, smiled at Naomi, and followed Galen.

The sun was just showing light in the east over a long green flat of pasture that led down to a small creek a hundred yards from the barn. Mist came up from the creek and layered the grass. The horses were making their way to the edge of the pasture. They already knew the routine—the morning hay would soon arrive.

Galen stood by the back door of the barn, one hand on the hay cart, watching the horses move through the mist as if walking on air.

"Well, look at that," Jimmy whispered as he walked up to him. "Never seen anything so pretty before, have you?"

"You talk too much," Galen said softly. "Just watch—you don't have to talk."

And so they stood and watched the horses head to their breakfast. Stood and wasted five or six minutes, and it was the first time working on Galen's horse farm that Jimmy had ever seen such a thing. His sullen boss, just standing when there was work to be done.

Imagine that. Galen King had a romantic streak.

Sammy was a continual worry, Mim thought. This morning at breakfast he asked if he could bring a friend for supper and of course her mother said yes. Maybe two friends, Sammy asked. And her mother seemed even more pleased. She was always encouraging Sammy to make friends. She worried he was too dependent on Luke. He asked Bethany, in his sweetest voice, if she wouldn't mind making her very excellent peach crumble for dessert. That was how he said it too. Her very excellent peach crumble. How could she say no to that? Then he went and got ready for school without being told. All during the school day, Mim kept an eye on him, wondering if he might be coming down with something. Cholera or the plague or dropsy.

Right at suppertime, Sammy came through the privet dragging Galen King by the elbow sleeve. Naomi followed behind. Galen looked all cleaned up, hair combed, face and hands scrubbed. He wasn't the smiley type, but his eyes seemed to twinkle when he said hello to her mother. When they were all in the kitchen, Sammy cleared his throat real loud, as loud as Bishop Elmo did at church, and said, "Bethany, Galen King has come to court you."

All heads swiveled to Galen. His mouth opened wide and his eyes quit sparkling.

Bethany dropped the excellent peach crumble right into the sink.

"What?" Naomi said. "Why, Galen, you never told me! You never even hinted!"

"How could he?" Luke yelped. "He never knew!" He started laughing so hard that he doubled over, holding his sides.

Mim's mother bent down and put her hands on Sammy's shoulders. "Son, sometimes we can get things confused."

Sammy looked up, eyes filled with hurt. "But . . . but . . . ," he sputtered, "Mammi Vera said the exact selfsame thing, and nobody yelled at her for it!"

"I never said any such thing," Mammi Vera said, waving those accusations away. "Nothing good comes of matchmaking. I'd just as soon poke a sleeping bear."

"You did! You said so!" He looked at Rose. "I heard her say it! In the kitchen the other night—she was talking to you about it. She said Galen was happier than he'd ever been." His head swiveled toward Bethany. "And she said that Bethany should stop pining for Jake. Cuz he's Car Amish. And you agreed. You said you didn't think Jake was sweet on Bethany the way she mooned over him."

Mim saw Bethany flash a dark look at her mother and she felt a tight knot in her stomach. Sammy kept on blathering! On and on and on.

"Sammy," her mother said, "it's kind of you to think about others, but it's best to let folks do their own matchmaking."

Mim thought Luke was going to die of laughter. He was rolling on the ground, literally rolling, gasping for breath. Head held high, glaring at her mother, Bethany swept around him and bolted up the stairs. Luke just kept laughing, like a wild hyena. Sometimes, he was just appalling.

"Luke, if you don't get yourself up off that floor and stop acting like a silly fool," her mother said, "I'll get the switch and you won't be sitting down for a week of Sundays. And don't think I won't do it."

Luke stopped rolling back and forth, but he didn't get himself up, despite that threat. Finally, Galen picked him up under his arms and sat him on a chair. Luke quieted down straightaway, brought up short by Galen's firmness.

Then Galen said he was grateful for the offer of dinner, but perhaps another evening might be best and he tipped his hat and took his leave. Naomi followed behind him.

Dinner ended up being a sad and quiet affair. The kitchen clock ticked loud in the silence. Only Chase seemed un-affected, checking under the table like he always did to make sure there wasn't something left for him. Sammy didn't un-derstand what he had done that was so wrong. "I was just trying to help!" burst out of him once or twice. Her mother said they could talk about it later, in private.

Without Luke's big ears and big mouth, was what she meant. Mim gave Luke a look of disgust and he returned it, crunched eyebrow to crunched eyebrow.

Bethany finally came down to eat but was, understandably, sulky. Sammy sat on the other side of Bethany, drawing up his small shoulders in a shrug as he sniffed back tears. Sammy meant well and Mim felt sorry for him. A few days ago, he had asked Mim a bunch of questions about courting. How did a fellow do it? What should he say? He was especially curious about the ages of people. Did they need to be the same age to court?

"No," Mim had said. "Dad was a lot older than Mom."

That knowledge was new to him and pleased him to no end. At the time, Mim thought he had a crush on Teacher M.K. A lot of the boys did. Not Danny, of course, but many others. Now she realized what was on Sammy's mind. She wished she could have set him straight before he embarrassed both Galen and Bethany. But then, it was hard for anyone to figure out the reasoning a boy follows.

One thing Mim knew, she would never let *anyone* know all the thoughts she had swirling in her head about Danny Riehl.

By Wednesday, the skies had cleared, leaving the air washed clean and the earth saturated from rain. Rose had been up most of Wednesday night. Her young mare, Silver Girl, had dropped her foal early and the colt was too weak to stand up. Rose was determined to save it if she could.

The sun was barely climbing in the sky when Luke ran to her in the barn stall, tracking in mud from his boots. The mare startled.

"Haven't I told you to walk up to horses?" Rose scolded.

"I'm sorry, Mom," Luke said, more excited than sorry. His eyes were fixed on the newborn colt.

"You were supposed to make up your bed before school," Rose said.

"I never did understand that," Luke said, eyes sparkling, "when I'll just be getting back into it tonight."

Rose frowned. "Seems like all you do is hang out the window looking for something to distract you from chores."

Luke wasn't paying her any mind. He had his palm laid out flat for the colt to sniff. The mare pinned her ears back in warning, not wanting him to mess with her baby, but Luke wasn't minding her, either.

His recklessness almost stopped Rose's heart at times—he was the kind of boy who would run out in the snow barefoot, bareheaded, oblivious to weather and risks. Sometimes, she feared for him, more than she ever did for Sammy. But she supposed most mothers shook their heads and worried about their sons. Boys seem to have to acquire common sense through bad experiences. The mare made a sudden move toward Luke and he stepped back, sticking his hands in his pockets. He looked like a ragamuffin under his shaggy head of hair.

It was hard to believe a little boy could catch a day's worth of play and dirty roughhousing by half past seven in the morning. "Luke, I need you to go get Galen next door. Tell him I'm having some trouble with a new foal." Before Luke disappeared, she added, "And then you've got to get yourself to school."

She heard Luke whistle for his brother as she walked over to the barn door. Sammy came flying out of the house, hatless, and raced to meet up with Luke to disappear through the privet. Sammy liked delivering messages as much as his brother.

A few minutes later, Galen arrived and eased his way into the stall, calmly and quietly, so the mare wouldn't spook. He looked the colt over. "I think you're going to need the vet."

Rose had feared that. She wasn't sure how she could afford it, but she didn't want to lose this colt.

Galen went down to the phone shanty to leave a message for the vet. When he returned, he let Chase into the barn, and suddenly an angry streak of gray burned across the center of the barn, tore past Galen, and disappeared in the yard.

"What was *that*?" Galen asked.

"That was Oliver," Rose said. "Fern Lapp gave him to Sammy. He's an old gray cat who hates dogs. He doesn't understand that Chase has no interest in cats whatsoever, even for chasing purposes."

"Well, I suppose a barn cat always comes in handy."

"Not Oliver. He's useless. He can't be bothered catching

mice and rats. He's just a big sulking, gloomy presence."
She watched the mare nuzzle her colt. "Not unlike Vera."
As soon as the words popped out of her mouth, she wished
them back. How could she have said such a thing? Thinking
it was one thing, saying it was another.

She looked up, expecting to see Galen frown. Instead, she
saw a big grin crease his face.

Galen returned home to finish feeding his stock, but later
in the day he went back to check on Rose's little colt, half
expecting it to be dead. But no—there it was, standing on
its wobbly legs. Rose said the vet had brought along some
bottles with nipples designed for colts that had trouble nursing, along with some powdered formula. He balked at first,
but then, Rose said, he guzzled that formula like sweet cream.

For a woman who had spent part of the night in the barn
nursing a newborn foal, Rose looked wonderfully fresh, bright
eyed, and beautiful. Her face was relaxed in a way Galen
had never seen it. The strain that always showed—the strain
of holding a household together, he supposed—had disappeared, making her look like a young girl.

Right now, although he couldn't say exactly why, he felt
uneasy.

Maybe he did know why.

He hadn't been able to stop thinking about Rose. It made
no sense. He hardly knew her—just a few minutes here and
there, as neighbors. He doubted all those minutes would even
add up to hours. After those few hours with her, what could
he know about her? It made no sense.

Random memories went flickering through his mind: the

delight in her laugh, her grace as she crossed the grass, and even the way she had picked up and held that little colt in her arms this morning. He simply couldn't get her off his mind. What was happening to him? Now and then, he'd had a vague interest in a female or two, but he had never felt this way about a woman. This time it was different. Why was it different?

It was Rose. Rose in the rain.

He had a quick recollection of the first time he truly noticed her, as someone more than a neighbor. Last fall, a brief downpour had blown through Stoney Ridge without warning. Sheets of rain came pouring down, in biblical proportions, a nightmare on the roads. Someone was playing with the hose up there.

From his barn, Galen had seen Rose struggling with a flapping sheet on the clotheslines. Most women would have considered the wash to be a lost cause and run for the house, but not Rose. Her skirt was so wet it was plastered to her legs, and in the struggle, two or three pillowcases that she had already gathered up blew out of her hand and across the yard, which had begun to look like a shallow pond. Galen hurried to retrieve the pillowcases and then helped Rose get the wet sheets off the line.

Rose was soaked, as wet on the top as on the bottom, and the flapping sheets had knocked the pins out of her cap, causing it to come loose. The wash was as wet as it had been before she hung it up in the first place. She was taking sheets off the line that would just have to be hung back on in fifteen minutes, and it must have been out of pure stubbornness, since the sun was breaking through the clouds to the east of the storm. It baffled Galen as to why anyone would have a penchant to fly directly in the face of reason. Even worse, Galen was helping her do it as if it all made some sense.

In a strange way, he completely understood her logic. This woman would not quit. He had never met anyone with as much determination. As much as he had.

By the time he helped Rose finish pulling down those drenched sheets, the rain was diminishing and the sun was already striking little rainbows through the sparkle of drops that fell. Galen had walked on home, water dripping from the brim of his hat. He couldn't get that image of Rose struggling with the sheets out of his mind. He felt like a hooked fish, absolutely smitten. The thing was, Rose Schrock wasn't fishing.

The day finally came when Galen left Jimmy in charge. It was a weekday, which suited Jimmy nicely because it kept those little Schrock boys contained in the schoolhouse. Galen wanted to see some new horses brought in from Kentucky before they went to auction on the weekend. Jimmy did the chores with will and skill, whereas Luke and Sammy had marginal will and little skill. Sammy, Jimmy had to admit, tried his best. Luke—not so much.

Jimmy was determined to make a success of this day and prove to Galen that he could take on more responsibility. Just yesterday, he was helping Galen work a three-year-old gelding that was ready to be sold. "He's like me," Jimmy said, watching the gelding ignore all kinds of distraction that Galen was tossing at it.

"How's that?" Galen asked, waving a flag at the gelding. "Lazy, you mean?"

"Mature, I mean," Jimmy said. "He doesn't get excited about little things."

Galen rolled his eyes.

"When are you going to let me train a horse, start to finish?" Jimmy asked.

"When you're ready."

"I am ready."

Galen ignored him.

"Why are you so hard to convince?" Jimmy asked. "I can't seem to convince you of a single thing." His gaze was fixed on Bethany as she left Naomi at the kitchen door and crossed the yard, disappearing through the hole in the privet that led to Eagle Hill.

"That's not true. You've convinced me of one thing for sure," Galen said. "You're foolish about women. I expect Bethany won't have anything to do with you because she knows you're too fond of ladies. Now, would you mind getting back to work?"

Now *that* was not necessary. Three things bothered Jimmy about Galen. First, he didn't think Galen ever had any fun. Second, Galen didn't do a single thing that couldn't be predicted. Third, he wasn't easy to talk to. Jimmy didn't say anything more to him for the rest of the afternoon, though he didn't think Galen even noticed.

And then Galen did something that was both fun and unpredictable. He told Jimmy that he would be putting him in charge of tomorrow's training. *Nice!*

Jimmy was not going to let Galen down. The day had been going well, almost perfectly, up until the moment when that blasted filly Galen was so fond of took a nip at his hand and drew blood. After he led the filly into her stall, he looked through Galen's workbench to find some bandages. The day was only half done and he needed something to wrap his hand. He thought about going to the house and seeing if Naomi could help, but felt she might surely pass out from the sight of blood. She was *that* frail. Jimmy would rather leave chores half done than tell Galen that he had caused his sister to faint.

"Some horse trainer you are."

He whirled around and faced Bethany, standing by the workshop. He held up his hand. "That filly has an evil streak."

"I was visiting with Naomi and saw it happen from the kitchen window. You'd better let me see it."

That meant she'd been watching him. *Nice!* He held out his hand to her, unconcernedly, and told her it didn't hurt, which it did. She scolded him and insisted on bandaging up his fingers. "It's going to need some hydrogen peroxide. You'd better come with me over to the house."

Jimmy followed behind her, pleased. He had a new appreciation for that diabolical filly. That was the thing about Thoroughbreds—hot-blooded, strong-willed, feisty, moody, breathtakingly beautiful, poetic in their movement. Most preferred warmbloods or drafts—they wanted a horse they could depend on. Steady, solid, reliable. But for all of the problems of Thoroughbreds, Jimmy liked their unpredictable, high-spirited nature.

He grinned. He could have been talking about women.

In the kitchen in Eagle Hill, Bethany cleaned the wounds on Jimmy's hand and wrapped the fingers carefully.

"How do you like being an innkeeper?"

She kept her head down but glanced at him. "That's the very thing I was talking to Naomi about when that filly took such a serious disliking to you. It's not as bad as I thought it was going to be. Of course, we've really only had one guest. She is a grand lady, though. She taught me how to make genuine steeped tea the other morning. From loose leaves, not from a bag."

"Have you given any more thought to quitting the Bar & Grill and working at the Sisters' House?" Jimmy said.

She whipped her head around to see if Mammi Vera's door was shut. "Lower your voice. Stop talking about that!"

"All right, let's talk about something else. Have you changed your mind about going on a picnic with me to Blue Lake Pond?"

"I'd be delighted." She smiled at him and he smiled back. "We'd all be delighted. Me and Mim and Sammy and Luke and Rose and Mammi Vera."

His smile faded.

"You seem to keep forgetting that I have a boyfriend."

"I keep forgetting because I've never seen hide nor hair of him." He leaned back in his chair. "Now, what makes this bloke so much better than me?"

"Well, for one thing, Jake has ambition."

Jimmy raised his bandaged hand. "What do you think caused this?"

"I'm not talking about hard work. Jake has plans for the future."

"And I don't?"

"Nothing that lasts longer than five minutes." She tied the last bandage. A war whoop outside pulled their attention to the windows. "Luke and Sammy are home from school."

"Those brothers of yours need a firm hand," Jimmy said.

"Oh bother. What did they do now? No—never mind. I can't handle any more complaints today."

"That's another reason you need a new line of work. Customer complaints. Wouldn't happen if you worked at the Sisters' House. They're not the complaining type."

She frowned. "Stop talking about my line of work." She wrapped up the bandages. "Just how old are those sisters, anyway?"

"Pretty old. They've got their fair share of summer teeth."

"What are summer teeth?"

"Summer in their mouth. Some are elsewhere." Jimmy looked at her and made his eyebrows do that crazy up-and-down dance.

She covered her mouth but a laugh slipped out anyway.

"Maybe your brothers should work for the sisters. Maybe they could knock some sense into them." He picked up his hat off the table and grinned that mischief-loaded grin of his, when his eyes sparkled like he'd charmed the hair right off a cat. "They're wilder than the wind, and nagging them—especially Luke—does no good."

"Well, I try not to nag them," Bethany said, straightening her skirt.

"You nag," Jimmy said. "Galen and I can hear you all the way over at his place."

10

Rain began at midnight and continued until dawn and then on through the day. All evening, Mammi Vera was reminded of the terrible blizzard of 1993, when it took days to dig out and find the road. She told Bethany the story twice.

"You say the same things, over and over," Bethany told her, but her grandmother went right on repeating herself. Last night, reading to the older woman by the oil lamplight, Bethany held Mammi Vera's rough, aged hand—webbed with blue veins and brown spots. She had such a fondness for her grandmother. She liked older people better than babies. Older folks had interesting stories to tell. Babies only cried.

She thought about Jimmy Fisher's suggestion to work for the ladies in the Sisters' House. She wondered why Jimmy was steering her away from working at the Grill. He had said, more than a few times, that she was playing with fire.

That comment struck her as odd. Jimmy Fisher seemed to be the daring sort—the type who liked to play with fire. After all, the job he loved best, he said, was gentling wild horses. Her thoughts drifted to Jake. Where was he? The letter he sent was so brief and unromantic, filled with complaints about a minor misunderstanding with his cheap landlord. When would she hear from him again? Had he stopped loving her? For a moment Bethany wondered whether life was happier with men, or without them.

It was lightly sprinkling as Rose walked up the hillside behind the farmhouse, but she didn't mind the mist. She enjoyed these quiet moments as the sun started to light the sky. She liked walking apart from the farm, listening to the sounds over the area. A coyote howled, and another coyote answered back. The sound made her shiver. She hadn't given the sound of a coyote a second thought until she became a sheep owner. She knew what a coyote could do to a sheep—it lunged straight for the throat, so the last thing a poor little sheep saw was the spilling of its life's blood.

She stopped for a moment as she saw one of the eagles pass overhead and soar along the creek. It was still too dark to see if it was the missus or the mister. Sometimes she wished she could be such a bird, just for a short time. She wondered what they saw, high in the sky with their night vision, and she envied them their freedom. Maybe it wasn't as free as it seemed, she thought, when its sole purpose was to find food.

But her sole purpose lately didn't feel too far off from that. She ought to get back soon. She had bread to bake, clothes to wash, and a million and one other chores that needed to be done. And then, of course, there was caring for Vera. Rose sighed.

Looking over the horizon at dawn never failed to fill her with a sense of her smallness, contrasted to God's bigness.

Her problems and worries seemed to shrink under the dome of the sky.

A twig snapped behind her and she whirled around. "Galen!" She smiled.

"No moon this morning." His greeting seemed quiet, intimate.

"What are you doing up here?"

"Checking traps. A coyote has been sneaking in and snatching Naomi's hens."

She looked around. "Did you find it? Or rather, did the coyote find the trap?"

"No. Too wily."

They walked along the path, silent companions, each with their own thoughts. There was only the sound of Harold, the rooster, crowing that morning had arrived.

"How is Naomi doing lately, Galen?"

He lifted one shoulder in a half-shrug. "Same cycle. She feels better, then does too much, and she'll get walloped with another headache and has to take to her bed."

She could see he loved his sister in his unspeaking way—continually warning her about her health or trying to keep her wrapped up from the cold. Naomi's migraines were a puzzle. Doctors couldn't quite pinpoint what triggered them or how to avoid them. They started when her parents had passed.

Galen was the eldest in his family of three boys, three girls. His parents died awhile back, first one, then the other, and Galen stepped into the role of patriarch. The other siblings had married, moved on, started families.

"What about Vera?" he said. "Any improvement?"

"None." Rose sighed. "If anything, she's getting worse.

More confused, weaker on one side. She tries to hide it, but I'm awfully worried about her."

"She's blessed to have you."

"I wish she thought so."

He pretended to look serious, but his eyes gave him away. Sparkling green those eyes were, and crinkled at the corners. "One of my sisters used to say that every time she talked to Vera, she came away feeling like she's eaten a green persimmon. You know how they make your mouth pucker up?"

That unexpected comment made her laugh, and him as well. But the quiet that followed brought an awkwardness with it, as if they both felt wary of the closeness their shared laughter had stirred. "Galen, I don't know what we'd do without you. Teaching the boys about horses, helping me get the inn ready. You do a lot for us as a neighbor."

"A friend, you mean."

Down below, Rose saw the sheep wander in the fold, bleating. "I hope that coyote keeps its distance from my sheep."

"Remind me again why you want to raise sheep."

"I didn't set out to raise them. Someone drove up in a truck one day and asked if we'd take them off their hands. Said they were tired of them."

"And you said yes?"

"I . . . well. I was worried what might happen to them if I said no." She looked down the hill at the fold with five fluffy sheep. Sometimes, she just sat and watched them. They slowly munched and dozed their way around the pasture, passing the time in the way they loved best. "They're not the brightest, but they are sweet."

He stared at her in that intense way he had, and she could feel the color building in her cheeks. Then the creases around his mouth softened in a smile. "Well, everybody knows you are the lady to help people. And creatures." He gave her a curt nod and set off toward his farmhouse.

As Rose made her way down the hill, Galen's words came back to her. *You are the lady to help people.* It was pleasing to know what people thought of you, but worrying too. You couldn't help everybody—nobody could—because the world was too full of need and troubles, a wide sea of them, and no one person could begin to deal with all that. And yet, even if you were just one person, you could do one thing. You could say yes to five little sheep and give them a home.

Despite Bethany Schrock's opinion, Jimmy Fisher did have ambition that lasted longer than five minutes. But it was not to inherit his mother's farm to become a chicken and egg dealer like his brother, Paul, who didn't mind living his life in a groove etched out by their mother. Jimmy had different ideas for his life. He wanted to become a respected horse trainer, just like Galen King.

He listened carefully to Galen—though he knew his taciturn boss thought otherwise—and he had discovered that horses coming off the Kentucky racetracks were breaking down. Too many horses were bred for one quality—speed—at the expense of others. They were weedy and unsound.

Jimmy decided that he should help out mankind and create a superb Thoroughbred bloodline. He developed a plan: he would stop dating girls and start saving his money. And he would attend local spring mud sales held at county fire stations on Saturdays, looking for the perfect foundation stallion to start his superb bloodline.

Amazingly, he found the horse on the first Saturday at the Bart Township mud sale.

It was early. The auction wouldn't get started for a few more hours, but there was a crowd milling around a certain stall that piqued Jimmy's interest. He made his way through the crowd to get closer to the stall and see what folks were oohing and aahing over. Inside was the most striking-looking horse he'd ever seen—a chocolate palomino stallion with a flaxen mane. He tried to gather as much information about the horse as he could without having the owner notice him. Bright eyes, a long arch to his neck, thick cannons, hooves in good condition, sound teeth that revealed he was a young colt. And he was definitely a stallion. He could just imagine what Galen King would have to say if Jimmy bought a gelding as the foundation of his breeding plan. No thank you! He did not want to have to be on the receiving end of Galen King's disdain any more than necessary.

The owner noticed him and sidled over to him. "Beautiful creature," he said. "I hate to let him go."

"Then why are you selling?" Jimmy asked.

"I've got some bills to take care of." He rolled his eyes. "But . . . a man's got to do what he's gotta do." He stuck out his hand. "Jonah Hershberger."

"Jimmy Fisher." He shook his hand and noticed that it wasn't the palm of a typical horseman: calloused and rough. This was a man who didn't use his hands for a living. In fact, he looked like he didn't get outside much—he had pale skin, was small-boned and slender, blue eyed, with shingled mahogany hair. The indoor type. Mennonite, he guessed, with a name like Jonah Hershberger. Hard to tell his age but he didn't wear a beard so Jimmy assumed he wasn't married.

Jonah Hershberger nodded his head toward the horse. "You can check him out."

Jimmy ducked under the rope gate and walked slowly around the stallion. Perfect conformation—large eyes, broad forehead, knife-edged withers, sloping croup, lean body, good depth of girth, beautiful coat. Jimmy lifted each hoof and examined it. The horse was calm, at ease with handling. "Does he have a name?"

"I call him Lodestar."

Perfect. Absolutely perfect. He knew what that word meant: a guiding light. Lodestar bumped Jimmy gently with his nose and he was hooked. This horse was meant for him.

Jonah Hershberger looked around, then lowered his voice. "Look, I can tell you know horses."

Jimmy nodded. He did.

"I'd rather Lodestar go to someone like you, someone who would give him a good home, than let him go on that auction block."

"How much? How much do you want?"

"I haven't signed any papers with the auctioneer yet, so if you can get him out of here before the auction starts, I'll let him go for $1500."

Jimmy inhaled a sharp breath. "The thing is, Jonah, I don't quite have that much. Not yet. I could give you a deposit and make payments. I've got a steady job. I'm good for the money."

Jonah hesitated. "I don't know. Like I said . . . I got these bills to take care of."

"It would just be for a few weeks, maybe a month—I get paid on Fridays. I'm good for it. Ask anybody around here. They all know me."

"How much can you get me today?"

Just how much was in Jimmy's checking account? Last time he looked was . . . blast! He couldn't remember. He had never been much of a money manager—mainly because he just didn't care much about it. "I could write you a check for $500."

"Make it $750 and you've got yourself the finest stud north of Kentucky."

He looked over at Lodestar, who stretched out his neck now, lifting his head, looking calmly at Jimmy through big round dark eyes. What was it about the meeting of eyes that created a connection? He'd never felt such a bond with an animal before. It's like Lodestar was meant for him and they both knew it.

But he remembered Galen's constant refrains—*Never let your heart rule your head. You make a purchase with your stomach.*

Jimmy's stomach felt just fine.

"Okay," Jimmy said, grinning. "I'll be back in thirty minutes with a friend who has a trailer."

"Hold on," Jonah said, laughing at Jimmy's delight. "I've got a trailer hitched to my truck. Throw in an extra twenty-five bucks, and I'll deliver him right to your barn."

Jimmy's grin spread from ear to ear. "It's a deal!"

Later that afternoon, Jimmy confessed to Galen that he had bought a foundation stallion for his future stud farm. He braced himself for a lecture on impulsive purchases, but Galen surprised him with only interest. In fact, he wanted to go over to Jimmy's farm to meet Lodestar. As they drove the buggy down the road that led to the Fisher chicken and egg farm, the buggy horse pricked its ears, then started to speed up, prancing on the road. Not a moment later, a dark object came hurtling through the woods, leapt over a fence, blew past them, and disappeared into the trees on the other side of the road.

It took all of Galen's attention to keep his buggy horse from bolting. His fists were clenched around the reins so tightly that his knuckles were white. When the horse finally stopped straining, Galen relaxed his grip, little by little. He edged the gelding sideways over to the side of the road. "What was *that*?" he said, mystified.

"A horse, I think," Jimmy said, peering into the woods. He gave a snort. "Somebody's gonna be sorry they left a barn door open."

Wait. *What?*

"That was Lodestar!" Jimmy swung out of the buggy and ran into the woods, calling Lodestar's name. He stopped and listened, hoping to hear some sound that the horse was near. The woods were silent.

Slowly, Jimmy walked back to the buggy and climbed in.

"You're sure that was your new horse?" Galen said. "It blew past us pretty fast. I couldn't tell if it was a bear or a buck."

Jimmy hung his head. "I'm sure."

"Let's go to your farm and double-check." Galen clucked for the horse to move forward and drove down the road, turning into the Fisher driveway. Jimmy's eyes immediately went to the paddock where he had left Lodestar grazing just a few hours earlier.

Empty. The paddock was empty.

11

In the warm kitchen of Eagle Hill, Bethany washed dishes, suds up to her elbows. Mim dried and put the dishes away. Seated at the kitchen table, Luke was reading his essay to them.

"'Noah and his wife, Joan,'" he read, "'lived on the Ark for a long time.'"

"What makes you think Noah's wife is named Joan?" Bethany asked. "I don't remember reading what her name was in the Bible."

"Everybody knows that. Joan of Ark."

Bethany and Mim burst into laughter. Luke ignored them and went back to his essay. "'The ark came to its end on Mt. Error Fat. It is still up there, teetering on the top of the mountain, just waiting to be discovered by *National Geographic* magazine.'"

"Luke, where did you get that information?" Bethany asked, scratching her nose and leaving a spot of suds there.

"I made it up," Luke said, looking pleased. "What do you think?"

"Luke, you can't make up facts!" Mim protested. "You research facts. Facts are true. Made-up facts are not true."

"Unless you happened to have interviewed Mr. and Mrs. Noah," repeated Bethany, scouring out the soup pot, making Luke smile.

"Can I say I did?"

"No!" Mim and Bethany shouted.

After Luke and Mim went upstairs, Bethany finished up the last of the dishes. She was standing at the sink, her hands immersed in soapy water, when she noticed movement outside, half in the darkness, half in the square of light thrown out from the window.

Her heart skipped a beat. *Shootfire!* She smacked her hands to her cheeks. *Oh my. Oh my! He's come for me!* "Jake! Jake Hertzler."

He didn't hear her; he was staring in through a window now, as if searching the room. She waved a hand, signaling to him, and he startled, hesitated, then smiled.

She dried her hands before opening the kitchen door, and tried to appear calm as a cucumber, as if the arrival by night of Jake Hertzler lurking in the darkness was nothing unusual. As soon as she had closed the door, she ran into his arms. "You've come. You've finally come!" She was floating, lighter than air. She loved him, loved him so much! Her relief was so great, she felt dizzy with it. Jake had come for her!

Jake put his hands on her shoulders and gently pushed her back. "Bethany, I'm here for Tobe's sake."

Her chin jerked up. He hadn't even seen her in months and months . . . and he was worried about Tobe? About *Tobe?* "Well, that's a fine way to greet your girlfriend."

He glanced into the kitchen. "Keep your voice down. Tobe's in trouble. He needs our help."

"Have you seen him?"

"Yes."

"Where's he been?"

Jake took his time answering. "He's been with your mother."

Bethany's head snapped up. "WHAT?"

"Hush!" he clamped his fingers over her mouth. "There's something I need your help with. Tobe said he left something important in the basement. But when I looked in the windows—"

"You peeped in the basement windows? There's a paying guest in there!"

"Relax. She didn't see me. But obviously, stuff has been moved out of the basement. Where would it be now?"

She shrugged. She was still reeling over the news that Tobe was with their mother. She had no idea where her mother lived. Somehow, Tobe had tracked her down and was living with her? "I . . . I don't know. I could ask Rose."

"No!" Jake snapped. She stiffened and he noticed. His face softened as he added, "I don't want Rose to find out about this. It'll only make things worse for Tobe."

"But she should be told if he's in some kind of trouble. She'll know what to do."

"Legal trouble, Bethany. I'm trying to help him stay out of jail. We can't get Rose involved in this—not yet. Not with the SEC lawyer sniffing around. It puts her in a tight spot. She'd have to turn him in or she could be in trouble herself. You understand, don't you?" He wrapped his arms around her and pulled her to his chest. "I'm sorry, Bethany. I'm trying to do all I can to help your brother. Now I want you to think hard for a minute. Where would things be that were stored in the basement?"

She breathed in the familiar scent of Jake: Old Spice shaving cream and peppermint gum. He always smelled so good and looked so good—unlike most of the farm boys in Stoney Ridge who wore the barn on their boots. She wished she could stay in his arms forever. "What are you looking for, anyway?"

"Most importantly, two black books with red bindings."

"Books?" She pulled back to look right at his eyes. "Tobe didn't read."

"These are ledger books. For Schrock Investments."

"What's the next most important thing?"

He hesitated. "I'm looking for a key. But I'm not sure Tobe took it. I couldn't find it after the SEC cleaned the office out."

She tilted her head. "What kind of key? For a car?"

"No. Smaller than that." He shook his head. "Never you mind. The books are what I really need. What Tobe needs."

"Where will you be?"

"I'm on the road a lot—interviewing all over, trying to find a job. But everyone seems to have been an investor in Schrock Investments or their grandmother was—it ain't good. It's been tough, you know."

She rolled her eyes. "Tell me about it."

He softened at that, and leaned in to kiss her on the lips, gentle and sweet, then he jerked his head back and glanced in the kitchen windows when he heard the sound of the boys yelling to each other. "I'd better go." He kissed her again, before she could object. "Start looking for those books."

Shootfire! "Jake! Wait! You can't just show up and disappear like a spook. I want to know why my letter got returned!"

He grimaced, ashamed. "I hated to let the apartment go. Couldn't make the rent. I'm just staying on friends' couches."

"Well, how am I supposed to reach you if I find those books?"

"Good point." He took a piece of paper from his pocket and scribbled a number on it with a small pencil. "This is my cell phone number."

Her eyes narrowed. "When did you get a cell phone?" *And why didn't you bother calling me on it?*

He read her mind. "I got it for job interviews—but it's the kind with limited minutes. Call me the minute you find those books." He kissed her again. Then again and again, until the sound of her brothers' footsteps thundering down the stairs jerked him away. "Trust me on this, honey. You find those books and we can help Tobe clear his name." And he vanished into the shadows. She waited awhile, hearing his footsteps head down the driveway. In the distance, she heard a horse whinny and Silver Queen answer back from the barn. Then she heard the sound of Jake's truck drive off.

Honey. *He called me his honey!* Bethany hugged herself with happiness. He still loved her. Of course he did. Why had she ever doubted?

She inhaled the sharp night air, feeling a surge of pleasure. Then it passed and in its place rushed a thought that filled her with discomfort: Tobe has been staying with their mother. She wanted to know more, and yet she didn't.

On Monday morning, Jimmy Fisher woke up a determined man. He marched into Galen's kitchen and helped himself to a mug of coffee. "Where's Naomi?" he asked.

"She's not feeling too well this morning."

Jimmy pulled out the kitchen chair and dumped three teaspoons full of sugar into his coffee cup.

Galen finished buttering his burnt toast. "Any luck finding the horse?"

"No, no sign of him." He took a long sip of coffee. "But I am going to find Lodestar and get him back. Yesterday, I went to all the neighbors and told them to keep an eye out for him. If you can spare me for a few hours, I'm going to staple posters on telephone poles and street signs. Someone's bound to have seen him. I was even thinking about taking out an ad in the paper, maybe adding a reward."

"Well, I hope you do find him. But there are other horses in the world."

"None like Lodestar. You haven't seen him. When you do, you'll know what I mean."

"If he's that fine a horse, someone will find him and keep him."

"Now, Galen, that's the difference between you and me. You're negative. I'm positive. You're pessimistic. I'm optimistic. You think people are all bad. I think there's good in them. Someone will find him and return him to me."

Jimmy snatched his hat off the wall peg and jammed it on his head. "I'm going out to look for him. I'll be back in a few hours." That horse was his destiny. He was going to find Lodestar. He was going to prove Galen King wrong.

Every few days, Rose stopped by the phone shanty to pick up her messages. She knew from experience that she couldn't handle it more often. At first, her message machine was filled with pleas from people who had invested with Dean's company. The first few months, after it all broke open, she would listen to the messages and her stomach would churn all day long. These people had trusted Dean with their life savings. So many people had been left penniless. Futures had been destroyed. Family homes had been foreclosed on. They begged Rose to return the money they had invested.

Didn't they understand there was no money?

She took down the information and wrote letters to each person who called, explaining the situation. She tried to include some cash in each letter—$5 or $10 or $20. There was a part of her that wanted to scold these people for trusting so easily, for getting tempted by high returns on their investment. What made them think that Schrock Investments could beat the market? In a brutal recession? It made no sense.

Today, she was relieved to see there were only a handful of messages. The calls were coming less frequently now and in a way, that made her sad too. They had given up hope of getting their money back. She wished she could tell each one, "I haven't forgotten! Just give me some time. I'm going to repay you, if it's the last thing I do." She picked up a pencil to take down notes from the messages. She had to listen carefully to the last one before it made sense. Then she listened to it again. As soon as her mind grasped what the message meant, she ran down the long driveway and pounded on the basement door. "Delia, something's happened! Something terrible."

Delia opened the door, an alarmed look on her face. "What's wrong? Come in. What's happened?"

Rose had to stop and take a deep breath after running from the shanty like that. "My first guest at Eagle Hill was a woman named Lois. Tony and Lois. She left a message that she had met you at . . . a gas station . . . and told you to come here. She had bright red hair—truly red, not orange-red—and orange lipstick."

Delia nodded. "Yes. Yes, I remember her. She helped me pump gas."

"She said that you seemed upset and looked like you needed a quiet place to be."

"That's exactly right. She's the one who told me about your inn. Has something happened to her?"

Rose sat down on the couch. She took a deep breath. "She said that your picture is all over the television. As a missing person. The news said your son reported you as missing . . ."

"My son? My son, Will?"

"Yes . . . that your son is on every news station pleading for some information about where you might be."

"Oh no." A trace of color rose under Delia's fair skin. "I should have called Will. I should have let him know. It's just that he's going through midterm exams and Charles didn't want to let him know about our . . . marital problems."

"Charles. Is your husband Dr. Charles Stoltz?"

"Yes. Why?" Then, impatiently, "Why?"

"Maybe you should sit down for this."

Delia sank to the sofa and Rose sat beside her. "Lois said she just heard on the news that your husband has been taken to the police station for questioning. She said that there's concern he might have something to do with your disappearance . . . that apparently he is having an affair." She lowered her voice. "Lois said there is speculation growing that your husband killed you and has hidden your body."

"Oh my," Delia said. "Oh my." She covered her face with her hands, but for just a moment. Then she let them fall to her lap in a gripping fist. "I should get to a phone. I need to straighten this all out."

Rose bit her lip. "Lois already did. She said she called the police to let them know where you are."

Delia looked sick. "Please tell me this is a bad dream."

The sound of a siren was heard in the distance, getting louder and louder as it came up the road. Rose and Delia went to the window and watched a police car with a flashing red siren pull up the driveway. "As a matter of fact," Rose said, "I think you're wide awake."

Delia Stoltz spent the next two hours at the sheriff's office in Stoney Ridge, on the phone with the Philadelphia police, explaining that her husband was innocent—sort of, she wanted to add, but didn't think it would be wise to complicate the situation. It was already far too complicated. "My husband did not kill me and hide my body," she said in a wry tone. "I just didn't happen to mention to him where I was going."

As soon as the sheriff allowed, she called her son, Will. She felt terrible when she heard the relief in his voice.

"I'm coming down there," Will said. "Don't try to talk me out of it. I'm leaving now."

"No, Will—you've got exams to get through. I'm fine. I really am. I'll call you each day if you like. I can't get service out at the farm, but I'll drive into town. I'm sorry I didn't let you know where I was. But what made you think I went missing?"

"Dad called me, thinking you might have come to Ithaca. I started phoning your friends to see if they knew where you were. None of them had heard from you in weeks. You weren't returning any of Dad's or my phone messages. Dad said not to worry, but that only made me worry all the more.

I mean, it's not like you, Mom. Dad is hard to get hold of, but you're always available. My imagination started rolling . . . too many CSI shows, I guess. So I called the police, thinking they might be able to locate your car or check with any hospitals to see if you might have been in an accident. Suddenly, it turned into a missing person's report, then I was interviewed for the evening news, then someone at Dad's office tipped off the police that Dad was having an affair with his attorney . . . and things got carried away."

Delia rubbed her forehead. What a mess. "I'm sorry to have caused you concern. I just needed a little time to catch my breath. So much happened, so quickly."

"Mom, I didn't know about Dad and this attorney bimbo."

"I just found out myself a few weeks ago. The day I found out about the cancer, in fact."

There was a long silence. "Wait. *What?* You have cancer?"

Delia squeezed her eyes shut. How could she have blurted that without thinking? She kept her voice calm and steady. "They found a lump in my breast and took it out. I'm sure they got it all." She wasn't at all sure.

"What did the doctor say? Were the margins clear? Anything in the lymph nodes?" Will's voice started to crack, which made Delia's eyes fill with tears.

"I . . . haven't gotten the results yet. I'm sure it's all fine." In fact, with each passing day, she felt a sense of growing dread about those results. She glanced at her wristwatch. It was too late to call today, but she would drive into town and call tomorrow.

"Does Dad know?"

"No. Not yet. I will tell him, Will." Her voice was firm. "Let me do that."

"So he's having an affair with his lawyer while you're recovering from cancer surgery." His voice was filled with disgust.

"To be fair to him, he didn't know, Will."

She heard Will call his father an unmentionable word and she cringed. She didn't want to become that kind of a woman—who told her son too much and turned him against his father. It wouldn't take much, she knew—Will and Charles always had a fragile relationship. "Listen—this is between me and your father. Not you and him. Nothing has to change between the two of you."

"Nothing has to change?" Will snorted. "Everything has changed! Dad destroyed our family. Life will never be the same again. Every holiday—Thanksgiving, Christmas—will be divided between parents. I've got plenty of friends from split-up families." He paused. "Look, Dad's . . . tomcatting . . . isn't as important as your cancer. You've got to find out the results of the surgery. I don't know when you're planning to come home, but you can't ignore this."

"You're right. I can't."

"I'll come down to Stoney Ridge. I'll tell my professors that my exams are just going to have to wait."

"Will, I'm going to be fine." She said it firmly, a mother to a son. "I can handle this. I won't have you jeopardizing your future because of me. You stay put at Cornell and I'll call you with the results. The minute I hear. Until then, no news is . . . no news."

She heard him exhale loudly. "Either way? You'll tell me the truth? The absolute truth?"

"I promise."

"Mom . . . do you think you and Dad can fix this?" Something in his voice reminded Delia of Will as a little boy, wanting a Band-Aid or a hug to make the hurt go away.

"Maybe. But I want you to know that I will be fine. And so will you. I love you. Now . . . go study."

Delia didn't leave the sheriff's office until he assured her that Charles had been released from questioning. She thought about calling Charles but knew he would be furious, and she couldn't take any more upset today. She still felt shaky from that call with her son.

Her mind drifted back to Will's question: Could this marriage be fixed? She was still trying to figure out when it had broken, and why.

Delia thought about a dinner she had at P.F. Chang's with Charles just last month. It was their favorite restaurant. He had left the table four times to make urgent phone calls and returned edgy, distracted. Delia had seen nothing unusual about it at the time. He was often edgy and distracted, though he had become far more so in the last month, since the malpractice suit.

Charles had a patient, a middle-aged woman, who had come to him with an enormous aneurysm pressing against her brain stem—a very dangerous situation. The brain could be surprisingly forgiving and tended to accommodate aneurysms or tumors as long as they grew slowly. Not in the brain stem with its tight pack of nerves. He explained all that and more to the patient, concerned she didn't understand how serious the situation was. The aneurysm had to be dealt with before it proved fatal. Charles persisted and she finally agreed to the surgery. The procedure was successful.

Delia remembered that evening—how satisfied Charles had been as he described wrapping coil after coil around the large aneurysm. She could tell he was pleased with himself. He had saved the patient's life.

And then the hospital called. Delia had never seen a look of fear on Charles's face until he hung up from that phone call. He didn't move for a long moment, and she heard him say, "Oh God, please no." The patient suffered a massive stroke and was having difficulty speaking.

The patient's husband ended up slapping a malpractice suit on Charles—his first. The husband insisted that his wife did not understand the risks of the surgery and that she would never have agreed to the procedure if she had known she might have ended up impaired. She didn't mind dying, he said, but she would mind living with such loss of function. And that was when Charles connected with Robyn Dixon, the attorney who represented him.

When Delia first learned of the lawsuit, she thought it might even be a good thing. Charles was so proud, taking on riskier and riskier surgeries. He thought he could do anything and do it well. He'd had very few failures in his career. He needed to remember that even he had clay feet.

Robyn Dixon convinced him to countersue, based on the fact—and it was a documented fact—that the patient had signed an agreement to have the surgery and therefore was duly informed of the risks. The countersuit claimed that the patient was causing him undue professional harm.

Delia had tried to talk Charles out of a countersuit. The poor woman and her husband had suffered enough.

Charles wouldn't hear of it. "It's never easy making decisions in matters concerning life and limb. Every surgery has its risks. She knew that. Bad outcomes are part of the medical profession. I'm only human."

If Charles really believed that, then why didn't he just admit he might have minimized any risk in his eagerness to have the patient agree to the surgery? He frightened the patient into thinking the aneurysm might kill her, but did he help her to understand that her life might never be the same, even with the surgery? In this situation, Delia thought his impatience and arrogance had interfered with his judgment.

But wasn't that the fatal flaw in Charles's character? He was never wrong, never at fault.

As Delia drove back to Stoney Ridge, she listened to her messages. There were quite a few from Will and Charles, increasingly frantic as they wondered where she was and why she wouldn't return their calls. She listened to two calm ones from Dr. Zimmerman's receptionist, asking her to call to schedule her follow-up visit, and then the voice mail said the box was full. She was just about to erase them all but decided to leave it full. She didn't want to hear anything more today. Not from anybody.

She pulled into the driveway and stayed in the car for a moment. Delia dabbed her eyes with an already damp tissue. Her face crumpled, and she started weeping softly.

Far above her flew the eagle couple, swirling in a courting ritual, skimming the distant trees, disappearing beyond the ridge. Their life was so simple. Why then did human beings not keep theirs simple too? Love, marry, till death do us part?

She was startled by a tap on her car window. Rose was waiting to speak to her. Delia didn't know what she was going to say. Ask her to leave, perhaps? She wouldn't blame her at all.

Until that phone message was left by Lois, Delia knew Rose had no idea why a stranger had arrived at Eagle Hill and collapsed like a rag doll. She was far too polite to ask, but now, it must have all become clear. She wondered what Rose told the family: Delia Stoltz's husband had left her for another woman. And a happenstance meeting with a stranger at a gas station convinced her to come here for her nervous breakdown.

Well, wasn't that the truth?

Delia opened the car door and stepped out.

"I need to take something over to the neighbor's," Rose said. "Would you like to come with me? Get some fresh air? It's a beautiful day. Not a cloud in the sky."

For the first time in hours, the tight, pained feeling in Delia's abdomen lessened a little. "I believe I would," she said with a hint of a smile.

So Rose and Delia took a loaf of extra bread over to Galen and stayed to watch him work his horses. They leaned against the top of the corral fence, transfixed by Galen's calm manner with very high-strung Thoroughbreds. Delia looked up. A dome of the lightest blue filled with air, with swirls and eddies of wispy clouds. She breathed in deeply, and felt the sweet air fill her with a buoyant optimism. Life, for just this moment, was good.

"I've been bringing fresh bread to Galen every other day, to thank him for tolerating the boys' help with his horses," Rose whispered. "Mostly, it's my excuse to spy on the boys and make sure they're behaving. But I do like to watch how Galen works with those prickly horses. He gets a look on his face as if he has a vision of what the horse will be like, once trained."

An Amish couple drove up in a buggy with a beautiful gelding tied behind them. Rose and Delia watched from afar as the husband explained to Galen that this horse had been a gift to his wife. The gelding had been a reliable horse, he was told from the previous owner, but now was behaving unpredictably in traffic.

The woman was quite upset. "I don't want to get rid of him. But I can't seem to get him to mind me. He bolts at the slightest thing."

Galen walked around the horse, stroked his neck. "The problem is you don't understand him."

"But I love this horse," the woman said. "I'm very kind to him."

"I didn't mean that you're mistreating him," Galen said. "Just the opposite. Horses from the racetrack are taught to go forward and run, no matter what. As long as they're headed in the right direction, forward, the trainers don't care how they behave. They don't want to kill the drive to win the race. So that's what the horse is trying to do now. Win the race."

The husband took off his hat and scratched his head. "What can you do to change that?"

"I need to work with him so he doesn't think running is the right choice. If he's in doubt or encounters the unexpected, he needs to pay attention to you."

The couple left the gelding in Galen's care. Delia overheard him tell Jimmy Fisher that most of the time the horse's training was just fine, and his job was about retraining the horse owners.

Delia wished Will could watch Galen work with these horses—he would find it fascinating, like watching a horse whisperer. Just being around Galen was very calming to the spirit.

She wondered what Rose thought about Galen. She was nice and polite to him, and he was as pleasant as could be to Rose, but now and then he seemed to look at her in a wondering sort of way. Why was that?

It was the kind of discussion Delia would have had with Charles over dinner, and he would vaguely answer as if he was listening to her, which he wasn't.

But there was the rub: there were so many things she wanted to tell Charles. Every day she thought of something new.

12

Call Jimmy Fisher what you will, but don't call him a quitter. He made a list of all of the spring mud sales that would be held in Lancaster County and decided to go to each one, every Saturday, handing out posters that described Lodestar. Someone, somewhere, must have seen his horse.

What he didn't expect was to find Lodestar at the very next mud sale of the season over at the Bird-in-Hand fire station. He had tied up his horse and buggy, picked up the posters he had printed, turned around and . . . there he was! None other than Lodestar. He dropped the posters back in the buggy, picked up a lead rope—something he had kept in the buggy in case he'd found Lodestar—and bolted to the stall where the horse was held. The chocolate brown horse looked healthy and cared for, which relieved Jimmy.

Jimmy stared at him, transfixed. This horse was regal—tall, elegant, confident. Jimmy held out his hand and the horse's ears perked up, thinking there might be a carrot. Lodestar edged his way over toward Jimmy and sniffed his open hand. With his other hand, Jimmy clipped the lead onto Lodestar's harness.

"Just what do you think you're doing?"

Jimmy spun around to face Jonah Hershberger. "You sold me this horse, square and fair."

Jonah tilted his head. "You're the one who didn't keep him in a place that could contain him."

"You put him in that pasture!"

"Temporarily. I was just doing you a favor by delivering the horse to you. Door-to-door service. It was your job to keep him from getting out. He's a stallion! All he needed was a whiff of a mare in season and he's out the door. If you're going to have a stud farm, you're going to have to pay attention to those kinds of things."

Jimmy frowned. That was a point he couldn't dispute. He hadn't given much thought to the mechanics of having a stud. Galen constantly chewed him out for not thinking into the future. "How did you find him, anyhow?"

Jonah looked at Jimmy as if his lantern seemed a little dim. "He found me. He's smart like that."

Dang! That *was* smart. Jimmy *had* to have this horse. "Look, I really need this horse."

Jonah sighed. "Then why did your check bounce?"

It bounced? Oh, boy. Jimmy was afraid of that. He wasn't exactly sure how much he had in his account when he had written that check to Jonah. He was hoping there had been enough. "I'll cover it."

Jonah looked at Lodestar. "You've put me to a lot of extra trouble." He rubbed his chin. "But there's something about you I like. I guess you remind me of me, a few years back. Okay . . . get me the deposit in cash this time, and we'll try it again." He stuck out his hand.

Jimmy looked down at it, looked over at Lodestar—what

a magnificent beast!—and shook Jonah's hand. "Deal. I'll be back in an hour." He would get to the farmers' market and borrow the money from his brother, Paul. It was pretty generous of Jonah to give him a second chance, and to only ask for the deposit too. He was afraid he would want the entire amount, cash on the barrel. As he untied his buggy horse from the hitching post, he grinned. He thought about the large humble pie Galen King would be eating after Jimmy informed him that Lodestar was in his barn, safe and sound and ready to be the cornerstone of Jimmy Fisher's Stud Farm.

And if his brother was in a friendly mood and could be quick about lending him the cash, he might have time to stop in the Stoney Ridge Bar & Grill and check up on Bethany Schrock. He could tell he made her nervous—she always dropped or spilled something when he was around—and he got a kick out of that.

As Saturday evening wore on at the Stoney Ridge Bar & Grill, Bethany felt more and more uncomfortable. First, she had told Rose she would be home by eleven and she wasn't entirely truthful to her about where she would be. She said she was taking a book over to M.K. Lapp's, which was the truth, though Rose gave her a funny look. Bethany should have thought of something besides a book. Everyone knew she didn't read much. And she certainly couldn't add on that she was working a late shift at the Grill.

What bothered her more than telling a half-truth was the group of men hanging out by the bar, drinking steadily, playing darts. Barflies, her friend Ivy called them. The Grill had a different clientele at night than during the day. On the wall was taped a full-page, full-length newspaper page of Osama bin Laden. "Go for the eyes," she heard them say as they threw the silver-tipped, evil-looking darts at the portrait. How awful!

Bethany steered clear of the bar as much as she could, but she had to walk past it to get in and out of the kitchen. One fellow, in particular, kept calling out to her in a slurry voice, "Hey, dollface, what's your hurry?" He sidled over to the end of the bar by the swinging kitchen door, trying to get her to talk to him as she passed by with a giant tray loaded with food for her table. "What time you get off tonight, sugar?" His comments took a turn for the worse as the evening progressed and his beer glasses emptied, and so did Bethany's temper. She had one more table to serve coffee, dessert, and collect the tab, then she would be done with her shift and could go home. But Slurry Voice made a critical mistake. He pinched her bottom as she walked out with a trayful of hot coffee mugs.

"Shootfire!" Bethany spun around, sending her tray toppling onto Slurry Voice. Hot coffee spilled over his shirt and pants.

"HEY!" Slurry Voice screamed, jumping back. He knocked into the man standing behind him, who shoved him away. Slurry Voice slipped on the hot coffee puddled on the ground and bumped into the back of someone else standing at the bar. A chain began of irritated barflies, overreacting, almost like a game of dominos—but it all seemed to be happening in slow motion.

At least, it seemed like slow motion to Bethany. Mouth agape, she stood frozen in the middle of the mess, staring at what was going on around her.

Someone approached Bethany from behind. Hard fingers dug into her arm and she was spun around abruptly, steered to the door. As she tried to slip out of this person's grip, he only hung on tighter. "You need to get out of here," an unpleasantly familiar male voice said. "I've got my buggy outside."

It was Jimmy Fisher, telling her what to do! What's he doing here, anyway? Outside by the buggy, she yanked her arm out of his grasp.

"I'm taking you home."

She glared at him. "What are you doing here?"

"I stopped in earlier today and found out you were working the late shift tonight. Had a hunch you might not realize what a Saturday night looked like at the Grill, so I decided to drop by."

She scowled. "How long have you been there?"

"Long enough to see what was going to happen after your shift ended."

"It hasn't ended! I still have customers in there."

"Doubt it." People were pouring out of the restaurant, eager to leave the chaos.

Bethany turned to him with a scowl. "You had no right to do what you did."

"What *I* did? How about pouring hot coffee down the pants of a customer and starting a brawl?"

She ignored that. "I could have handled the situation myself."

"Goodness, you're sassy. You beat any woman for taking the starch out of a man."

"I'm merely honest," Bethany said.

Jimmy practically lifted her into the buggy, then climbed in on the other side and snapped the horse's reins.

When a car passed by them, the headlights lit up the interior of the buggy. Her clothes! She was wearing her English clothes. She didn't even have on a prayer cap. Her Plain clothing was tucked in her cubby back in the restaurant. She would have to be as silent as snow as she entered the house. It was late, past midnight, but Mammi Vera was often awake during the night, prowling around the downstairs, fretting. Bethany hoped she might be sound asleep. Some things, she knew, were best left unexplained.

"Bethany, listen to me. I like excitement as much as anyone, maybe more than most. But you're way in over your head here. You need to quit."

In that instant, all her aggravation at Jimmy Fisher tumbled back. Here he was, telling her what to do again. She didn't speak to him the rest of the way home. Too furious. Too embarrassed, mortified at the thought of a creepy drunken man pinching her bottom. Too mad at herself. She never saw those things coming. They happened too fast. One minute, she's serving coffee, the next, she started a small riot.

If Jimmy hadn't been there . . . well, who knew how the evening might have turned out? She shuddered.

That was the thing about Jimmy Fisher. He had a way of making her feel as if her bonnet was on backward.

Jimmy Fisher was looking forward to church this morning as never before. He wanted to tell Galen that he was dead wrong about Jonah Hershberger. Lodestar was in a locked stall in the latched barn. And when he had stopped by the Stoney Ridge Bar & Grill and learned that Bethany would be working the late shift that night, he returned at the end of her shift . . . sensing she would need a little extra help. And he had been right—she was facing a very dicey moment. Best of all, he was sure she might be talked into going out with him sometime, if he ever had a little extra cash.

In the last twenty-four hours, he had made significant strides toward maturity and long-term thinking—two areas that topped the list of Galen's complaints about him.

He splashed cold water on his face and shaved so quickly that he nicked himself twice. He grabbed his shirt and took the stairs two at a time, stopping by the back door to jam his stocking feet into his boots. He hurried down to the barn, eager to check on Lodestar. As he came around the corner, he saw something that made his heart beat a little faster. The barn door was opened by about two feet. He gave it a push and walked inside. The sun was just rising on the horizon and cast a beam of light from the open door, down the interior aisle of the barn. Jimmy walked slowly down the aisle, holding his breath. When he got to Lodestar's stall, the door was wide open. The stall was empty.

The rising sun crested the tops of the hills that surrounded Galen's ranch. It had turned the clouds around it a coral pink and cast a pale yellow light over the fields that were just greening with the first shoots of spring.

Jimmy burst through the kitchen door of Galen's house and found him seated at the kitchen table, sipping coffee. Naomi was dishing up scrambled eggs by the stove and offered him a plate. He shook his head. Too upset.

"It happened again, Galen. I found Lodestar. Then he ran away again. I woke up this morning and he was gone. The barn door was open."

Galen chewed and swallowed a mouthful of scrambled eggs as if he had all the time in the world. "You latched the stall?"

He scowled at Galen. "Of course!" Of course he did. "I'm sure of it." He remembered latching it, then double-checking it. Didn't he? Could he have been so conscious of it that he neglected to actually do it?

"You'd be amazed at how wily some horses can be." Galen finished off the rest of his scrambled eggs. They were just the way Jimmy liked them—buttery, sprinkled with salt and pepper. His stomach rumbled.

Naomi brought over a plate of steaming waffles. "Didn't Dad have a buggy horse that could unlatch a gate with its lips?"

Galen laughed and helped himself to a waffle. "We had to get a combination lock, but that only worked until he learned his numbers. Finally wised up and got a key lock."

Jimmy wasn't listening. Deflated, he was in no mood for jokes. That must have been exactly what Lodestar had done. He should have spent the night in the barn, watching him. How could he have had that horse in his grip a second time, only to lose him? What were the chances he would get him back a third time?

"I'm going to get ready for church," Naomi said. Before she left the room, she turned and said, "Jimmy, if you change your mind about breakfast, you just help yourself."

Galen poured warm maple syrup over his waffle. "Where'd you find him?"

Jimmy watched the syrup run into the pockets of Galen's waffle. Maybe he should reconsider breakfast. Naomi was a fine cook and it was hard for a man to think straight on an empty stomach. "The trader had him. Said the horse had made his way back to him."

Galen froze, fork suspended in the air speared onto a bite of waffle. He put down his fork and made a small sighing sound, as if he'd heard this story before.

"What?" Jimmy took the plate of remaining waffles and poured maple syrup on top. Just the smell of the crisp waffle, smothered in melted butter and maple syrup, was lifting his spirits.

"Jimmy, you're never going to find that horse again. Even if you do, you'll never keep him."

Jimmy finished swallowing his bite. "What makes you say such bleak and gloomy things? This is why folks are scared of you, Galen."

Galen lifted his dark eyebrows. "You need to start thinking less like a man blinded by love and more like a horse trainer. There are plenty of other horses in the world."

"None like Lodestar."

"I'll help. We'll find another. Might take some time, but we'll get you a stud."

Jimmy finished off the waffles and eyed the bowl of scrambled eggs. He was definitely feeling more cheerful after eating something. If he had been smart enough to track Lodestar down a second time, surely he could find him a third time. "You are wrong, my friend, and I am going to prove it to you."

It was strange, thought Bethany, that you could go to sleep thinking one way, and awake the following morning thinking quite another. And so it was with her opinion about working at the Sisters' House. "I've changed my mind," she would say to Jimmy Fisher after church later today, if she could talk to him without anyone noticing. After all, she had her reputation to uphold. "I'll work for those old ladies."

Seated in a swept clean barn across from the men on wooden, backless benches, Bethany happened to steal a glimpse at Jimmy Fisher and was struck senseless by those blue, blue eyes. But as Bethany was here to worship God, she tried not to think about the color of Jimmy's eyes, or how he had rescued her last night from near disaster at the Stoney Ridge Bar & Grill and then acted like he was a knight in shining armor, which he wasn't. Then he caught sight of her peeking over at him a second time and gave her an audacious wink with a smile dipped in honey, which made her blush despite her best effort to keep her composure.

That Jimmy Fisher was no good and low down, with a bad character to boot.

He just sat across the room grinning like he always did, prouder than ever that he had made her flustered.

She lifted her chin a notch and turned her attention to the minister, who was preaching of days long ago, of a time when the Plain People suffered terribly for their faith. Sometimes Bethany listened to these old familiar stories. Sometimes she just let the words float around her while she drifted away on her thoughts. A barn swallow fluttered through a missing board to disappear into its nest in the rafters.

The minister was preaching now of how some of their ancestors had been driven from their homes and chased across Europe. Some had been burned alive, others whipped or stoned. Tongues were severed, hands and feet. She shuddered. She couldn't imagine feeling so passionate about something that she would be willing to be tortured for it, and that left her feeling guilty. Even today, the minister explained, there were hardships to suffer. Even in this land of plenty, the place where they had come to hundreds of years ago, to find freedom to worship God. Even here, there was pain, there was loss.

That, Bethany understood.

Her hands curled into a tight ball in her lap. Whenever she thought about her father, feelings of anger welled up inside. How could he? How dare he? He hurt so many people who trusted him. How could he have betrayed Rose and Tobe? And Jake too? All innocent people who cared about him. And then . . . he died. Rose insisted it was an accident, but Bethany had plenty of doubts. Death was an easy out. Her father was the very opposite of these martyred ancestors, who were willing to suffer for what they believed to be right and true. Her father . . . he was a coward.

So was her mother, for that matter. They both vanished when life took a sharp turn.

The minister's slow, singsongy voice was winding down to an end. Much time must have passed while Bethany's thoughts stayed on her father. She tried to shake off the unsettled feelings those thoughts left her with and push them away—that was why she didn't let herself think about him very often. Her gaze fell to her lap. She put a pleat in her apron with her fingers, then smoothed it out with her palm. She could smell the coffee brewing for the fellowship meal after the service. She listened to the chickens clucking in the yard through the open window, to the baas of the goats and the bleats of the sheep out in the pasture. During the silent and solemn moments of waiting for the minister to dismiss everyone, Bethany pulled her thoughts and feelings back together, like cinching a rope. It was much more enjoyable to think about Jake. Jimmy too.

After church, Bethany walked out of the cool darkness of the barn and blinked against the sudden wash of sunlight. Naomi waved to her to help serve tables. The women always served the men first. After the men had eaten, Naomi and Bethany grabbed a clean plate and sat next to each other at the end of the table. As Bethany spread church peanut butter over her bread, she asked Naomi if she had ever been kissed by a boy.

Naomi held her hands to her mouth, shocked. "Heavens, no!"

Bethany handed her the slice of slathered bread.

"Have you?" Naomi whispered.

She nodded.

"Oh, Bethany! Before you are married? Or even promised to someone? Oh my." She looked terribly concerned.

Suddenly, Bethany felt like a fallen woman. She often felt such pricks of conscience around her friend. Naomi was so pure and innocent and good and Bethany was so . . . tangled up and filled with doubts. "Well, it was the day I told Jake Hertzler that I was moving away. We were upset, you see, and didn't know when we would see each other again."

Naomi's face grew studious and she looked back at her plate. "Of course," she said at last, and sighed with relief. "Of course, it was a terribly emotional time. You were both overcome with sorrow. I'm sure it wasn't anything more than that. Just a heartfelt goodbye kiss."

Bethany nodded righteously, but she couldn't look her friend in the eyes again. She wondered what Naomi's reaction would be if she knew that she and Jake had kissed quite a bit, sometimes as passionately as if he was saying goodbye before heading off to sail the seven seas. As recently as a few days ago.

Some things, she decided, were best left unsaid.

13

Barn swallows darted in and out of the ceiling rafters. Galen had a mare's left rear hoof up on his thigh and was scraping caked dirt out of it with a hoof pick. Last evening, he noticed the mare looked a little lame and he wanted to check on her first thing this morning.

"Hello, neighbor."

Galen straightened up at the sound of Rose's voice. It was Monday, it was early, and he was in need of a shave. He wished he'd had a little warning that she was coming by.

Then he checked himself. Since when had he started worrying about what he looked like? Rose had seen him plenty of times looking pretty bad. Why did it suddenly matter? It shouldn't.

But it did.

He looked over the mare's neck at Rose and wondered how she was able to look fresh and pretty at this hour. He had a bunch of sisters—they sure didn't look like that at the crack of dawn. "Morning, Rose."

He could feel her eyes on him as he exchanged the hoof pick for a brush and began to run it over the mare's neck and withers. "Something on your mind on this rainy morning?"

"That coyote took down one of my sheep last night. An eagle was working on the carcass." She was trying to sound matter of fact, but Galen saw her shudder. It was a gruesome thing, what a coyote could do to a sheep. "I was hoping Jimmy wouldn't mind helping me move it before Sammy wakes up. It was his pet sheep."

Galen put down the hoof pick. "I'll take care of it."

"Isn't Jimmy here?"

"No. He's too busy chasing a horse he'll never catch."

"What do you mean?"

Galen straightened. "Two Saturdays ago, Jimmy decided he was going to be a horse breeder. He bought a colt off a trader that he thought would be his foundation stallion. Just like that." He clicked his fingers together. "No vet check. No paperwork about the colt's bloodlines. Not even a bill of sale." He shook his head. "My grandmother Jorie used to keep charts and graphs of her Percherons' traits, trying to find just the right match."

"Jimmy's learning a lot from you. Maybe it'll all turn out just fine."

"Oh, I don't think so. The horse is gone."

Her eyes went wide. "Gone? What happened?"

"Jumped the paddock and took off. That was the first time. The second time—he slipped out of his stall."

"Twice? The horse has gotten loose twice?"

"Twice." He lifted his chin. "Doesn't that sound a little fishy to you?"

"What do you mean?"

"There's an old scam called 'The Runner.' The trader sells the horse to a naïve buyer, but he's trained the horse to return to him with some kind of signal—a whistle or a clicker. Then he scoops the horse up in his trailer and sells him to the next easy target."

She looked at him, eyes wide. "Poor Jimmy."

Galen rolled his eyes. "Save your pity. That boy needs to learn everything the hard way. This is a lesson he'll never forget."

Disappointment showed raw in her face. "Galen."

"What?"

"He needs you. You could help him."

"What?" The word came out as a tiny squeak. He cleared his throat and tried again. "What? He hasn't been asking for my advice."

"Still, he's just a boy."

"He's twenty-two. Maybe twenty-three. Plenty of Amish boys have married by that age."

Her head snapped up. "You weren't."

Galen set his jaw at a stubborn tilt. "No. But I was entirely different—"

"Boys need time to grow up and become men." She ran a hand down the mare's long neck. "Jimmy reminds me of Tobe."

Galen gave a hard, short laugh, which caused Rose to give him a sharp look. Tobe Schrock? Jimmy Fisher reminded her of her stepson? If that were true, they might be waiting a very long time. Tobe Schrock had never impressed Galen. The last time he had seen him was a few days before he vanished into thin air. Dean Schrock had brought a goat home for the little boys but hadn't thought to buy feed for it, so he sent Luke over to borrow a bale of hay. When Galen reached the barn, he struggled to get the door open with the hay bale on his shoulder. Inside the barn was young Tobe Schrock, idle as usual, though there was plenty of work to be done. He sat on a wooden barrel playing a game of solitaire, using an upturned nail keg for a table. He glanced up at Galen, not even bothering to get off his duff to open the barn door. It evidently didn't bother Tobe to play while others worked, a fact that annoyed Galen. He was tempted to kick the barrel and send him sprawling. He hadn't, of course, but he had sorely wanted to.

"You of all people should be able to understand Jimmy. He lost his father when he was young, and his mother, well, you know what Edith Fisher is like. He's trying to become a man and he needs you in his life. You should be helping him find his way in the world, not feeling smug like he deserved what he got."

How was it suddenly Galen's fault that Jimmy did something stupid?

"Promise me you'll talk to him."

Galen wasn't about to make any such promise. Since when did the future of Jimmy Fisher become his responsibility? He was minding his own business when Deacon Abraham interfered—he hadn't even wanted an apprentice in the first place. And now Rose made it sound like it was his job to be a father figure to the boy.

"Sense gets wasted on people until they learn to ask for help. Jimmy has to learn. It's part of life," he said, knowing how callous his words sounded to her.

"I just don't understand you men. You won't listen to anyone's good advice, especially if it comes from a woman. You're all alike. Stubborn and proud and independent and unbending. Just like . . ." She seemed about to say more, but thought better of it and clamped her lips shut. "Sometimes," she added, "you have to keep talking until a person listens."

Her gaze met his over the horse's head. The silence between them took on a prickly tension, like a strand of wire pulled tightly between two fence posts.

As she turned to leave, Galen reached out and grabbed her sleeve. Her eyes were fixed on the hand that held her. In as gentle a voice as he could manage, he said, "I'll make sure that coyote doesn't trouble you again."

"It's part of life," Galen had told her.

What part? Rose wanted to ask. The part where a sweet little sheep had its belly ripped open by a vicious coyote, where a mother-in-law turned into a child, and a boy lost his dream of finding the perfect horse? How difficult did life have to get before someone stepped in? To come alongside and make it better. So much for living the Plain life, where one never needed to face life alone, never needed to be afraid.

Being Plain never meant being perfect, she could hear Bishop Elmo's voice say. Just yesterday in church, he had said it again. *Only God is perfect.*

She didn't expect perfection, but this hardness Galen had for Jimmy, for Tobe—it nettled her. How could Galen possibly understand? Rose thought. He wasn't married. He wasn't a parent. He hadn't raised a boy to become a man, only to discover that he had turned into somebody else entirely.

In many ways, Galen went out of his way to help her, as a neighbor, as a friend. But there was a part of him that remained aloof, separate, a little cold. It seemed nearly impossible for him to share his thoughts, his feelings. Sometimes, he seemed to her like a walnut that couldn't be cracked open with a sledgehammer. When she tried, like she just had, she saw the expression in his face change in a flash—surprised, confused, then annoyed—before he stiffened up like wet leather left in the sun.

It dawned on her that she didn't know how old Galen actually was, that he might be closer to Jimmy Fisher's age than to hers. Imagine that. Not all that much older than Jimmy Fisher. And yet, they were worlds apart.

On Monday morning, a day full of problems stretched in front of Bethany. First, she was going with Naomi to the fabric store to get some material for a new dress. Naomi went straightaway to the solid colors, but Bethany stopped by a lightweight fabric of bright blue waves. She stroked the printed fabric and was amazed at how soft it felt, as soft as the velvet nose on Rose's new colt. She felt a pang of longing.

Normally, Bethany didn't spend much time thinking about all the things she had given up after moving in to her grandmother's home: cell phones, cars, and lights that flipped on and off with a switch. There was usually a way to get the same thing done, even if it took a little longer. But it was another story entirely when it came to printed fabric.

Naomi came up behind her and said, "I can't imagine why any woman would wear a fabric like that. Men would stop seeing the real beauty of a woman if she were dressed in that."

Of course. Of course it would seem like that. Naomi would never understand why Bethany loved those prints. She was too good and pure and innocent. And she was right too. The Lord looked on a person's inside, but people—men, especially—looked on the outside.

Bethany wouldn't stay Old Order Amish forever. When Jake was ready to marry, she would return to the Mennonite church, become baptized, and be with him.

Just a little longer. Then she could wear all the prints she wanted to.

Bethany took a deep breath and walked over to the plain solid colors. She asked the shopkeeper to cut seven yards of a serviceable plum-colored fabric. As Naomi was getting her fabric measured and cut, Bethany walked by the wavy blue cloth one more time. What was it about that blue color that made her smile? The sight of it made her happy. Where had she seen it before? Then an image popped into her mind. It was the color of Jimmy Fisher's eyes.

Naomi dropped Bethany and her scooter off at the farmers' market and went home. Bethany waited until Naomi's buggy was out of sight, stashed her scooter behind the dumpster, and hurried to the Stoney Ridge Bar & Grill. Her friend Ivy met her at the door, eyes wide. "What on earth happened here on Saturday night?"

"Nothing!" Bethany said. "Well, other than a drunk fellow pinched me and I left early, but I had finished my shift." Almost finished.

Ivy seemed skeptical. "The manager wants to talk to you."

Bethany walked into the main room. Her jaw dropped when she saw the condition of the dining room. Chairs were overturned, tables were knocked on their sides. Ted, the manager, was bent over, sweeping up broken glass.

"It looks like a tornado swept through this room!" Bethany said, righting a chair.

Ted straightened to look at her. His voice turned to smoke. "An Amish tornado."

She swallowed. "Um, did this happen after I left on Saturday night?"

Ted gave her a look as if she might be one brick short of a full load. "Bethany, this job . . . it isn't right for you. Your paycheck is waiting for you up by the cash register."

Bethany could see the decision was made. She crossed the room to the cash register, stepping gingerly around broken bottles and stale puddles of beer, to find the envelope with her name on it. Ivy handed her a brown paper bag filled with clothing from her locker, then hugged her goodbye.

Bethany walked back to Ted. "What about my tip money from Saturday night?"

"Ah yes." He dug into his own pocket, pressed a tip into her palm, then closed her fingers around it. "Here it is." He turned around and went back to sweeping.

A one-dollar bill looked back at her.

Delia unpacked a few groceries in the little kitchen of the guest flat after she returned to Eagle Hill from a trip to the Bent N' Dent. She didn't want Rose to feel she needed to provide meals for her. Breakfast was enough.

As she tucked some apples in the fridge, she thought of the scene she had observed at the farmhouse last night. She had taken a walk up the hill behind the house to watch the sunset. As she came down the hill in the deepening dusk, her eyes were drawn to the only brightly lit room in the farmhouse—the rest of the house was dark. It was the living room, where Rose and the children were gathered around a board game at a table. Vera sat in a rocking chair nearby. Delia paused for a moment, touched by their pleasure over such a simple activity—laughing together, sharing a bowl of popcorn, eating sliced apples, having a wonderful time. Even Vera. A buttery glow from the kerosene lampshine in the room made the scene reminiscent of a Norman Rockwell or Thomas Kinkaid painting. It was so beautiful it hurt to look at it.

She couldn't help but compare what this farmhouse might look like if it were filled with a typical American family: every light in the house would be on and each adult or child would be in a different room, probably facing the cold glow of a television or computer. Maybe that wasn't a fair assessment of most Americans, but it would have been true of Delia's home.

Delia heard a knock at the door and went to open it, assuming it was Rose.

There stood Charles. His gray-green eyes looked icy cold. "May I come in?"

She took a deep breath and tried to keep her hands from shaking, told herself she could do this. She stepped away from the door.

Charles walked in and looked around the small room, then spun around to face her. "Did you realize the police hauled me off to the station for questioning? They accused me of doing away with you. Accused me of being a wife killer. *Me!*" He thumped his chest with his fist. "Did you think of that when you decided to vanish?"

She closed the door, then lifted her chin. "Of course I didn't. I should have told someone I was heading out of town. I never dreamed there would be such a fuss."

"And why here, of all places?"

"Why should that matter? Why should it matter where I've been?"

He narrowed his eyes. "Maybe it's a passive-aggressive

way to try to get to me. Make a dig at my upbringing? Try to help me remember my humble roots?"

Charles's childhood was something he never discussed. He was raised Old Order Amish and left as a teenager to pursue college and a career in medicine. When she met him, he was a surgical resident. He told her he was estranged from his family—that they didn't believe in higher education and were ashamed of him for wanting more out of life than farming. Charles always said the word "farming" like it was a terrible disease—something to be avoided. Contact with his family over the years was minimal, despite Delia's encouragement. He even attended his parents' funerals alone, insisting Delia and Will would be bored. She didn't push Charles on the subject. It wasn't worth it. Besides, it didn't make any difference.

"Do you realize that this was the town where Will interned for the game commissioner when he was kicked out of college? What were you thinking?"

She knew.

Maybe, subconsciously, that was the reason she had jumped so impulsively at Lois's suggestion. After Will had spent that spring on an Amish farm in Stoney Ridge, there was a change in Charles, a softening. He had even contacted his siblings to catch up on their news. That softening lasted until Will decided on vet school. Charles didn't think being a veterinarian would be enough of a challenge to his son. But Will's mind was made up, and Charles hardened again.

This time, Delia wasn't going to budge. She was going to hold her ground. "Sit down. I will explain, but I'm only going to say this once." Charles was a large man and tall, his stance a little threatening. She motioned to a chair but he didn't move to it, which didn't surprise her. "Not everything is about you, Charles." She sat in the chair by the window and folded her hands. Surprisingly, she felt remarkably calm. "I have breast cancer."

Charles sank slowly down in the chair.

"The day you told me that you were leaving me was the day I found out about the cancer. I was coming home to tell you, but your news trumped mine. Since then, I've had a lumpectomy. And I also found out that the . . . object of your . . . affections . . . is Robyn Dixon. I saw you in the car together, at the lawyer's office when we were scheduled to meet. That's the reason I left. I'm sorry it caused you a little inconvenience and bad publicity."

He seemed to be fighting to make sense of what she was saying. "Are the . . . were the margins clear?"

"I don't know. Dr. Zimmerman thought it was caught early, so I'm hoping so. I'll call in tomorrow and see if the results are in. I can't get reception out here, so I'll have to go into town."

She stood on wobbly legs and started for the door. "Now, if you'll excuse me, I believe we are finished with this conversation."

Charles didn't move. "Does Will know?"

She nodded. "We spoke on the phone."

He leaned forward in the chair and steepled his fingers together. "I'll call Zimmerman's office tomorrow. I want to see all the op notes and get the test results. There's a specialist in Boston I'm going to send you to."

"No. No, you won't. Dr. Zimmerman is an excellent doctor. You're no longer making decisions for me. I can take care of myself."

A muscle tightened in his jaw. "Don't be foolish, Delia. You have every reason to be upset with me, but—"

"I don't want you making any decisions for me. Not anymore."

He rose to walk toward her. She held up her hand as he opened his mouth to protest. "You must know why. I don't trust you, Charles. You have lied, you have cheated. You have destroyed our family. All that's left is mistrust. And sadness."

His throat moved up and down. For a moment, he looked away. On a shaky breath, he turned back to her. "I do have regrets, Delia."

"Regret." She gave a short laugh. "Like the regret you feel over the patient who had the stroke after the aneurysm surgery?"

Charles stared at her, his face settling into deep lines, and Delia stared back, her head held high, erect. "What does that have to do with us?"

She gave a short laugh. "Everything! You can't admit you make mistakes."

"I did not make a mistake in that surgery. But I do have regret for the patient."

"That's not the same thing as being sorry. Truly sorry." A flash of fury rose inside of her. "Has it ever occurred to you to apologize to that patient? Just to admit that you're sorry?"

"I said I had regret over that outcome!"

"No, your ego is bruised, but that patient's life is forever changed. So is her husband's life. You need to tell them how sorry you are. Sincerely sorry." She paused. "No, no. It's more than that. Not just a professional apology, without accepting any blame. You need to ask her to forgive you for not preparing her for the risks of surgery."

He looked at her as if a cat had spoken. "Do you realize what that would mean? What it could do to me, professionally? Legally? And it wouldn't change a thing."

"That's where you're wrong. I think that patient and her husband need something from you before they can move on with their life. I know you didn't intend to cause her any harm, but the fact is that she trusted you. She trusted you with her life. You need to ask for her forgiveness. You owe the woman that much."

For a moment Charles said nothing, and his mouth kept that tight, stern look. Then he sighed, rubbing a hand through his hair. "You're not being rational. I realize you're under a great deal of stress—"

"I believe we've both said enough," she said in a curt tone. She reached for the door handle and opened the door. "Please go."

She surprised him so, a stain of red flushed on his cheekbones. He looked at her now as if he'd never seen her before, as if she wasn't the Delia he had known for half his life.

Charles stopped at the threshold, reaching out a hand to Delia, but she flinched and he pulled it away. He headed out to his car. Before he climbed in, he gazed all around the farm. Then he gave his head a shake, as if he were dusting something off, and drove away.

As she saw the car disappear down the road, tears welled in her eyes. She had promised herself she wouldn't cry, but this was Charles and she had loved him so much. Her heart felt so bruised it was hard to breathe. *What happened to us, Charles? Our love was supposed to last forever.*

Maybe she shouldn't have said what she said. She shouldn't have blurted out that she had cancer, but the stunned look on his face was gratifying. She wanted to make him pay for the suffering he had caused. She wanted him to hurt.

She wished she could turn back time, to try to find the moment when they had started to lose each other, and to fix it.

More than anything, seeing him again, she realized she just wanted him back.

14

It was a beautiful afternoon in the first week of April, touched with a hint of spring. After Rose had helped Vera eat her lunch, she desperately needed some fresh air. It was strange how one person could change the mood of a room. Some could fill a room with excitement and energy. Jimmy Fisher was like that. Whenever he joined the family for dinner, which was happening more and more often, Rose noticed that everyone laughed more, ate more, lingered longer.

Then there were others, like Vera, who could drain off energy and joy, like siphoning sap from a maple tree. Her mother-in-law had a way of turning a sunny day into a dismally gray one. Well, she wasn't going to let Vera spoil this beautiful day.

Rose went out to the flower garden to pour clean water into the birdbath. Chase trotted behind her and ran off to chase a cottontail through the privet, the poor fool. He never caught a blessed thing, though he did his best. She noticed the "Inn at Eagle Hill" sign standing tall and stately at the end of the driveway. Galen had built it, Mim had painted it with her careful, deliberate penmanship, and Jimmy Fisher helped install it. It seemed so official to hang a shingle and the very sight of it brought delight to her.

She glanced over at the guest flat and noticed the curtains were still drawn. On Sunday, Delia Stoltz had a little spark back in her, but now, Wednesday, she seemed to be withdrawing into sadness again. Rose tried to ignore that spike of worry—the last thing she wanted to do was to grow attached to the guests.

But she just couldn't help it. She knew that Delia Stoltz needed Eagle Hill.

A few days ago, Rose saw Delia take a walk into the hills behind the farmhouse in the late afternoon. An unexplainable pity touched her heart as she watched Delia head up the path, head down, shoulders rounded, fragile and defeated. Yesterday, Rose walked next door to fetch the boys home for supper and couldn't pull them away until Galen had finished working with a jumpy horse. Galen displayed utter calm—a wonderful example for her sons to observe, especially Luke. When she returned home, Mim and Vera had informed her that Delia Stoltz had entertained a visitor in the guest flat. The male type—but he didn't stay long, they said. Vera commented on how fine looking the man happened to be, despite being English. Twice, she said it.

Rose had a hunch that fine-looking man might have been the doctor looking for his lost wife. She thought she should check on Delia, but the evening got away from her. Here it was a day later, nearly three, and she still hadn't had a moment to tend to Delia. Once the boys returned from school, the day was over.

Rose knocked gently on the guest flat door. When there was no answer, she opened the door and softly called Delia's name. The blinds were drawn to keep out the daylight, and it took a moment for Rose's eyes to adjust to the dimness. She found Delia curled up in a corner of the sofa, surrounded by a litter of crumpled, damp tissues.

Rose walked across the room to the window and pulled the cord on the window blind. Delia's eyes blinked rapidly as the bright noonday light streamed through the glass directly into her eyes. Rose's heart went out to her; she was a pitiable sight. "Delia Stoltz, you don't seem to me to be a woman without a backbone."

Delia remained still, facing her for a very long time, and then Rose saw tears well in her eyes and spill over onto her cheeks. "I know you want to help, but you don't know what I'm going through."

"You're right. I don't." Rose sat on the sofa, uninvited. "So tell me."

Delia felt uncomfortable confiding in Rose, wondering if, behind that wide smile and those thoughtful gray eyes, she might be secretly judging her. But if she was, she gave no sign of it. After a few minutes, Delia felt more relaxed in her presence. She thought she might start crying again, but curiously, finally, she was out of tears.

Soon, everything spilled out. Drained and exhausted, she covered her eyes with one hand. "I'm alive. The cancer is gone, I hope and pray. I know I should be grateful for that, but I don't feel grateful. I feel completely lost." She opened her eyes, looking for answers in Rose's patient gaze.

Rose stood. For a moment, Delia thought she was going to put her arms around her and tell her it would be all right, and that would have made Delia furious. It wasn't going to be all right.

Instead Rose went to the little kitchen, picked up the trashcan, and started to fill it up with tissues. Then she went into the bedroom and made up the bed, tucking the sheets in so tightly Delia would have to pry them loose to get back into bed.

When Rose finished, she came back into the main room. She leaned against the doorjamb and folded her arms across her abdomen. "My husband had a knack for numbers and accounting. He started an investment company and, for quite a few years, he was very successful. More and more people heard about Schrock Investments. Dozens of our friends and relatives invested their life savings in the company. Then the recession hit and Dean had trouble keeping up those high returns. So he turned to riskier means to pay dividends. He was sure he could recoup the losses. But it all caught up with him. A year or two ago, everything started to fall apart. Everything.

"Dean had put our home up for collateral with bank loans and lost it. We had to move in here with his mother. The investors started to catch wind of Dean's problems and tried to pull their money out—but there was no money to pull out. It wasn't there. Dean declared bankruptcy. Not long after that, the police came to the house and told me Dean's body was found drowned."

Delia was stunned. "Your husband took his own life?"

Rose lifted one shoulder in a half shrug. "We don't know. We truly don't. He'd been having some racing heart troubles over the last year and refused to see a doctor about it. It was a very hot day, but why had he gone swimming in an unfamiliar pond? He wasn't much of a swimmer. The police declared it an accident—that he was a drowning victim, they said. I hope it was an accident."

"Didn't you have an autopsy? That might have answered your questions."

Rose looked down at the ground. "I refused it. Maybe that was a mistake. I don't know. Maybe I just didn't want to have my questions answered." She walked to the window and looked outside at the boys, pushing a wheelbarrow filled with hay toward the goat and sheep in the pen. "If Dean took his own life, our church believes he would lose his salvation. It's the ultimate way of turning against God. Of saying that God couldn't help a person out of a bad spot. I guess I felt it was better not to know why he died." She spun around to face Delia. "But then there's God's mercy too. Dean was stressed to the breaking point. I can't help but believe that God would understand. I pray so. I pray it every day."

Delia wasn't sure how to respond. She had never given suicide much thought other than pity. A terrible, terrible pity. She'd certainly never concerned herself about the afterlife.

"I was left to pick up all the pieces for Dean. I'm doing all I can to pay investors back what was owed to them. But this will follow me until the day I die. I want to make sure it doesn't follow my children." Delia saw her hands tighten into fists as she added quietly, "I will not let that happen."

"You have every right to be angry."

"Oh . . . believe me, I was. And I can be—it doesn't take much to flare it all up again. Whenever I get a call from that Securities and Exchange Commission lawyer with another twist and complication, I churn with feelings of anger all day long. But I know I can't live like that. I can't live on the precipice of anger. Husband or no, the world keeps on turning. I have children who need raising and a mother-in-law who needs tending to.

"So on those days, when anger returns, I go back to the beginning. I ask God to help me forgive Dean for not being all I wanted him to be, to help me forgive him so I can move on." Rose gathered a few dishes from the coffee table and put them in the kitchen sink. She turned on the hot water faucet and poured dish soap into the sink, swishing her hand to stir up bubbles. "Life doesn't always turn out the way we wish it would. Maybe we all have to get to the point in our lives when we face that fact. But I do know that God brings good things out of bad events. I've seen it, over and over. God doesn't waste anything. Not a thing."

Delia closed her eyes. "I don't know how to get there. How to get past the anger and disappointment. I wish I did, I wish I were more like you, but I just can't seem to do it."

Rose turned off the hot water and faced Delia. "For me, that's when I pray the prayer that always works."

"What's that?"

She lifted her eyes toward the ceiling and raised her soapy hands, palms up. "Help."

Two cars drove into the driveway, one right after the other. Rose rinsed off her hands and grabbed a towel as she went to the window. "The first car is our vet. She's coming to look at the colt. He's not eating enough. I don't know who is in the second car. A young fellow."

Curious, Delia rose from the sofa to join Rose at the window. "Why, that's Will. That's my son." It was the first time in weeks that she felt a genuine smile tug at her lips.

"Would you look at that," Luke said, excitement in his face. He had just arrived home from school and was delighted to see strange cars in the drive. He loved visitors.

The boys were standing in the doorway of the guest flat, watching Delia and her son embrace. Rose scowled fiercely at the boys until they backed off. She shooed them away to give Delia and her son a moment of privacy.

"Why's he crying?" Luke asked, as they walked to the barn.

"He's just unnerved—he's come a long way and I imagine he's just overcome at seeing his mother," Rose said.

"But he's a man," Sammy said. "Men don't cry."

"Men have tears in them, same as you," Rose said.

She went out to the barn to find the vet, a young woman named Jackie Colombo. Silver Girl's colt still wasn't thriving, so Jackie had come up with a few other remedies to help the little horse gain weight.

"He's just born a little too early," Jackie said. "Like a premature baby. I'll show you how to mix up some high-calorie meal for him." She carried a sheaf of hay to a worktable and took a knife to it, cracking and chopping that hay into baby-size pieces, almost like grain. Then she mixed it with some oats and a little molasses and a chopped apple. She held a handful out to the colt and he snorted over it suspiciously, but nibbled at it. He dropped more than half of it as he tried to chew it, but he went after the stuff he'd dropped. By the time Jackie was packing up to leave, his little sides were starting to fill out.

Sammy came bursting back into the barn. "Mom, something's wrong with the missus eagle!"

"What makes you say that?" Jackie asked.

Sammy turned to the vet. "She's screeching and screeching."

Rose's heart stopped. "Sammy, where's Luke?"

"He climbed a tree to get a close-up view of the eagles' nest."

The vet stuck her head over the stall door. "That nest must be forty feet high."

"I know!" Sammy said, proud of his brother's prowess. "He's up there!"

"Why would he try to get near the nest?" Rose said. "You boys know how dangerous eagles can be."

"We been watching them. They head up north during the day to hunt. They haven't been coming back to the nest by the creek till the sun starts dropping." Sammy's eyes were as wide as a dinner dish. "Luke said the nest was at least six feet wide and made mostly of sticks. Some of the sticks are bigger than me, he said. In the center of the nest is a soft spot made of grass and wool. Wool—from our very own sheep!" He took off his black hat, looking sheepish. "I almost forgot. Luke said he was having a little bit of trouble figuring out how to get down."

Even in the barn, they could hear the screeching sound of an eagle in distress.

"Something must be wrong with her." Sammy waved his arm at the vet. "It's good you're here. You can fix her."

"I wouldn't have any idea what's wrong with her," Jackie said.

"I do," said a man's voice. "She's defending her home. She's trying to warn you off. We'd better go get your brother out of that tree before she starts making a run at him."

They spun around and saw Delia's son standing at the barn door.

From her window, Delia watched Will escort the attractive young veterinarian to her car after the little boy was rescued from the tree. The two stood by the car, lingering. If Delia wasn't mistaken, she had noticed a spark or two between Will and the vet as they discussed the eagles. Of course, get Will on the topic of birds and he lit up like a Christmas tree. But wouldn't that be something—to have him find a girlfriend here, on an Amish farm? She smiled and dismissed the thought. Will always had a girl or two buzzing around him. Never anything serious, except for that one Amish girl, Sadie something-or-other, who had broken his heart. Delia only knew that because Will wouldn't discuss Sadie—he was pretty talkative about the other girls who had come and gone. Mostly gone. She hoped he would get serious about a girl someday. She was counting on grandchildren.

Earlier today, Will had finished a midterm exam and driven all afternoon to get here. For the first time, she saw not her son, full of boyish charm and mischief, but a competent and determined man.

Will told her he was going to stay with her until she was ready to return to civilization. "Even though you say you don't need my help, I want to hang around until you're back to your old self." He said the next part so firmly that she wondered if he was as confident about her recovery as he sounded. "You're going to get well, and I want to be there to help you do it. Is that such a terrible thing for a son to want to do? Help his mother, who's spent her whole life helping him?"

"No," she had said quietly. "Of course not, but I don't want you sacrificing the final stretch of your education just because of me. You're so close to the end. You need to finish and move on."

They agreed to a bargain. He would stay with her until she received the results about her lumpectomy. If the margins were clear, nothing in her lymph nodes, he would return to school. If they weren't, well, then they would decide together about next steps. She glanced at her watch. As soon as Will said goodbye to this lady vet, they should get into town so she could try to use her cell phone to call the doctor's office before it closed for the day. She finally felt ready to hear the results. It helped to have Will by her side.

She saw Rose herd those two boys up to the house. Rose moved lightly and quickly, Delia noticed, whether in the yard or in the kitchen. Often, she sang.

How she envied Rose. Just a week or two ago, if someone were to tell her that she would find herself envying an Amish widow, she would have laughed at the thought. Charles didn't speak much about his upbringing, but the truth of it was that she didn't ask about it. She wasn't interested. She didn't even ask Will many details about his spring on an Amish farm. If anything, it had embarrassed her to think her husband had been raised Plain, that he had looked like one of those little boys with black hats on. But there was something to this life, to these people. Maybe that's why Will had been so enamored with them. There was peace here.

Rose was a peaceable person. Delia repeated the word a few times. *I like that word peaceable,* she thought to herself. *It's what I would like to be.* She would try to be more like Rose.

Husband or no, the world keeps on turning, Rose had said. Add cancer to that list, Delia thought. Cancer or no, husband or no, the world keeps on turning.

During the rescue, for a few minutes or even longer, Delia had forgotten she had cancer. Forgotten that her husband had betrayed her. Maybe that's how emotional healing took place. Not all at once, but five minutes here and there. Hopefully, another minute each day. Perhaps by this time next year, she would hardly think about Charles.

As she pondered that, the strangest thing happened. A large news van with a satellite dish on top pulled into the driveway.

Will waved a hasty goodbye to the lady vet and came to the basement door. "That's another reason I thought it would be best if I come. The newspeople are still on this story about the disappearance of the doctor's wife. I saw a TV interview this morning with a scarlet-red-haired lady named Lois—she said you were tucked away at a charming new Amish inn in Stoney Ridge. She said you needed your peace and quiet, so everyone should leave you alone." He looked over at the news van. "So, of course, they came."

Vera sat at the kitchen window and watched Bethany hurry off to visit with that neighbor girl, Galen's sister. What was her name? Vera couldn't recall. She dismissed that hanging question and turned her attention back to her darling grand-daughter. Even as a child, Bethany always did tend to flit through the house like a bird, too full of energy to sit still. Just like Dean had.

Vera adored Bethany, always had. She smiled, or at least she tried to smile. Her thoughts drifted to Rose, cruelly setting the washstand mirror near her bed this morning. Vera had turned and caught a glimpse of herself in the mirror. The image of the droopy side of her face mocked her and she burst into tears. Rose quickly took away the mirror—but it didn't lift the sadness weighing on Vera's heart.

She couldn't believe what Bethany—dear, dear Bethany—did next. She realized how upset Vera was. She rubbed Vera's back and said it was the most precious smile in all the world, crooked or not. That's what the sweet child said about her, right in front of those children and in front of that mean-spirited daughter-in-law.

The most precious smile in all the world.

Vera sat up straighter and sighed. "Nothing has worked out like I thought it would." One little comment in a let-ter—inviting Dean to come live with her after she learned that his house had been foreclosed—and things had started to happen, things Vera couldn't see the end of.

When Dean had told her they would accept her offer to move in, she thought it would mean no more worry. No more loneliness. Rose and Bethany and that feisty one could tend to her like daughters should tend to mothers and grandmothers.

But Rose and Bethany didn't tend to her like she thought they would. Rose didn't neglect her in any way that Vera could put her finger on, and the children were good to her, minding her when she asked, but there were many times when she felt left out of the life of her own household. Rose was completely absorbed with the constant demands of those children—and Vera didn't particularly like children. They were noisy and messy. Sweet Bethany immediately started working at that farmers' market. All day, nearly every day. She was sure that Rose was behind that. Rose worked those children too hard. Bethany, mostly.

When Bethany told her that she wouldn't be working at her job any longer, Vera was thrilled. When she expressed delight that Bethany would have time to tend to her, Rose said no. She said Bethany needed to find a job outside the house. *Insulting!*

It was a worry that Vera's tiniest suggestions were never appreciated. And then she had these awful strokes, and it seemed all she ever did was worry.

Rose would tell her there was nothing to worry about and then mangle Scripture in that way she had, quoting an English Bible when the Amish only used the Luther Bible: "'Do not worry about tomorrow, for tomorrow will worry about itself. Each day has enough trouble of its own.'"

Each day had trouble enough of its own. You didn't have to be a preacher to know that was true. But a thing may be as true as death and taxes and still be hard to put into practice.

But for today, Rose would remind her, they had enough. And enough was as good as a feast.

Enough. Enough to keep food on our table and a roof over our heads.

Wasn't that what Rose was trying to do with this notion of turning the farm into a . . . what was it? What did you call a place where you rented out rooms? Oh . . . it didn't matter.

What worried her most was that Rose was disgracing the family and didn't seem the least bit ashamed about it. And she just completely ignored all of those horrible reporters who wanted to know more about the doctor's wife. She'd like a minute or two with those reporters and tell them what she had to say on the subject: that doctor's wife should just scoot on home, that's what Vera thought.

No one in Stoney Ridge had ever run a—what was it? . . . a boardinghouse?—from their home. She'd heard of such liberal Amish a few towns over, but never in Stoney Ridge. Vera shook her head. Dean's memory deserved far more. He would never have allowed his family home to become a . . . way station for travelers.

Vera struggled to find the word that Rose now used for this farm—the very farm where Vera had lived since she was born. Where her parents had been born. Bed and Bath? Bed and Butter? It was hard for her to remember so many things at once. It never was before. She stared at her right hand. Useless thing. *Come, now. Move. Open just a little.* Just the fingers, could she make a fist? What good was she without her hands? She couldn't roll out pie dough or make noodles. She couldn't pin hair. Sew, knit, garden—those were all lost to her. Such simple, everyday activities and things. How many hundreds of pies had she baked? How she'd loved to brush Bethany's long hair and pin it in a tight bun.

Vera stared at her right hand again. She noticed the half-done quilt tucked in a basket in the corner of the kitchen, where it had sat since she took sick. With that right hand, hadn't she knotted comfort quilts for sick folks and prisoners and orphans?

Rose had left the *Budget* out for her to read, turned to scribe letters from friends in Ohio and Indiana. Trying to determine what the newspaper said had nearly driven Vera crazy. The letters were all jumbled up for her. She'd read stories to Dean as a child. Now she would have to be like a child and have others read to her. Terrible!

Vera did appreciate what Rose did for her. She did. She had messed her bed this morning and Rose didn't say a word. She had brought her the mirror to distract her and quietly changed the sheets. Vera overreacted to the mirror because she was embarrassed about messing the bed. She knew that about herself.

She also knew that Rose was trying hard to find ways to keep the family together and solvent. But Vera couldn't let emotions cancel out her common sense. She refused to go soft over this terrible idea of turning their home into a Bed and . . . Brothel? No, no, that didn't sound right.

Besides, no one knew Rose like Vera knew her. They didn't hear the roof-raising argument Rose had with Dean on the evening before he died. Poor, dear Dean. Vera came from a generation of women reticent to argue with men. Vera always felt Rose was hardest on Bethany and the other one—the boy, that one who looked just like Dean. The one who ran away. Tobe! That was his name. He ran to get away from Rose, Vera was convinced of that. Why else would the boy have run?

Speaking aloud to the empty kitchen, she declared, "Why won't God heal me? Haven't I been serving him right along? Why me?" She no longer had anything to offer. And even worse, Rose wasted time to have to tend to her as an invalid. Vera had to ring a bell and stop everything if she needed anything at all. It was a terrible thing to have to be such a burden to others. A terrible, terrible thing.

Vera picked up the bell with her left hand and rang it as loud as she could.

Chase seemed to be patiently waiting for Delia to return from town. He greeted Delia and Will's car with his crooked dog smile, as if he knew what she knew. When Delia climbed out of the car, she reached down to pat Chase. The silly dog lifted his head to meet her hand and wagged his tail like a whirligig. Then he collapsed in a fury of friendliness.

Rose walked out on the porch of the farmhouse and waved.

Delia couldn't hold back her news. She cupped her hands around her mouth and shouted, "The cancer is gone! They caught it in time. It hadn't spread, not even to one single lymph node."

Will was grinning from ear to ear. "Rose, I think that sign of yours is spot-on."

Rose walked over to join them. "What do you mean?"

"That phrase, under 'Inn at Eagle Hill,'" Will said.

"What phrase? I haven't seen the sign close up yet—and now with those reporters, I don't want to go anywhere near the road." Rose turned to Mim, who had come outside to see what all the excitement was about. "Mim, what did you write underneath 'Inn at Eagle Hill'?"

Mim started blinking rapidly. "A Latin phrase: *Miracula fieri hic.*"

"Do you have any idea what it means?" Will said.

"No," Mim said, her face pinching with worry. "I read it in a book and liked how it looked."

Will grinned. "It means 'a place where miracles occur.'"

15

It was starting to become a habit for Jimmy Fisher to appear, magically, right at suppertime at Eagle Hill. Rose always invited him to stay and, of course, he always accepted.

Tonight, about the time Jimmy was due, Bethany pinched her cheeks for extra color. She peeked out the kitchen window and saw him approaching, one hand on Luke's shoulder and the other on Sammy's, steering them along the path from Galen's. Clearly, they had gotten into some kind of mischief over at Galen's. It was written on their faces. She hurried out to the porch and scowled at them before sending them in to wash up for supper.

"Those two boys are headed down a dangerous and slippery path," Jimmy said. "They pay me no mind."

"Join the club."

Jimmy had his eyes on the road where a news van was parked. The large satellite dish on the roof of the van was facing Eagle Hill. "What's going on over there?"

"Something to do with the doctor's missing wife, who was never missing in the first place. But never mind about that. I need to talk to you about something." She bit her lip. "Okay. I'll take it."

He gave her a sideways glance. "What exactly is the 'it' you're talking about?"

"That job at the Sisters' House."

"You're going to have to interview for it. I'll certainly put in a good word for you, but they're persnickety ladies."

Well, that was unsettling news. She thought she had the job if she wanted it.

He sat on the porch step and pulled off his muddy boots, one after the other. "I thought you were happy at the Stoney Ridge Bar & Grill."

She gave him her silkiest smile. "I was. I am. I'm just thinking of trying something new."

Jimmy rested the heels of his hands against the porch flooring and slanted her his superior look. "Liar."

Those blue eyes were much too perceptive. He was right, she was lying. She never lied! Well, hardly ever. Jimmy Fisher had a way of making her say things, do things, that were not herself. "Fine. I lost my job over that tiny little misunderstanding on Saturday night."

"From what I heard, it turned into a rip-roaring brawl."

Shootfire! How did he always know so much? "Are you going to help me get the job or not?"

"I'll do what I can, seeing as how you're so sweet and polite about it." Then he smiled at her, a sweet smile this time, and went inside the house like he owned the place.

Jimmy was an odd fellow, always good-natured and cheerful. His grin was like a flash of light. It was like the sun coming up at dawn; it changed everything.

When Rose woke early for her walk, she stopped abruptly as she came down the front steps of the porch. She was stunned to see that there was double the number of news vans out front than there had been last night. Hours after the first one showed up yesterday, Eagle Hill was crawling with reporters.

One reporter had walked right into the house while Rose and Bethany were scrubbing dinner dishes, reached into his black shoulder bag, pulled out a camera that he hung around his neck by a strap, took out a lined notepad, and laid it on the kitchen counter. He looked around the kitchen, squinting, and scratched his chin. "Somebody called the news desk and told him about your bed-and-breakfast. My editor thought it was a good human-interest story for the weekend section, so here I am."

Fortunately, Galen happened along to return Luke's forgotten hat, sized up the situation, and politely escorted the man off the property.

Then the game commissioner arrived, tracking the eagles that were building a nest on the farm. He shooed reporters farther away and ribboned the farm with yellow caution tape. The reporters camped out across the road and set up to film short clips for the evening news. The Inn at Eagle Hill sign featured prominently in the foreground.

Rose ordered her family to stay in the house. She was grateful to Delia's son for being willing to talk to the reporters and the game commissioner, whom he seemed to know. It was baffling—all that had happened in the last few days. When Monday morning arrived, she had thought she was facing a typical week. The children went to school. Vera complained about Rose's housekeeping. Luke came home from school with a note from the teacher that he had done something foolish. Nothing unusual in any of that.

Suddenly, her house was surrounded by predators. All

because a woman with a famous husband needed a little time to herself.

Delia had offered to leave right away, but Rose wouldn't hear of it. God had brought her to Eagle Hill for healing. Rose was sure of that now, and she didn't want to see her leave until she was good and ready to go. No doubt, she told Delia, the reporters would move off as soon as another story broke.

But that was before one of the reporters translated the Latin saying about miracles that Mim had painted on the Inn at Eagle Hill sign. The story grew bigger. And bigger. It had been picked up on the internet, Bishop Elmo told her last night, when he dropped by with a brush and paint and politely asked her to remove that Latin saying. With every news account, the Inn at Eagle Hill became more peaceful, more beautiful. A place where miracles abounded. Ready for the picking, like ripe cherries on a tree.

On this morning, Wednesday, the reporters were still staked out on the road, so Rose went the other way, toward Galen's property. Usually, Chase liked to come along with her, but he was sleeping in Mim's room—probably curled up right on her bed—and she didn't want to disturb them. She took a hillside path that her boys had carved and stood at the top to take in the sight. The air was so crisp and clear that the rising hills in the distance weren't layered, but alone and separate.

Rose relied on these quiet moments. She needed to get off by herself and listen to the sounds of the country, to pray and to think. She was accustomed to feeling pressed from dawn till dark, bound in by the small but constant needs of others. Not until she felt fortified again—felt that she could lead the family—would she return to the farmhouse.

Here, high in the hills, she could relax and pay attention to other sounds. There were sounds, she thought, that belonged just to early morning. The country talked quiet: one human voice could drown it out, particularly if it was a voice as loud as Luke and Sammy. On a still day, those boys could be heard at least a mile, even if they were more or less whispering.

A mourning dove called in the distance, and somewhere in a nearby tangle of bushes, its mate trilled out a reply. The eastern sky was red as coals in an oven, lighting up the hillside. She watched the process happily, knowing it would only last a few minutes. The sun spread reddish-gold light over the trees, making them look like they were on fire. It would be gone soon, and the day would begin. A sunrise was tribute enough to the glory of God.

She saw Galen on the far side of the hill, rifle tucked under his arm. She waved and called out to him. "Any luck?"

At the sound of her voice, he turned, spotted her, waved, and crossed over to meet her. "He was in the trap."

What a relief! She would sleep easier without that mournful howl of the coyote. At least one thing in this day was starting out right. She tilted her head. "Galen, just how old are you?"

He looked surprised. "Thirty-one. What's that got to do with a coyote?"

She grinned. "Just wondered."

He took a step closer to her. "So how old are you?"

"Thirty-six. Thirty-seven come August."

He whistled two notes, one up, one down. "Practically ancient. Closing in on Vera's age."

Rose smirked. "Well, I hope I am not that ornery."

"No. There's a difference between strong coffee and bitter medicine."

She laughed out loud. "Galen King, you are a sore trial and a wonder. Both." Then he held her gaze and she blushed.

Galen was not as handsome as black-haired Dean, but there was something about him. In so many ways he was gruff and abrupt, but in his way with Rose, he was always gentle and she could always count on the truth from him. A true friend. "Remember when I told you the eagles' nest would be a blessing to us?"

He nodded.

"The police chased those reporters off the property and warned them to stay away because the game commissioner complained that they would disturb the eagles. So . . . blessing number one."

A corner of his mouth lifted. "Number one?"

"Yes. Something about those eagles choosing our home makes me feel blessed. A sign that God is with us."

"But God is always with us, Rose, whether we think it or not."

"Yes, but sometimes it's nice to have a reminder."

A blast of cold wind came over the ridge and Rose shivered. Galen reached out and adjusted the collar of her coat—Dean's old coat. Warm, calloused hands brushed against her neck as he pulled up the collar and straightened it. "I won't let you chill." He rumbled the words in a soft, deep voice.

Rose lowered her gaze. "I'd better get down the hill in case Vera is ringing her bell." On the way down the hill, she pressed her hands to her fiery cheeks. How could such a simple gesture feel so intimate?

Galen felt uncertain. He exhaled a deep breath as he watched Rose hurry down the hill. He tried to reason out what had just happened. His heart was pounding like a teenager's, an odd staccato that echoed in his ears.

It troubled him that Rose skittered off just now like a frightened cottontail. He thought of what Jimmy Fisher had scolded him about recently—that the more he stayed apart, the more his presence made folks nervous.

"It's hard for normal people to relax around you, Galen," Jimmy had said. "You've never been relaxed yourself, so you don't know what you're missing."

The last few months, he felt as if he had been missing something in life.

His wants had always been simple. When his mother passed, and then his father was called home, he willingly took on the mantle of seeing his younger siblings to adulthood. He never resented that obligation. He was a man who felt responsibility keenly. He took great satisfaction in his work as a trainer of Thoroughbreds. It was challenging, interesting, and useful to the community. And sometimes, on a warm summer afternoon, he did like to catch a couple of cooperative fish, griddle size.

Was that enough? It had been. It used to be.

Sometime during lunch recess, when the students were playing a game of softball, Danny Riehl left a note in Mim's desk. It read "Be at the phone at 5 PM tonight. DR"

So Mim was at the phone shanty at 4:30. The phone call came in at 5:00 p.m. on the dot.

"Hello," she said, waiting to answer until the third ring. She didn't want to seem too eager. Bethany was always telling her that boys didn't like overly eager girls.

"Hello," Danny said. "You can see the moons of Jupiter tonight. Through my telescope. Around ten. I'll be there, at the hill behind the schoolhouse, I mean. Then I could walk you home. Or not," he added quickly.

Stargazing with Danny Riehl!

"Okay," she said.

"Okay," Danny said.

Then the phone went dead. Danny hung up without saying goodbye. As soon as Mim put the phone back in its receiver, the phone rang again.

She waited for the third ring. "Hello?"

"Goodbye," Danny said and hung up.

There was one bright spot about not having to work at the Stoney Ridge Bar & Grill: Bethany had more time to hunt for Tobe's books. She had searched the house through, but to no avail. The attic was all that remained. No one ever went into the attic, which probably meant the books were there, hidden beneath cobwebs. She shivered. She hated spiders. Hated mice. But then she cheered up—the books were in the basement up until a month ago, when everything had been shuffled around to make room for the inn. How many spiders could have found those boxes? Surely, not many.

She took the largest flashlight she could find and climbed the rickety stairs to the attic. Standing in the middle of the attic, she turned in a circle and shined the light on the walls and floor: old furniture, grimy trunks, dusty boxes that had been stacked in place for years. But then the light shined on boxes that looked new. They weren't dusty, and they had Rose's handwriting on them. Her heart beat fast. She ripped open the tape on the boxes. Inside were Luke and Sammy's baby clothes, shoes, some drawings Mim had made in school, a Mother's Day card signed by Tobe, the first nine-patch quilt square Bethany had made, which looked more like triangles. It was terrible! Why had Rose saved *that*?

In the last box was a bundle of letters tied in a blue ribbon, addressed to Rose, written by her father, dated before they were married.

Tears pricked Bethany's eyes at the sight of her father's graceful handwriting. She wouldn't cry. She wouldn't.

Taking care, she put the letters back in the box and folded the box top. In her mind, she crossed off one more room on her mental list. Tobe's books were not in the attic.

A beam from a thin moon streamed in the window. It fell across Mim's bed and onto the rug. She lay on top of her bed, fully dressed, until she heard the bongs of the grandfather clock in the living room hit half past nine, then tiptoed downstairs. The house was dark, silent. She grabbed the flashlight her mother kept by the kitchen door before she quietly slipped out, then hurried to the hill behind the schoolhouse. An owl hooted and she stopped short, then laughed silently at herself. She stood for a moment, listening to the saw of the crickets, the gentle purr of the creek, the soft soughing of the wind, and her heart felt full.

High on the hill behind the schoolhouse, she saw Danny stooped over the telescope, peering through it. She called out to him and he straightened, then waved.

When she reached him, he stepped back from the telescope so she could peer into it.

"What am I looking at?"

"Jupiter. You can see the four moons."

She squinted her eye and saw small dots of bright light all in a row and horizontal with the face of the planet. "I think I can see those moons. I actually can!"

"Those are the same four moons that Galileo saw with his first telescope five hundred years ago. Now scientists know that Jupiter has over a dozen moons, but I can only see the four with this telescope."

She stepped away so Danny could have a turn. He peered through the small lens and turned a few knobs on the long tubes of the telescope.

"All of the moons orbit the planet in the same plane, but at different distances and speed, so each night they're different. Tonight's a good night to see them."

She gazed up at the dome of the sky. "What's that bright spot. A star?"

Danny kept peering through the telescope. "If it's in the west and it's lying low, it's Venus." He straightened up to see where she was gazing. "Pretty soon, we should be able to see Mars coming up in the east. Mars looks red compared to the brightness of Venus."

Here, standing next to Danny in the crisp night air, with the black velvet sky dotted with diamonds, it was hard to feel as if anything could be wrong in the entire world.

Danny walked Mim all the way back to the end of her driveway, which she thought was very gallant. One more fact to add to her list about Danny Riehl. He was a gentleman.

They stopped to watch a little bat bounce through the air, taking bugs for his supper.

"Did you finish writing your vocabulary sentence?" Danny asked.

It was due tomorrow. Mim had been working at it all week, thinking of it nearly as often as she thought of stars and planets. And Danny. She recited it out loud to him: "The sibilant sound of the snake, eyeing the ort by the porch steps, was drowned out by the pother of my sudorific siblings, who refused to kowtow to danger."

"I like it," Danny said. "It's very clever and smart. And it succeeds at meaning nothing."

That was another true fact to add about Danny. He was incisive. A very incisive boy. It meant smart and insightful. Besides collecting facts, Mim collected words. In the very second when she looked toward him, he looked toward her. Then each turned away.

"I might be leaving Stoney Ridge," Danny said, scuffing the ground with the top of his shoe.

Leaving?

"Going where? When?" Mim wondered, her eyes bigger than her head. "You don't mean moving away?" *But . . . but . . . but . . . what about me?* She felt a pinch of panic in her tummy.

"My parents are talking about moving to a new settlement. Someplace in the south. My dad's cousins live there and said there's lots of good land that isn't expensive. They want us to come too. My dad wants to go, but my mom isn't sure." He bent down to tie his shoe. "One good thing is that it would be close to NASA. That's the headquarters for astronauts. You can see spaceships and moon rocks if you visit. I'd like to see NASA. My dad said that maybe we could go there sometime." He straightened and poked his glasses up on the bridge of his nose.

Mim felt another pinch in her tummy. Would Danny still

want to be almost-an-astronaut if he saw moon rocks and spaceships? Or would he want to be a full-fledged astronaut?

Mim walked up the porch steps feeling very droopy, very down in the mouth at the thought of Danny going away. She felt like crying, and her mind was a pinball machine of exasperation with herself, with all of life. She tiptoed upstairs and flung herself into bed, but couldn't sleep. So she went to the window and opened it, propping her elbows on the sill. She looked out over the farm, listening to the sounds of night, letting her thoughts roam at random.

She tried to imagine what her mother would say if she told her that Danny, the boy she loved, was going away. If she knew that Danny wanted to be almost-an-astronaut. If he didn't come back from NASA headquarters, not ever. "You'll manage," she could hear her mother say. "Life will go on."

But Mim saw change coming, and that was always a worry.

16

Delia wondered if life was returning to normal for Charles, if he was proceeding with the legal separation. She told Will to go ahead and let his father know that her cancer was gone after he was back at school. She wondered what that news would mean to Charles. Relief from guilt, she supposed.

Trying to be more like Rose had not been going quite as well as Delia had hoped. She still wanted to wound Charles. She wanted him to hurt as badly as she hurt. She needed to work on this. Even though Delia didn't know her well, Rose didn't seem to harbor such evil thoughts toward her late husband. Or toward that sharp-tongued mother-in-law, either. Delia could hardly tolerate more than a brief encounter with Vera. She reminded her of a librarian who spent her days shushing people. Whenever Delia happened to see her in the yard or at the farmhouse, Vera would fling darts, such as, "Mercy, are you still here?" or "Isn't it time you scooted on home?"

Delia didn't want to scoot on home.

Before Will left, he had asked her how long she intended to stay in Stoney Ridge and she hadn't had an answer for him.

She had the strangest feeling about this subject—as if she shouldn't leave. Not yet. She wasn't sure what it meant or where that gut feeling came from, but it felt as if a journey had begun for her and she still needed her travel documents. That sounded crazy, but that's how she felt. There was something she needed to get—to receive—before she left.

Delia had come to admire the genuineness of these Amish people. Their faith in God, especially. She had always perceived God as belonging in a compartment, like a piece of a pie that made up a life. Rose spoke about God as if all of life belonged to him. God was the piecrust, holding the pieces of life together. In fact, the strength of Rose's faith was part of why Delia had gone back to church last week. Rose seemed so happy and at peace even though she had been cast some serious blows. She hoped a little of what Rose believed would rub off on her.

When Delia was first getting acquainted with Rose, she seemed so calm and content that Delia honestly thought she might not be all that bright. She was embarrassed to admit it, but it was true. Most smart people she knew, including Charles, were forever complaining about the state of the world. They had all kinds of opinions on all kinds of subjects, but she'd rarely seen any of them do anything besides complain. As far as they were concerned, the world was bad and getting worse.

Rose didn't seem to trouble herself about the condition of the world. She was the kind of person who didn't discuss problems—she quietly set to work to solve them. And she had plenty of problems: her animals, her children, her cranky mother-in-law.

Rose was clearly a very intelligent woman. Delia's friends, no doubt, would have scoffed at the simplicity of the Amish life. After all, an eighth grade education? She could just hear the disdain drip from their voices. They valued higher education—the higher, the better. They would start to question the veracity of Rose's contentment—believing she was an oppressed woman who had no choices.

Rose was anything but oppressed. She spoke her mind and then some. It surprised Delia to see how she refused to answer those reporters' questions. She went about her business and acted as if they weren't even there—which, in a way, was worse than showing anger or upset. Being ignored was the very worst thing of all.

Of that, she had no doubt.

On the way home from school, Mim would stop and get the mail from the mailbox. It was her job, hers alone, always had been, and she gave Luke and Sammy the what for if they beat her to the mailbox. Soon, Luke would be taller than her. Getting the mail first was one of the few ways she had to remind him she was older than him.

The mailman handed Mim a large bundle of mail, bound with rubber bands. She was astonished. Ordinarily, the mail contained a bill or two, a letter, a *Budget* newspaper, and some advertisements. As she walked up the driveway, she pulled off the rubber band and sifted through at least ten letters, addressed to Mrs. Eagle Hill Inn or Mrs. Miracle.

When Mim got to the house, she found her mother in the kitchen, washing the floor. She stopped at the threshold and waited until her mother noticed her.

"Where are the boys?" her mother said, a worried look on her face.

"They went straightaway to Galen's. Jimmy's setting off firecrackers today."

Relief covered her face. "Oh good . . . this floor will have a chance to dry." Half the floor was slick with soapy water.

"Is Mammi Vera awake?"

Her mother sloshed some soapy water on the floor and spread it around. "Not now. She's napping." Just then, a rat-a-tat sound came from next door. "Well, she *was* napping until Jimmy Fisher started his fireworks."

Mim helped herself to a chocolate chip cookie. Then she remembered the mail. She pointed to the bundle of letters she set on the counter. "Here's the mail. A bunch of letters are addressed to Mrs. Miracle."

Puzzled, her mother tossed the scrub brush on the floor and stood. She opened one letter, then another, then another. Then she shook her head and dropped the letters on the counter. She didn't even open the rest. "It's all because of those reporters." She pushed a lock of hair off her forehead. "I guess we can be expecting another visit from the bishop."

"What do the letters want? Reservations to stay here?"

Her mother bent down, picked up the scrub brush and dipped it in the bucket of soapy water. "No. They're asking for advice. They think the inn spits out miracles like a soda pop vending machine. They think we've got the solutions to all their problems."

Now *that*, Mim thought, was intriguing. "Are you going to answer the letters?"

"I should. I need to put a stop to them. I don't want folks to think of this inn as anything more than a nice place to stay. But with your grandmother needing extra help, I don't know when I'll have the time to write them back."

Mim watched her mother slosh some soapy water on another section of the linoleum and scrub in circles. "Maybe I could help."

Her mother stopped scrubbing and looked up. "Really? Would you, Mim?" A big smile covered her face.

Mim loved her mother's smile. It was like the sun coming out and filling the room with light.

"All you need to tell people is that only God makes a miracle. That's all. You don't need to try and solve their problems."

Oh, but Mim loved to solve problems. "If I can use your typewriter, I'll answer the letters." She didn't think her own handwriting looked grown-up enough, though she did have the best handwriting in seventh grade.

Her mother beamed. "It's yours to use! That would be an answer to my problem, Mim."

Her mother was gazing at Mim, her head tilted in a question. "Mim . . . is there—" Mammi Vera's bell started to ring.

"I'm thirsty!" Mammi Vera called out in a creaky voice from her room behind the kitchen.

Mim's mother turned her head toward the back room. "Would you mind seeing to your grandmother so I can get this floor finished?"

Mim took off her shoes to tiptoe across the wet kitchen floor. The letters would have to wait. But as soon as Mim had finished tending to Mammi Vera, she slipped up to her mother's room, found the typewriter, and carried it straight to her room. She sat on her bed, cross-legged, to read through the letters. Fascinating! She felt as if she was peeking into people's lives, but not in a nosy way. With permission.

Dear Mrs. Innkeeper,

I read about your Inn in the newspaper. My boyfriend forgot my birthday. Should I forget his?

Please write back.

Signed,
Forgotten in Delaware

Dear Mrs. Miracle,

I could sure use a miracle. Two years ago, I joined the Army so that I could see the world. I've seen it. Now how do I get out?

Sincerely,
Trapped in Tennessee

Dear Mrs. Innkeeper of Miracle Inn,

I have a new job, starting next week. But I will need to be late to work on the first day. Maybe the second day, too. When should I tell my new boss?

Very truly yours,
Rhonda from New
Hampshire

Dear Mrs. Miracle,

I signed up for a class on "The Brain and Aging Well" at my community center. Then I forgot to go. They won't give me my money back! Any suggestions?

Sincerely,
Outraged in Harrisburg

Problems, problems, problems. Her mother had told her not to try to solve these people's problems. But their problems were so easy to solve! And Mim hadn't actually agreed to what her mother had recommended, so technically, she wasn't doing anything wrong. She stared at the typewriter. Very carefully, she put in a fresh sheet of paper. She thought a moment, her fingers frozen above the keys.

She took a breath. And then, with two fingers, very slowly, she began to type.

Dear Forgotten in Delaware,
I am sorry your boyfriend forgot your birthday. Here is my advice: wrap an empty box in gift paper and give it to him for his birthday. And then I think you should suggest that you will both do better next year.
Sincerely,
Mrs. Miracle

This was fun.

Dear Outraged in Harrisburg,
There is a lesson to learn in every circumstance. I think you are missing your lesson. Do not worry about getting your money back. The next time "The Brain and Aging Well" class is offered, sign up for it again and be sure to mark it on your calendar. Take the class again, Outraged. And again.
Yours truly,
Mrs. Miracle

A door slammed. It was the exuberant sound of her brothers as they returned from Galen's. How much time had gone by? Mim rolled the last letter out of the typewriter. Carefully, she folded each one and tucked them into envelopes, addressed them, put a stamp on them, and put them safely in her pocket to mail.

It was already dark by the time Bethany had a chance to get out to the phone shanty to pick up messages. She'd told Rose she would check messages each day for her, seeing as how she was out of work, but she had a hope there might be a message from Jake. She called him as often as she dared—every other day, sometimes every day. She knew it wasn't considered proper to call too often and she never left a message—that would be far too bold. The call went straight to voice mail and she liked listening to his voice, but then she hung up so he wouldn't know she had called. She still hadn't found those books he wanted.

Today, to Bethany's shock, the message machine was full—people who wanted reservations at the place of miracles. She rolled her eyes. For days now, there had been all kinds of ridiculous newspaper articles about the Inn at Eagle Hill, starting with Delia Stoltz's disappearance and discovery, then the bald eagles' aerie. But details were always mixed up: one woman said she heard a lady's cancer disappeared while she was staying at the inn. Another one said she read that a marriage on the brink of divorce had been healed. The strangest one was a fellow who said he wanted to study the energy flows of the farm and see if that's why it produced miracles.

Energy flows? Miracles? Sheer craziness.

Bethany wrote down all the names and numbers for Rose, grateful these people weren't her problem. Delia Stoltz had certainly been a nice enough lady to host for the first guest, but Bethany still wasn't comfortable with the idea of strangers at the farm. Especially weird ones, like the energy flow man. Creepy.

Mim looked forward to getting to the mail each day, sifting through letters to Mrs. Miracle and tucking them up in her room before her mother saw them. Her mother had only asked her one time about the letters she was responding to—a few days ago when she couldn't find any stamps. "Have you used up an entire roll of stamps, Mim?" her mother had asked.

Mim froze. "Well, you said I could answer the letters."

"That's true."

"You said you felt concerned that people were looking to Eagle Hill to solve their problems."

"That's true. I did and I do. But I thought the letters had finally dwindled down. Seems like we haven't gotten any in a few days, have we?"

Just as her mother was about to ask her another question, Mammi Vera's bell started to ring and her mother's attention turned to see what she needed.

Crisis averted.

She did not want to be put in the position of lying to her mother. Lying was wrong. But she also did not want to stop receiving or answering the Mrs. Miracle letters. People counted on her to help solve their problems. She couldn't let them down. She felt important and that was a new feeling for her.

Today, she opened the mailbox and saw that the mail had already been picked up. Oh no! She hadn't anticipated that wrinkle. She ran down the driveway and into the house. Her mother stood by the kitchen table, sorting clean socks from a laundry basket. "Hello, Mim."

"Hello." Mim's eyes darted around the kitchen and landed on the stack of mail piled on the counter. She casually crossed the room to sift through the letters. She picked up three letters addressed to Mrs. Miracle.

Her mother was watching her. "You'd think they'd stop writing after a while, wouldn't you?"

Mim shrugged.

"It's not too much for you to answer those letters, is it?"

Mim waved that thought away. "No trouble at all. It helps me improve my typing skills. I'm up to 15.5 words a minute."

"You'd let me know, though, if it was getting to be too much. Wouldn't you?"

"Of course," Mim said, a little too happily.

Delia heard a knock on the door and opened it to find Rose, standing with a stack of stiff, sun-dried towels in her arms. She handed Delia the towels with a gentle smile and said, "Looks like it's going to start raining soon."

Delia put the towels on the table and motioned for Rose to come in.

"Have you told your husband that your cancer is gone?"

"My son was planning to tell him."

"I'm sure he'll be relieved."

Would he? She didn't know how Charles felt about her anymore.

Rose looked at Delia. "Do you think there's any chance for your marriage to be fixed . . . for things to be made right?"

Delia was quiet for a moment, thinking. "I know you mean

well, but you make it sound easy, and it's not. At this point, I wouldn't even know how to begin to make it right."

"Sure you do, Delia. You begin with forgiveness."

"Forgive Charles for having an affair? For breaking up our family?" She crossed her arms against her chest. "Forgiving Charles won't bring him back, Rose. It won't change anything."

"I'm not saying it will, but I have no doubt you'll be surprised by what forgiveness can change." Rose walked over to the door and put her hand on the knob, then hesitated. She turned back to Delia. "I know what it's like to be married to a difficult man. A man who is too smart for his own good and hard to love because of it. I know what it's like to suddenly lose him. I know about regrets and grief that few would understand. But I also know that every marriage takes two people. I made my share of mistakes." A slight smile tugged at her lips. "Dean made more, mind you, but I made a few myself." She opened the door. "After you sort all that out, you can ask God to forgive you. And he will, Delia."

Delia curled up on the sofa after Rose left, mulling over her words. She had blamed Charles entirely for this affair. Was it possible that she played a part? She couldn't deny that they had been drifting apart the last few years, and the truth was, she hadn't really minded. As his work demanded more, she was happy to fill that space with activities that interested her. He had asked her to travel with him to some medical conferences, but they were so boring for her. Still . . . she could have gone to a few of them, especially when he was scheduled to speak.

Maybe . . . Delia could have tried a little harder to stay

close, to understand the world of neurosurgery he lived in. It was so far beyond her understanding that she had stopped listening. Stopped trying.

But Robyn Dixon knew that world.

Delia leaned her head against the back of the sofa. It was clear that, somehow or other, Rose had found a peace with her circumstances that Delia hadn't. But still. It was a complicated issue.

Maybe that was the problem. Maybe it wasn't as complicated as she had assumed.

Delia decided to fix herself a cup of tea to ward off the chill of the rainy April afternoon. She filled the teakettle with water and set it on the stove. She turned on the burner and waited for the water to heat up, then poured the hot water through the infuser, watching the water change color and taste. Maybe that's what it was like with God—he infused a situation with love and forgiveness.

What was it Rose kept saying? That Delia just needed to ask for help. She set the infuser in the kitchen sink and held the teacup and saucer in her hands. What did she have to lose? She closed her eyes and said a silent prayer.

God, I know there really isn't any reason for you to listen to me. I haven't done a very good job of listening to you these past sixty years, so a part of me feels hypocritical to come to you now, with a crisis. I wouldn't blame you a bit if you ignored me, but I pray you won't. Rose says I have to forgive Charles so that you can forgive me, and I want to. I'm just not sure I can, not unless you help me. Please, dear Lord, please help me. I've always thought of myself as strong, but I'm not strong enough for this. I just can't do it. Help me. Please help. Amen.

Just as the "amen" was forming in her mind, she heard a car pull into the driveway. Her eyes flew open and she crossed the room to look out the window. Tea splashed into the saucer and the breath went out of her.

It was Charles!

17

S top twisting my arm off." Vera flashed Rose a frustrated look.

Rose patiently continued exercising Vera's right arm. "Jehoshaphat, you're as prickly as a jar of toothpicks today."

Vera felt she could tolerate many things, but not having her moods waved away. She sat at the kitchen table, a truculent expression on her face. She had just completed reciting the litany of wrongs she felt Rose had committed as a wife to Dean, her dear boy Dean, starting with how she had tempted him away from his church to go to the liberals, which resulted in so many additional temptations, and ended with Rose being responsible for Tobe's running away.

She saved her best for last. "And what about Dean's passing? You've never admitted to the despair you drove him to. That despair led to his death."

A long moment of silence followed, Finally, Rose lifted her head and looked Vera right in the eye, giving her a stern look. "Vera, I know that your life did not turn out the way you hoped it would. I know that. But you need to get your mind off your troubles."

Patronizing. How dare Rose treat her like she was a child!

"As soon as we finish these exercises, I'll make you a cup of tea. Tea has a way of making everything seem better."

Tea! As if a cup of tea would cure what ailed her.

"Now try to work your shoulder," Rose said. "Up and down, side to side, and in circles."

Vera reached out, but her arm refused to budge. She tried to make her arm work, just a simple wiggle or twitch . . . yet nothing whatsoever happened. The weakness was getting worse. *No. Oh no. Father, don't let this be real.* Her eyes filled with tears as she tried and tried to move her arm.

Rose stood behind her and started to gently exercise her shoulder. "Vera," she said softly, "we will find ways to make things work. I'm going to do everything I can to help you get back to where you used to be."

Vera knew exactly what Rose was referring to—leaving her to fend for herself, like she'd had to do since Dean had up and married Rose and gone off to the liberals. She'd be alone again.

What will I do if Rose decides to leave? What will happen to me then?

As shakes started to overtake her, Vera couldn't say whether it was from anger or fear. Both!

Delia opened the door to Charles but didn't say a word.

"I came by to . . . to talk to you." Charles took a deep breath. His voice was shaky and she noticed his hands were trembling. "Will called me. He said the margins were clear. Is it true?"

"Yes. You didn't need to drive all the way out here."

"Well, I couldn't get anything out of that idiot Zimmerman."

Delia stiffened. "He's not an idiot. He was respecting my wishes."

The wary, belligerent expression came back to Charles's face, and he drew back a little, taking on that stance of his that always reminded Delia a little of a prizefighter. She knew that look so well. She started to close the door in his face.

"Wait! Delia, just give me five minutes. I just need five minutes. Hear me out, then I'll leave and I won't bother you again."

The sooner it was over, the sooner he would be gone. "Come in," she said, half order, half request.

He walked into the large room and sat on the sofa, eyes fixed on the ground. His hands were clasped together on his lap; now she saw them tighten involuntarily. "It's not easy for me to talk about some things."

"I've always known that about you," Delia said. "That's why I've never pressured you to talk."

She watched his body change—from ready-to-snap tension to dropping his chin on his chest. And to her total surprise, Charles began to cry. Huge sobs and heaving shoulders. The works.

Charles . . . was . . . crying! She didn't know what to think or what to do. He sat on the sofa, weeping. Her authoritative, in-control-of-every-situation, brilliant neurosurgeon husband was crying so hard that she had to keep feeding him tissues. "I'm scared, Dee, for the first time in my life, I'm really scared. I just feel . . . adrift, I guess. That's it. It's like I woke up to find myself sitting in a boat in the middle of the ocean. I've got no sail, no oars, and no idea where I am. I don't know what kind of man I've turned into."

Just an hour ago, she would have danced a jig to see Charles's remorse, but she didn't feel that way anymore. She wasn't interested in exacting revenge or placing blame. How astonishing! Rose had reminded her that, even in the midst of tragedy, it was possible to find unexpected blessings if you only asked for God's help. Hers had been exactly that, a newfound ability to let go of the past and the bitterness she'd harbored toward Charles.

They sat there in the basement of an Amish farmhouse while Charles told her he was miserable without her.

But . . . she wasn't to be fobbed off so easily. "And so you decided to come back to what was familiar—to a time when you knew who you were?"

"Yes. No! Dee, it was a mistake. Robyn, moving out of our home. I'm sorry. I understand now what I put you through. And I'm just so sorry. When I was suddenly faced with losing you . . . I think that's when I started to realize what I'd done. What kind of man I'd become."

She was doing the very best she could to be empathetic, compassionate yet detached. After all, tears didn't wipe out the damage that had been done.

"I drove all the way here to tell you I've ended things with Robyn. It's over. And I want to ask if we could get back together. I'd like things to be the way they were before."

She drew in her breath sharply; she had *not* expected this. She was listening intently, her heart lifting with every word. These were the very words she had wanted to hear. The very words. But the truth was, she didn't want things the way they were before. Everything had changed. She had changed. She recovered her poise quickly. "I don't want to go back to a marriage of two ships passing in the night."

Charles stared vacantly out the window, though it was impossible to see anything through the rain and fog that clouded the glass. "I guess I can't blame you, Dee. But I just want you to know I meant what I said. I'm sorry for everything. I don't expect you to forgive me."

And to her surprise she said quietly, "This isn't just your fault, you know. There were things we both could have done differently. I'm sorry too."

"Well, maybe, but when the going got tough, I was the one who called a lawyer, not you."

That was true.

"Delia, I thought about what you said—about the difference between having regret and being truly sorry. Before Will called to let me know your test results—I spoke to the patient who was suing me for her stroke. I apologized to her. To her husband too." Charles's voice choked up. "That was all they wanted to hear. That was it. They dropped the malpractice suit."

Delia was stunned. Never, in her wildest dreams, could she have imagined such a conversation. Never.

"I don't know when you're planning to return home—"

Delia stepped in quickly. "I don't know that, either."

"Maybe, if it would be all right with you, I could come out and visit you. We could go out to dinner and just . . . talk. Would that be acceptable?"

She smiled. "Entirely acceptable." They were a long, long way from reconciling, from becoming a family again. But it was a step in the right direction. Then something occurred to her, out of the blue. "Before you go, could I ask you to pay a house call on Rose's mother-in-law?"

Outside, rain fell softly, nourishing Rose's recently planted strawberries in the dark, wet garden earth. She hardly noticed.

Vera was having a bad spell, and when a knock came on the door, it startled Rose. When she opened it, there was Delia, looking pleased, with a man by her side. A fine-looking man. Her husband.

"Rose, this is Charles. I thought it might be a good idea if Charles were to meet Vera."

Rose stepped onto the porch, pulling the door closed behind her. Charles put his hand out to shake Rose's. She looked down at his hand before taking it, then she didn't release it.

"It's not a good night for visitors." Rose lowered her voice. "Vera's having a bad night."

"That's why I wanted Charles to meet her," Delia said. "As a doctor."

Rose turned and opened the door and let them both into the kitchen. Vera sat in a chair, hiccupping, tears streaming down her face in misery.

Charles turned to Rose. "Has she had medical attention?"

"Yes, of course. The doctor said she was having mini-strokes."

"What medication is she on?"

"Coumadin."

"Does she get episodes of singultus very often?"

Rose looked at him. "Single-what?"

"Swallowing disturbances," he said.

"Hiccups," Delia clarified. "And yes, she does."

Rose nodded. "More and more. For longer and longer stretches. And the weakness in her right side is spreading."

Charles crouched down by Vera and tried to straighten out her right hand. "Do you have a tingling sensation in your hand?"

She nodded.

"Dizziness? Headaches?"

"Some."

Charles patted Vera's hand reassuringly in a way that was touching to Rose. From the way Delia had described him, she would have assumed he was a stern man, but here he was, tender and kind, to a complete stranger. "I'd like you to get an MRI to help pinpoint the problem."

"What's that?" Vera asked.

"Magnetic Resonance Imaging. It's a technique used to take pictures of soft tissues in the body."

"But why?"

"Strokes can be misdiagnosed. There are many other things that share symptoms of strokes, but they aren't strokes." It seemed like a stone had fallen into the room. No one moved. No one breathed.

Vera stared hard at Charles. "Such as?"

Rose saw Delia and Charles exchange a glance.

"We can talk about it more after the tests are concluded," Charles said.

"What else could it be?" Vera said, in between hiccups. "What else? Do I have Old Timer's Disease? I do, don't I?"

Charles looked confused. "Old Timer's?"

"She means Alzheimer's," Rose whispered.

Distress clouded Vera's face. "That's what you're thinking, isn't it? That I'm losing my mind!" She started to wail.

Charles hesitated, but the look on Vera's troubled face couldn't be ignored. "No. I doubt it would be Alzheimer's. It's more likely to be operable—maybe a brain tumor—"

Those two words were like the crack of doom.

Vera wailed louder.

—⊙◊⊙—

Jimmy Fisher must have gone right to work. A day later, Bethany received a written invitation from the Sisters' House, asking if she would come for tea to discuss the opportunity to work for them. There was a postscript at the bottom of the letter: "Do you have a steady eye and good aim? Do you like rituals?"

Bethany marched right over to Galen's barn and found Jimmy in the workshop, repairing a harness buckle. She waved the letter at him. "Are these sisters truly sane? Am I safe going over there?"

Jimmy roared with laughter and said yes, the sisters were both safe and sane. A little eccentric, perhaps. "You should go. If nothing else, you'll have a great story to tell."

None of that prepared Bethany for what actually happened. The Sisters' House was two-story, framed and old, in need of fresh paint, surrounded close in by a small picket fence that was also in need of paint. The grass in the yard needed mowing as well—or would as soon as the weather warmed up.

The sisters met her at the door, five of them lined up in a row, all in their eighties. You never saw such an elderly group of ladies, and Bethany thought Mammi Vera, at sixtysomething, was ancient. Very prim and ladylike, with white hair piled like swirls of whipped cream at the back of their heads, tucked under their gossamer prayer caps.

"I've been expecting you," Ella, the eldest, said. "Right on time . . ." She spoke in a quiet, intelligent voice, but right away Bethany noticed she had the habit of dropping off her words in midsentence, as if she had forgotten what she was going to say.

"She always claims she knows when a person is coming,"

Ada, the second eldest, whispered to Bethany. "She claims she knows everything."

Lena, the third eldest, led Bethany into the living room. Bethany felt stunned by the condition of the room. It was filled with furniture, stacks of books, overflowing boxes. Every nook and cranny was steeped with some kind of clutter: newspapers, books, boxes filled with quilting material, baskets full of yarn, junk mail, bills. Even the walls were covered, floor to ceiling, with old calendars. Most Plain families had . . . well, plain homes. A rug, some perfunctory furniture, maybe a calendar or two on the wall. Sometimes a picture of a bird. But walls were mostly bare. This home looked like nothing Bethany had ever seen.

One of the sisters—Sylvia, the youngest—caught the look of shock on her face. "It might seem a wee bit disorganized, but we know where everything is."

Ella bobbed her head. "We do."

"We're facing a bit of a sticky wicket, you see," Sylvia said. "We're supposed to have church here and some of our relatives said they would help us clean things out. But we don't want them to help. Last time they helped, we couldn't find anything for weeks."

"Months," said another sister.

"Years," said another.

Bethany exhaled. "When are you scheduled to host church?"

The sisters looked at each other. "Whenever we can get the house tidied up, I suppose," Sylvia said. "Deacon Abraham said we didn't have to rush. But he'd like us to take a turn. It's only fair, he said."

"That's true," Ella said. "It's only fair."

Bethany looked around. Tidied up? That was an understatement. This house was buried in clutter. It was drowning.

They emptied stacks of old *Budget* newspapers off the sofa and sat down to tea—excellent tea, made by Fannie, the fourth eldest, which Bethany thought even the oh-so-proper Inn at Eagle Hill guest would approve of.

"Can you make a good cup of tea?" Fannie asked. "We don't drink coffee. But we do love our tea. Real steeped tea. Not the cotton ball type."

"As a matter of fact, I can." Delia Stoltz had shown Bethany how to make tea one rainy morning after she had brought down the breakfast tray. At the time, Bethany listened politely to the tea steeping lesson, but inside, she was thinking, my lands, Delia Stoltz was a grand lady. Now, she was grateful.

"And have a prune," one of the sisters said, thrusting a bowl of wrinkled prunes at Bethany.

Another sister nudged her. "Never pass up a chance at a prune."

Bethany swallowed hard.

Then things took an odd turn. Or rather, even more odd. The sisters sat along the sofa, in order of their age, and peppered Bethany with questions, one after the other, right down the line. "Do you have fine penmanship? Are you trustworthy? Are you punctual? Do you get nervous if you're confined in small, dark places? Can you keep a secret?" Bethany's throat went bone dry. These ladies might be certifiably crazy. She barely put her teacup down when Ella said, "Sisters, I believe she will do . . ." Then her voice trailed off, distracted by something in her head.

Ada peered at Bethany over her spectacles and picked up where Ella left off. "I believe you're right, Sister." The three other sisters nodded in agreement, capstrings bouncing up and down, along with their chins.

Bethany was still very unsure of what exactly they were proposing.

Sylvia, the youngest, was the only one who seemed to sense Bethany's confusion. "We'd like to offer you the job. Of course, take all the time you need to make your decision. A minute. Two minutes. Whatever you need."

While Bethany's head went round in perfect circles, the sisters assumed her silence meant acquiescence. As they walked her to the door, she was told to return in a week's time—because it would take them that long to get used to the idea of having someone in their employ—to wear work clothes, and to not be late.

18

Why her? Why did bad things always happen to her? Vera lay in bed early on Sunday morning, startled by the sound of a door shutting. That would be Rose, slipping off to watch the sunrise. It was a habit of Rose's and an annoying one, considering Vera's bedroom happened to be on the first floor.

Last night, after the guest lady and her doctor husband finally left, Rose pointed out that Vera and the guest happened to be about the same age. "Well, I might look like her if I didn't have the troubles I do," Vera snapped back.

Her mind drifted back to her troubles. The doctor's words. Why did doctors always circle-talk and cross-talk and use hundred-dollar words? Why didn't he just come out and say she was dying?

Because she was. She knew she was. She had been old since she was thirty-five, when her dear husband died after a fall off the roof. She'd been teetering at death's doorstep since she was forty-seven, when her first daughter-in-law abandoned dear Dean and their two babies. Then at fifty, she took a step through the threshold when her son left the Old Order Amish church to take on a second wife and faced excommunication. She just hadn't gotten around to the actual dying part yet. When she stood over her Dean's coffin, she clutched the coffin rim and said, "Mine will be next. I'll be the next box they shovel the dirt on."

Deacon Abraham chastised her for saying such a thing. "Only the Lord knows the future," he said. True, but Vera had a gift for prophesying doom. And she was rarely disappointed.

What was the point of having another medical test? Besides, that test sounded like something out of a nightmare. Imagine getting rolled into a big tin can and have magnets turned on? There was no way in the world she could tolerate something like that. She must have looked like she just found out they were going to drop her in a pot of boiling lard, because the doctor hastened to add the test should only last for ten minutes. Ten minutes too long! She heaved a stretch-to-the-limits sigh.

If Dean were still alive, he would let her pass in peace, dignity intact. The very thought of Dean made her sadder still, if that were possible. Why had God taken Dean, but left her? It wasn't right for a mother to outlive her child. "Therefore shall his calamity come suddenly, suddenly shall he be broken without remedy," the proverb read. That was true. She was left broken without a remedy.

A little later, Vera locked eyes with Rose the minute she stepped into the kitchen from her morning walk. "I'm not going through with it. No matter what you and your fancy English friend say. I'm not doing it."

Rose crossed the kitchen floor to start the coffee. "I assume you're talking about the MRI." She measured scoops of coffee into the filter, then set it on the stovetop. "It's your choice, Vera." She walked up to Vera, seated at the kitchen table, and wrapped her arms about her. "You know that we need you around as long as the Lord sees fit. I need your help raising those children. I don't know what we'd do without you. Why, there's no telling what those two little rascal boys would turn into without their grandmother's fine influence."

"So true. So very true." Vera closed her eyes, squeezing them tight for a long moment. "Bieg der Baam wann er yung is, wann er alt is, kannscht nimmi." *Bend the tree while it is young, when it is old, it is too late.*

"Mim is just starting to turn into a young lady. She needs a grandmother to help her with that. And you don't want Bethany to end up with a liberal like Jake Hertzler, do you? When you've got someone like Jimmy Fisher buzzing around? And then there's Tobe. I haven't given up hope that he'll be home one day."

Vera chanced a look at Rose. "You'll mess it all up without me."

Rose kissed the top of her head. "I truly would."

A bird screeched, followed by a chorus of frantic cries. Rose hurried outside to see several birds in flight, along with a flock of crows excitedly beating their wings. Obviously they'd been disturbed by someone or something. As she turned away from the window, she caught sight of Mister or Missus Eagle—she couldn't tell which. It soared elegantly in the distance, circling the farm. For once, the word "awesome" seemed apt. Its beauty and grace were stunning. Hypnotic to watch. It didn't take long to realize there was no love lost between the eagle and the other birds.

Luke and Sammy came barreling outside to join her. They had heard the bird racket too. She hushed them and pulled them close to her. "Watch with your eyes, not your mouths."

The three of them stared at the sky until the eagle flew off. "Mom, did you hear there's an egg in the aerie?" Luke said.

Rose frowned at him. "How do you know that? Were you climbing trees again?"

"No!" Luke said. "Some of the bird-watchers told us so."

There was an avid group of bird-watchers that set up their scopes morning and night to watch the eagles hunt for food in the creek.

She grinned. "Well, that's good news. When do you think it might hatch?"

"Mim said it takes thirty-five days," Sammy said. "So that would be . . ." He started counting on his fingers.

Luke couldn't wait for Sammy's slow accounting. "In a few weeks."

"We'll have to mark that birthday on the calendar," Rose said.

"Don't get your hopes up," Mim said, standing by the kitchen door. "The chance of a baby bald eagle surviving its first year of life is less than 50 percent. That's a fact."

Luke's and Sammy's faces crumpled.

Jimmy knew that asking Galen for a cash advance wasn't going to be warmly received, but he didn't expect to hear Galen's churlish opinion about his judgment.

Earlier this morning, Jimmy had located Lodestar at the Bart Township mud sale. Jonah Hershberger was brushing him down in a makeshift stall. As soon as he spotted Jimmy, he threw the brush down and lit right into him, giving him a lecture that felt like the ones his mother used to give him—causing the very hair on the back of his neck to stand up straight.

"What's the matter with you, son?" Jonah bellowed. "Don't you lock your barns up at night? He's running loose all over the county! You've been awful lucky that Lodestar's a one-man horse. He can track me like a flea on a dog. But you—" he pointed his finger at Jimmy's chest—"you don't deserve a horse like Lodestar."

"But I do! I really do. I must have left the barn door open."

Jonah narrowed his eyes. "What kind of horseman leaves a barn door open?"

"It'll never happen again. You can count on me."

Jonah squeezed his eyes shut. "This goes against my better judgment." He opened his eyes and let out a puff of air. "But I've got to get this horse sold. Look . . . get me cash for the rest of the money you owe me and I'll give you one more chance." He stabbed his finger against Jimmy's chest with each word: "Last chance, Fisher. I mean it this time. Do. Not. Lose. That. Horse."

Jimmy promised to bring Jonah the remaining seven hundred and fifty dollars by noon—but that meant he would need to ask Galen for the cash. His brother Paul had made it clear that he was not Jimmy's bank.

An hour later, he pulled his buggy into Galen's yard and couldn't find him in the barn or paddocks. He ran to the house and Naomi let him in, pointing to the living room where Galen worked at his desk.

"Galen, I need to get an advance on a few weeks' salary. Cash."

Galen put down his pen and leaned back in his chair. "What do you need it for?"

"Can't you trust me?"

"No."

"I found Lodestar. I need to get Jonah the balance that I owe him."

"Jimmy, when are you going to learn?"

"I've learned my lesson. This time, I will keep the barn door shut. Locked!" He frowned at Galen's reluctance. "Why can't you just give me a little credit?"

"I'll tell you why, since you're finally asking questions and not just yapping your jowls. Have you ever heard of the Runner Scam?"

Jimmy shook his head. "What is it?"

As Galen explained the scam, Jimmy's head rocked back a little, as if he'd just been slapped.

"You've been swindled."

Jimmy shook his head. "You don't know that. How could you possibly know? You've never seen the horse. You've never met the trader. Maybe the horse just has a knack for getting out of tight spots. I'd do the same thing, if I was a horse."

Galen rolled his eyes, disgusted. "Everything you described about it fits the Runner Scam. A trader sells the same horse a half-dozen times over. As soon as folks get wise to him, he disappears."

Jimmy paced the room, back and forth, then swung around to face Galen. "Maybe you're right, maybe you're not. But I'm not letting this chance slip through my fingers. That's the difference between you and me. You're always watching life from afar . . . you never take any risks yourself. You let chances slip through your fingers all the time. You're crazy about Rose, any fool can see that, and yet you—" He stopped himself abruptly. He was crossing the line and he knew it by the warning look that covered Galen's face. He glanced at the clock on the desk and realized he needed to get back to Jonah by noon. "If you're right, you're not out any money. I'll work for you without pay."

Galen didn't move or make a sound, but Jimmy could feel something change in him. He finally stood, walked to the kitchen, opened a cupboard door, and took out a coffee can. "How much?"

The wind had come up hard in the night and Jimmy woke with a start when a door banged shut. For a split second, he wasn't sure where he was, then he remembered—he had slept in the barn on a cot in the saddle room—determined to keep Lodestar contained. A gust of wind banged the door shut again. Jimmy grabbed his flashlight and bolted down to the horse's stall. It was empty, the door wide open. Out of Jimmy's mouth burst an unrepeatable word that he saved for emergencies.

He heard something. He flung himself out the door so fast he bumped his shoulder on the jamb and cried out in pain. Outside, he scanned the farm, hoping to see Lodestar. It was a moonless night, pitch black, and he had to wait for the sough of the wind to still—but he was sure he heard something. There! He heard it again—the squeak of hinges as a trailer door shut tight and then the sound of a car pulling away.

He covered his face with his hands. He wasn't sure what hurt more—the fact that he had lost Lodestar for a third time or the fact that he was going to have to tell Galen he had been right all along.

Jimmy, a young man who considered himself unsusceptible to hoodwinking and swindling, had been hoodwinked and swindled.

"Mom, Mom, Mom!" Sammy came flying into the house, tears streaming down his face. "The baby eagle died! It died, Mom!"

Rose wrapped her arms around her youngest son. The bird-watchers had made the discovery and told Luke and Sammy the news as they went to school. It rankled Rose that those bird-watchers didn't think about the hearts of a little boy. Couldn't the news have waited?

After Sammy had finished his cry, she washed his face and walked him to school through the field, so they didn't have to talk to the bird-watchers. When they went into the schoolhouse, she noticed that Luke was slouched at his desk, looking sad. She also noticed that Luke's desk was exactly one stretched-out arm away from the teacher's desk. It surprised Rose that Mim hadn't informed her Luke's desk had been moved. Mim usually kept her abreast of Luke's crimes.

"I'm sorry Sammy is a little late today," Rose told the teacher, who understood there had been a crisis without needing an explanation.

As Rose walked back through the fields, she went up the hillside to watch the eagles. Missus Eagle was on the edge of the nest, her white feathered head bowed. Mister Eagle was at a distance in another tree. That was typical—it was rare to spot the two eagles together. Usually one protected the nest while the other hunted, then they would switch roles.

"I just heard."

Rose turned and saw Galen approach her. "What do you think happened? Do you think another bird attacked the eaglet?"

"Eagles don't have any predators. They're at the top of the chain." He stood beside her, watching the mother eagle on the side of the nest. "More likely, they're just inexperienced parents. They messed up. Maybe left it alone too long. It was cold last night. It might have chilled. Or starved."

"Do you think the eagles will leave the nest and not come back?"

"Maybe, but maybe not. Time will tell."

"I know I shouldn't give human emotions to birds, but doesn't she seem sad to you?"

"She does. She truly does."

At that moment, Mister Eagle flew next to Missus Eagle on the nest and tucked his head against her neck. It seemed as if he was trying to give her comfort. Heartbreaking! Rose turned away, buried her face in her hands, and her shoulders shuddered.

Galen moved so his chest grazed her back and wrapped his arms around her. Turning her chin slightly, she said, "How can the world be so beautiful and yet break the heart?"

Galen drew in his breath. There were moments in life when something had to be said, or be left unsaid forever. It wasn't the best time for it—he knew it wasn't—but he had to speak.

Twice, he opened his mouth to say the words; both times, words failed him. For a moment, he lost focus. He never lost focus. Never, though earlier, he'd lost his breath when he saw Rose coming toward him on the hillside, the hazy morning sunlight casting a glow about her. Sometimes out of nowhere the sight of her could snatch his breath and make his chest hurt. She was beautiful. Graceful and beautiful. He wanted to protect her from all the sadness in her life. The emotions shimmering in her tear-filled eyes tore at him, so he wound his arms about her, pulling her into the shelter of his very being. Finally, he said, "There are sad times, but there are good times too. Like . . . now."

She pulled away from him and turned to face him, puzzled. "Now?"

"Yes. Now." He cleared his throat. "This very moment. This is a good time. For me, anyway."

She turned her deep-gray eyes on him, calm and penetrating. "Galen, what are you trying to say?"

He had yet to take his eyes off her. "Rose . . . I . . . care about you. And what I want to know is this . . ." He cleared his throat again. "Would you let me court you? Sometime? Soon?"

She looked surprised, her mouth formed a small, tight O. Her eyes popped, then mysteriously, filled with tears. Were these sad tears, happy tears, angry tears, outraged tears, a little of each? He couldn't tell. He was relieved she wasn't leaping down the hill.

The moment stretched between them until finally she spoke. "Galen, I have children to raise and a farm to run, and I've got to make money to pay back those investors, and a son who seems to be facing serious legal problems."

He swallowed hard. "You take a lot of chances, and you stand up to them all. Why not take a chance on me?"

"Because . . . well, for one thing, because of our friendship. It means so much to me. I don't want to lose that."

"Why would we lose it? It's our foundation. I want to build on it."

She didn't speak for a long moment. "Galen, my husband broke my heart and then broke it again."

"But I'm not him."

She studied him. Indecision played across her features. At long last she set her jaw and lifted it, and his heart missed a few beats. To his surprise, she took his hand. He felt it, cool in his own, believing, for a moment, that she might love him the way he loved her.

"Do you mind if I wait a little while before giving you my answer?" she asked gently.

He did mind. He had hoped she would say yes at once. But he remembered his manners and took a step back. "Of course not. Take all the time you need."

Rose could hardly bear to see the pained expression on Galen's face after she told him she needed time to think. His voice had gone flat, no longer throaty, warm, inviting. He waited, but there was nothing more to say. She was not going to say yes on a whim. She had to go home and ponder his question. The silence fell heavy between them, thick and cold, and after a moment too long of it, he turned and left.

He had shocked her when he told her he wanted to court her. Shocked her . . . and yet . . . it hadn't shocked her at all. Their friendship had been deepening. Hardly a day went by when they didn't see each other, talk to each other. She counted on him in a way she didn't count on anyone else. Did she love him? Was this love? Did he love her? He looked so devoted, she felt almost weak. What had she done to deserve all this love?

Would she like to be courted by Galen King? *Well, why not?* A part of her answered back. *Really, Rose, why not? He's kind and caring and he's the best friend you've ever had. And he loves you. You know he does. You've known it for some time. You've seen it in his eyes.*

But then the practical part of her brain kicked in. Galen was much younger than she was. His life could be—*should* be—just starting with a young woman. Hers was inching toward the midline. His life was fairly uncomplicated. Hers was a big tangled spool of thread and she was just starting to figure out where the thread began. She had no idea where it would end.

Besides, there was a reason Galen had remained single. Hadn't she learned her lessons about independent men?

No. She should definitely not entertain any thought of being courted by Galen. Put those thoughts right out of her head. Banish them now.

On Monday three bad things happened. First, Mim received a B on last week's vocabulary sentence. Teacher M.K. thought she hadn't tried hard enough. Second, a horrid sixth grade boy, whom Mim considered to be a blight on humanity, told her she looked like a chipmunk in glasses. The glasses part didn't bother her as much as the chipmunk part. She was very sensitive about her teeth and took excellent care of them. Excellent. She did not want to be toothless when she was older, like so many of the people in Mammi Vera's church. Third, Danny didn't even look her way at church yesterday. Or today at school. Not once.

Mim wanted to talk to someone about Danny Riehl. Was

it significant that he didn't look her way? Was it possible that he thought she looked like a chipmunk too?

She thought about asking her sister, but Bethany thought of Mim as a little girl. She would tell her to stop wishing she were older than her years.

She thought about talking to Naomi, but lately Naomi had been so enthralled with Bethany that she hardly knew Mim was there. It wasn't like that when they first moved to Stoney Ridge. Naomi spent equal time with both sisters, which was only fair because, she acted like she was right between them in age. But when she turned eighteen, she seemed to think she was much closer to Bethany's age than to Mim's. She would only spend time with Mim if Bethany was at work.

Mim checked herself. What kind of advice would Naomi give to her? First, she would be shocked that she was even thinking about being in love with a boy. Second, she would tell Galen, straightaway, about Mim spending time on a hillside with that same boy. At night and unchaperoned. She wouldn't understand that it was perfectly innocent and they were only stargazing.

And what would Galen do? Mim smiled. Probably listen to his sister and quietly dismiss it. That's one thing she liked about Galen. Unlike most of the people in her life, he did not overreact.

She had a mental list of whom she would *not* talk to about being in love with Danny Riehl: any girl at school. Mammi Vera. Her brothers.

That left her mother.

Her mother was the one person Mim did want to talk to about Danny. Her mother would not overreact and she would not think Mim was too young to be in love. This afternoon, she was going to find a window of time alone with her mother and ask her about love. She reached home ahead of the boys and went right into the kitchen. It was empty. There was a note on the kitchen table:

Mim, Luke, and Sam,

I have taken Mammi Vera to Lancaster to get the MRI test. Delia Stoltz drove us over. We won't be home until late. Mim, start supper. Luke and Sam, feed goat, chickens, sheep, and horses. Boys—Mim is in charge until Bethany gets home. Mind your sister!

Love, Mom

The boys burst in behind Mim, tossed their hats on the bench by the back door, and started hunting for a snack in the pantry. It was like a pack of wild dogs descended on the kitchen. They stuffed cookies into their coat pockets and headed back to the door.

"Where do you think you're going?" Mim said.

"Eagle spying," Sammy said. Luke was already out the door.

She held up the note. "Mom wants you to feed the animals."

"We will!" Sammy said, his mouth filled with cookie. It was disgusting. "After the eagle spying." The door slammed behind him.

Mim looked around the empty kitchen. Everyone was gone. The house seemed eerily quiet.

Under normal conditions, Jimmy Fisher could snap out of a funk. But being a victim of a scam was not a normal condition. When he discovered that his initial check to Jonah Hershberger had indeed cleared—which meant he had paid for Lodestar one and a half times—he felt stupid, he felt duped, he felt angry. Mostly, he felt grief over losing that beautiful horse. There was something about that horse he just couldn't forget . . . or get over. Galen kept telling him there were other horses, but none were like Lodestar.

After Galen and Naomi went into town to run an errand, Jimmy put the horse he was exercising back in its stall and took a break. He pushed a chair in the sun, tucked his hat back, and started to whittle on a piece of wood.

"You aren't getting anywhere very fast, are you, young feller?"

When Jimmy looked up and saw Hank Lapp walk up the driveway, he snapped shut his whittling knife and dropped it into his shirt pocket, then hopped up to greet his elderly friend. There was no law against whittling, but he didn't want to get a reputation as an idler. Hank Lapp was Amos Lapp's uncle, a confirmed bachelor, a quirky, lovable character who ruffled everyone's feathers at one time or another. "What brings you around here, Hank?"

"MY BIRTHDAY PARTY, of course! I'm coming to invite you."

"Why, Hank, are you a hundred yet?"

"I'm crowding it, boy." Hank eased himself into the chair that Jimmy had just vacated. He leaned back and tugged his hat over his eyes. "Jimmy, do you know what men who live in glass houses should do?"

Oh no. He wasn't in the mood for one of Hank's lame jokes. "What should they do?"

"Change in the dark!" Hank chuckled so hard his hat fell in the dirt. He reached down to grab it, slapped it on his knee to dust it off, and plunked it back on his head. "Any luck finding that mystery horse of yours?"

"No." Jimmy threw the piece of wood on the ground. "Galen thinks I've been scammed."

"He's probably right. Galen's seen 'em all."

Jimmy was disgusted. "The two of you don't give me enough credit. It's like you think I don't even have a handle on life."

Hank yawned. "I used to have a handle on life, but it broke." He pushed his hat back and sat straight up. "I nearly forgot! I want you to put on a fireworks show for the end of my birthday party. It's a paying gig."

"Yeah? How much?"

"All you can eat. Tell Galen he's invited too. We're going to have fun."

Jimmy snorted, amused by the comment. "Galen never had fun in his whole livelong life. He wasn't made for fun. That's my department. That's why he needs me."

"Yes, but what's far more interesting to me," Hank retorted, "is why you need Galen King."

19

What a difference a week made.

Delia drove Rose and Vera to Charles's office to find out the results of the MRI. Charles had arranged for the test to be done at a local facility in Lancaster, then had the results sent to his office. Delia could see that Vera had never been so frightened in all her life. Getting an MRI had terrified her. Usually, an MRI took about ten to fifteen minutes. For Vera, it took nearly an hour. She had a fit of claustrophobia and needed to be pulled out of the machine, then she sneezed and that slowed it all down. She complained about everything—claustrophobia, the noise of the vibrating magnets. She had to wear earplugs, then earphones over the earplugs. And she had to be absolutely still—that meant no talking. A terrible thing for Vera to endure!

Rose stayed by Vera's side through it all. Delia knew Vera was grateful, though she would never let on. Even she could also see the decline in Vera since she had arrived at Eagle Hill. Her physical weakness and confusion were escalating, and whenever she felt stressed, real or imagined, the hiccups started up again.

Delia was so focused on Vera and Rose that she hardly

thought about the fact that she would be going to Charles's medical office for the first time since they had separated. She knew the office staff—had known them for years—and was warmly welcomed by them, but her mind was preoccupied with Vera.

When the receptionist asked them to wait in Charles's office, Delia assumed she would stay in the waiting room. "Please, come with us," Rose said.

So Delia followed behind them and went into her husband's office. On the desk and in the bookshelf were pictures of her and Will. When Charles came in, his eyes met Delia's and softened. He greeted Rose and Vera, then he sat at his desk and turned on the computer monitor to show Vera the picture of her brain.

"It turns out that you didn't have a stroke after all, Vera, just like we had discussed at your farm. But you do have a brain tumor." He turned the computer screen around and showed her the picture of her brain.

"I don't see anything," Vera said.

"It can be hard to see," Charles said. He ran a finger around the outline of the small tumor. "The tissue is one texture. The tumor is a different one."

"All I see is a gray blob."

"That's the tumor. It's grayer than the gray of your brain. It's called a primal tumor. Symptoms mimic a stroke so similarly that about 3 percent of primal brain tumors are misdiagnosed as stroke victims. In a way, you're very fortunate. Most brain problems don't give warnings. Aneurysms, for example, can hide in the brain like a ticking bomb."

Too much. He'd said too much. Delia could see Vera gasp at the words "ticking bomb."

Charles saw it too. "But lucky for you," he hastened to add, "your symptoms of aphasia and singultus and weakness have given us a heads-up."

Vera and Rose swiveled in their chairs to look at Delia for translation. "What's he saying?" Vera asked.

"*Aphasia* means having trouble with word recall," Delia explained. "Tip-of-the-tongue-itis. *Singultus* means . . . hiccups."

Vera's face pinched in fear. Her hands worked in her lap. "I knew it! I knew it. I'm dying!"

"No, no," Charles said, hastening to reassure her. "The brain tumor is located in a part of your head that is very accessible. I believe we can remove it."

"Brain surgery?" Rose said.

"I don't want my head split open and have people rooting around in it like a pumpkin," Vera said. "Tell him, Rose."

Rose reached over and held Vera's hand. "Let's find out more before we decide anything."

"Charles, is it benign?" Delia asked.

"We won't know until it's been removed and sent to the lab, but I'm cautiously optimistic that it's not malignant."

"What do them hundred-dollar words mean?" Vera whispered to Rose.

"Cancer," Rose whispered back and Vera shuddered.

Charles turned off the computer monitor. "Vera, I recommend we take care of that tumor. Soon. Very soon. I have every confidence that the tumor can be removed."

Vera fixed her gaze at him. "Can you guarantee that? One hundred percent guarantee that?"

Charles and Delia exchanged a look. She wondered if he was thinking about the malpractice suit. "No, of course not. No surgery is without risks."

"Then I don't want it."

Rose sighed. "What would happen without the surgery?"

Vera sat up straighter in her chair. "Maybe I can wait. Maybe it'll go away on its own. Like Hank Lapp's toothache."

"Hank had that tooth pulled," Rose said.

Charles looked like he was starting to run short on patience, which, at best, was never a leisurely path. "The tumor will continue to grow and eventually affect other regions of the brain. And then . . ."

"And then I'll die." Vera clapped her hands together over her chest. "I am ready to meet my Maker."

"Vera, before you do, let's hear more about the option of surgery." Rose turned to Charles. "If the surgery is successful, will her symptoms disappear?"

"Most should. And if it's benign, then she won't require any treatments—just follow-up scans. Physical therapy will help her regain her confidence in her strength and balance."

Rose turned to Vera. "I think we should consider it."

Vera huffed. "And how are we going to pay for this brain surgery? Have you thought of that?"

Rose, normally so capable, seemed at a loss for words. "Well, I . . . I'll speak to Deacon Abraham. I'm sure the church will help. We'll manage somehow."

"Charles will volunteer his services," Delia blurted out. Charles's eyebrows shot up. "He does it all the time. Bona fides. It means free. He's generous like that." She studiously avoided Charles's stare, but Vera did calm at that news.

Rose walked back and forth in the room. "When do we need to decide?"

"Right now," Charles said. "There's an opening for tomorrow morning. We had to postpone a patient's surgery because his blood pressure is too high. Delia can drive you over to the hospital now and get you settled in."

"You're going to do it?" Vera asked, the first, tiniest glimmer of hope crossing her eyes.

"My specialty is with vascular neuropathy," he said. "My job is to cut off the blood supply that feeds tumors and allows them to grow. The surgeon I have in mind for you is excellent. He's available tomorrow because of the canceled surgery."

Vera flashed a look of panic at Rose, who turned to Delia. Delia could see this was a new wrinkle. Possibly, a deal breaker. If Vera was going to agree to this, it hinged on Charles's performing the surgery. "But Charles, you have done this surgery. Hundreds of times."

"Yes, but . . ."

"And you've always said that every single brain surgery is unique. There are no two situations that are exactly the same when it comes to brain surgery. You've said that the reason you're such a good neurosurgeon is that you're prepared for every possible scenario. You've kept your skills current. I've heard you say that, dozens of times."

"Yes, but . . ."

"So you are familiar with this type of surgery?" Rose said.

His eyebrows shot up. "Of course. As Delia said, I've performed open brain surgery more times than I can count. But, just to be clear, I'm a specialist for an even more complicated type of brain surgery . . ." He looked at Rose, then at Vera, who looked back at him with eager anticipation. "I . . . but I . . ." He looked at Delia. She saw his expression slide from disbelief to confusion to acceptance. She knew him well enough to know what he was thinking. He hadn't expected this turn of events—but he was pleased, nonetheless. Charles had a great deal of confidence in himself and knew he was an excellent surgeon, but he was not immune to others' appreciation for his skills. In other words, he could be bought. "Yes . . . I could perform the surgery. Assuming Vera gives her consent."

Then all eyes turned to Vera, waiting for her to agree to the surgery. She sat quietly as she considered all that Charles had said to her. "Why? I don't understand why this is happening. Why would God do this to me? Why would he let me down?"

Rose crouched down beside her chair. "Vera, I know one thing. I know that God has never let us down. Not even when Dean passed. He has never abandoned us. It's not possible. God is good no matter what circumstances you're facing. We need to remember that, and to keep declaring that God is good, no matter what. That we know it to be true."

Vera nodded in agreement. "I need more faith."

"Then borrow mine," Rose said.

Those three words felt like an electric shock to Delia. Was that even possible? To borrow someone's faith? She'd been leaning heavily on Rose's faith since she arrived at Eagle Hill. Or maybe Rose meant that a person's faith could be inspired to grow just by observing the depth of another's faith.

Whatever Rose meant by that, it seemed to do the trick. Doubt and blame seemed to be pushed away, and peace rolled in. Vera turned to Delia. "Is he any good?"

"Vera, if I had to have brain surgery, I would insist that Charles perform the surgery." Delia looked at Charles. "He's the best, Vera. The very best."

Charles didn't even exhale when she said this. It was as though he was holding his breath, waiting to hear Delia's response to Vera. Then he let out a breath and turned his attention to Vera. "I have the skills to help you, Vera, and I love using those skills. I want to try to help you so you can get on with the rest of your life. But I can't guarantee a perfect outcome. No one can. All I can promise is that I will do the very best job I can."

Vera rose, a little wobbly. "Let's get this over with."

As Charles held the door for them, Delia was last out the door.

"Bona fides? I think you meant to say pro bono. That means free. Bona fides means in good faith."

She lifted one shoulder in a half shrug. "Same thing." She turned to him. "Charles—this family, well, I can't explain it, but they have become a very special family to me."

His eyes softened again. She had forgotten how he used to look at her in that special way. A just-for-her way. How long had it been? "We'll figure something out," he said.

"Thank you for agreeing to perform the surgery. I think that made all the difference to Vera."

He lifted an eyebrow. "I'd forgotten how the Amish can be surprisingly stubborn."

She arched an eyebrow back at him. "I hadn't."

Delia took Rose and Vera over to the hospital to get Vera checked in. Charles's office had called over to smooth the path—and still, it was daunting. She wasn't sure how two Amish ladies could have navigated the complexity of hospital administration without this kind of streamlining help. She could barely wade through it all herself.

As a nurse settled Vera into her hospital room—a private room, which she knew Charles had arranged—Delia spoke quietly to Rose. "Tell me how I can help. Would you like me to drive you home tonight? Or would you be willing to stay at my house here in town?"

"I think I should stay at the hospital tonight," Rose said. "Vera is frightened. This is all happening so fast." There was a pull-out bed in the corner. More like a padded bench.

"I can call the farmhouse and leave a message."

Rose frowned. She wasn't sure if the children would remember to check the messages for her. "Maybe you could call Galen. He has a phone in his barn. There's a better chance of getting through."

"Rose, would you like me to drive out tonight? I could let everyone know what's happening."

Relief flooded Rose's face. "Oh, Delia, would you? Then they could pray. And that would put their minds at ease."

Delia would have worded it differently. If she had information, then her mind would be at ease. And then she could pray. Information felt like control—but it really wasn't. Rose had it right. Prayer came first, then the peace. "Why don't you give me a list of things you and Vera will need for a few days."

"How long do you think she'll be in the hospital?"

"I don't know. Tomorrow will answer a lot of those questions." Assuming there was a tomorrow for Vera. Brain surgery was risky. "I'll go now. I'm just going to drop by my house and pick up a few things, then head out to Eagle Hill. I'll return first thing in the morning." At the door, she turned to Rose. "Maybe you should call Galen anyway. I think he'd like to hear about all this from you."

Later, as Delia drove west along I-76, she called her son Will.

"Isn't it amazing, Mom?" Will said after she had explained all that had happened in the last week.

"What?"

"The circumstances."

"Yes, your father definitely made this surgery possible for Vera."

"More than that. You're a big part of this. What about the fact that you happened to be at that particular Amish inn, and Dad happened to have met Vera. I mean, what are the chances? Seems like it's all part of a master plan. Like God is orchestrating all of this."

She hadn't thought of the last few weeks like that, but as soon as Will said it, something clicked into place for her. It *was* God's orchestration! She felt it deep in her bones—a feeling of love and well-being washed over her. God was involved in all of this, down to every detail. He loved prickly Vera, he loved strong Rose, he loved her—flaws and all. He probably even loved Charles. Tears welled in her eyes. She had to blink them back.

"It's kind of you to help them, Mom. A few weeks ago, they were strangers to you."

"They've become friends. Rose, especially."

"If anybody would have told you, a month ago, that you'd be moving heaven and earth to help an Amish family whom you just met, well, wouldn't that surprise you?"

She grinned. "I suppose you're right."

"You've changed. You used to be so determined not to let anyone get close. You're different now."

Delia hesitated, not sure how to respond. But Will was right, something had changed her. Or Somebody. This entire experience had affected her, and for the better. Uninvited and unwanted, cancer had barged into her life—as another woman had barged into her marriage—and turned it upside down. Thank God.

"Mom, years ago when I was in Stoney Ridge, living at Windmill Farm—I came away with a belief in God. I've let it sort of get crowded out. Gone dormant."

Crowded out. Dormant. That's exactly what she had done with God. Kept him there, but pushed off to the side of life. She hadn't needed God . . . until now. "Me too, Will. It's time to change that. I don't think God wants to be a bystander."

Will laughed. "Amos Lapp told me one time that if you weren't paying attention to God, then God had a way of getting your attention."

Wasn't that the truth? Hadn't this last month been a wake-up call for Delia? Awful events—yet, she wouldn't change a thing. If cancer and Charles's affair were what it took to feel this close to God, to have these kinds of conversations with her son—it was all worth it.

"By the way, if you happen to see that vet who was treating the colt, would you get her phone number for me?" He cleared his throat. "I have a question or two for her . . . about one of my classes."

She grinned. She *thought* there was a spark between those two! "I'll see what I can do."

20

Breakfast was scorched scrambled eggs, orange juice with frozen lumps that hadn't dissolved, and undercooked pancakes. There were rumblings of thunder and lightning, which meant the boys had to remain inside until school started.

And that meant that Mim couldn't concentrate on her book. Luke and Sammy were stomping around their bedroom, which was next to Mim's. They were like a hurricane, Mim thought. Those two would never stop joshing each other and trying to outdo each other. Finally, downstairs, Bethany had enough of the big thumping sounds. She told them to clean up their rooms and throw their collections out. Usually, Bethany barked commands that nobody obeyed. But she was serious about getting rid of those collections. She complained they were stinking up the whole upstairs and she couldn't stand them one more minute. Those boys collected all kinds of things—anything useless. Birds' feathers, pebbles, eggshells, snake skins, the skeleton of something that might be a bat. They were regular packrats.

The boys burst into Mim's room without a knock. "We

need you to make a sign for us," Luke announced. Sammy nodded.

"What kind of a sign?"

"We want to sell stuff."

"That's ridiculous. No one will buy your useless stuff. It's junk."

Luke was insulted. "They might."

She put down her book. "I'm all for you cleaning out your collections and I'm all for you making money, but you need to find a way to make your things desirable to someone else."

Sammy brightened. "Like . . . buried treasure?"

She laughed. "Oh sure! Just tell folks you're selling rare antiques and your junk will sell like that." She snapped her fingers in the air. She was joking.

The boys looked at each other, then their faces lit up like firecrackers and they vanished back into their bedroom.

"I was joking!" she called out.

Later that night, Mim lit the small oil lamp on her desk. There were definitely moments when she missed flipping a switch and having electric lights, but she couldn't deny that there was no pleasanter light than the soft glow of an oil lamp. She read once that whale oil gave off the nicest flame, but she didn't know where a person would buy whale oil.

She couldn't sleep tonight, not with her mother away in Philadelphia in a hospital with her grandmother. Too many worries bounced through her mind. Tomorrow would be a very big surgery for her grandmother. She might die. Mim hoped she wouldn't die, but she might. In such important matters, Mim always felt it was best to prepare for the worst.

She uncovered the typewriter and polished her glasses. Then she set to work on answering Mrs. Miracle letters. She found the questions about love to be the trickiest to answer. Love was a mystery. How could she try to explain the shaky-excited feelings she got whenever she was in close proximity to Danny Riehl?

Dear Mrs. Miracle,
My boyfriend cheated on me. Should I cheat on him to teach him a lesson?

Signed,
Angry in Arizona

Dear Angry,
I am sorry to hear that your boyfriend had such bad judgment. But no, you should not cheat on him to teach him a lesson. Two wrongs don't make a right. However, I do think you should break up with him and find a new boyfriend. A faithful one.

Very truly yours,
Mrs. Miracle

Satisfied, Mim pulled the letter out of the typewriter with a flourish and folded it. She typed the address on the envelope, put the folded letter inside, licked it, stamped it, and set it on her nightside table. Time for the next letter:

Dear Mrs. Miracle,
I would like to know, according to all your experience, if love can overcome everything.

Lonely in Love

Dear Lonely,
If love is true, it will overcome almost everything.
> *Sincerely,*
> *Mrs. Miracle*

Mim stopped and stared at the page. Wasn't that the answer to her own dilemma? If Danny were her true love, then even if he moved away, that wouldn't change anything, would it? She smiled. Mrs. Miracle had solved her problem. She took out a blank piece of paper, rolled it into the typewriter, and started typing . . .

Dear Mrs. Miracle,
My mother doesn't see me. She doesn't hear what I say. She thinks she does, but she doesn't. She is busy with my grandmother, my sister, and my brothers. I would welcome your exceedingly wise counsel.
> *Very truly yours,*
> *Miss Invisible*

Mim pulled the paper out of the typewriter and held it up. To see a problem in black and white made it seem less like a conundrum and more like a situation waiting for a solution. Almost like a math formula. Not quite, but almost. No wonder she was so inspired in her new role as Mrs. Miracle.

Rose felt such a shock at the sight of Vera getting wheeled out for surgery that she had to steady herself against the wall. The pre-operative area was a large, busy room. Nurses and doctors were rushing here and there, machines beeped, worried families gathered in clumps and murmured quietly, gurneys slid by with patients on their way to surgery. One of those gurneys held Vera. Seeing her mother-in-law with head shaved, tubes going everywhere, a big IV bag filled with saline by her side—the sight made Rose's stomach twist. For Vera's sake, she tried not to let on how she felt. It was no time to be weak. She squeezed Vera's hand as she walked alongside the gurney.

The orderly stopped the gurney at the operating door and gave a nod to Rose. "This is as far as you can go. Wish her well."

Rose leaned over and brushed a tear leaking down Vera's cheek. "I'll be praying the entire time and I'll be here when you get through it."

Vera squeezed her eyes shut. "Dean's the lucky one. He's missed a lot of heartache."

"He's missed a lot of joy too."

Vera opened her eyes. "I wish I could be as strong as you."

"Why, Vera, you're the strongest person I know," Rose said, in a gentle tone. "I couldn't manage without you. We've weathered all kinds of storms together. We'll get through this one too."

"Rose, I don't really think you're the worst daughter-in-law in the world."

"I know you don't."

A sharp little spark lit Vera's eyes. "The first one Dean brought home—she was the worst."

Rose sighed.

As the orderly pushed Vera's gurney through doors that led to the operating room, Rose decided to try to find a quiet place, maybe a chapel, to pray. To pray away some troubles that just weren't willing to leave.

Trust, from Galen, came slowly. When Delia Stoltz asked him if he would like to drive to the hospital with her, he hesitated. His mind raced through all the potential disasters that could occur in his absence with Jimmy Fisher in charge. He knew he kept Jimmy on a short tether—he thought the boy had a talent for horses, but he also knew his tendency toward the lazy when unsupervised. And if Bethany happened by, Jimmy couldn't keep his mind on the task at hand.

But Galen did see glimmers of maturing in Jimmy. In fact, he was learning so quickly and developing into such a skilled hand that Galen felt a little guilty for holding him back from more responsibility.

Still, leaving Jimmy Fisher in charge of his Thoroughbreds for an entire day? The boy couldn't even keep track of the one horse he had bought.

It was Delia who said just the right thing to convince him to set aside his worries and go to the hospital. "I think Rose might need to have a special friend like you by her side."

Galen looked at her sharply but didn't answer right away. He had never so much as mentioned Rose's name to anyone—how could Delia know Rose was on his mind? It was disturbing to him to have one's thoughts suddenly plucked out of the air. Women could smell feelings as a dog could smell a fox.

Would Rose be glad to see him? He wasn't really sure. But he knew he needed to do this.

A full day of waiting stretched out in front of Rose. To wait and wait. She hadn't eaten breakfast and was starting to feel a little weak, close to tears, as the what-ifs crept into her mind. What if Vera's brain was damaged in the surgery? What if the tumor was cancerous? What if she didn't survive the surgery? Vera may not be the easiest person to live with, but she was family. She was loved.

Sitting on that uncomfortable chair in the sterile room, Rose felt so alone. Tears welled in her eyes, and her throat ached. A deep sense of loss rose up in her, so forceful, woven of so many memories. Vera had a saying: Oh, das hahmelt mir ahn. *Calling to mind poignant memories with such vividness that they brought pain.*

Such scenes rolled through her mind: Dean's happiness on the day he brought Rose home to meet Vera, Tobe, and Bethany. The children's small faces, so hopeful as they looked at her, eager to have a new mother. Luke and Sammy as toddlers, wrestling like two bear cubs. Serious Mim with her arms filled with books. The children's shocked faces as they stood by their father's graveside, newly turned earth, the raw wind cutting through their coats—Mim hated wind from that day on. Bethany's stoic face—she never shed a tear for her father. Not that day, not since. Someday, Rose knew those tears of hers would need to spill.

But after the funeral . . . they all buried their grief and carried on. Got back to the business of living. That was the way of things.

Too much. Sometimes, it was just too much.

The whoosh of the automatic doors startled her and she raised her head. She hadn't known she was crying until she felt the air from the outside cool the wetness on her cheeks.

In strode Galen King with his black hat on, coming through the doors as if he walked through that hospital door every day of his life. In one hand was a cup of coffee, in the other was a brown bag.

"Are you all right?" he asked, peering at her with concern. "Are you okay, Rose?"

She nodded, still not quite trusting herself to speak. The truth was that she had never felt so glad to see anyone. All her nervousness and sadness squeezed right out of her. "Galen!" she said at last, whispering the words. "How did you get here?"

"Delia Stoltz drove me in. She dropped me at the door and went to park. She's going to go see if she can find out how the surgery is going." He handed her the coffee. "We thought you might need a little moral support."

She took a sip of the coffee. A dollop of cream, just the way she liked it. "I'm glad you're here, Galen. I have to admit I'm scared of today's outcome."

He looked at her with one of those quiet smiles that touched only his eyes and said, "You always seem as calm as a dove."

"That's on the outside," Rose said. "On the inside, I'm a bundle of raw nerves."

He sat in the chair next to her and stretched out his legs, crossing one ankle over the other. "There's no outrunning fear. It comes on you and you have to face it."

She just looked at him, then, taking her time and thinking. He held her eyes, then looked away, as if embarrassed. He lifted the brown bag. "Delia stopped by a store and bought a package of one-bite doughnuts."

He opened up the bag of cinnamon sugar one-bite dough-nuts and offered one to Rose. She found them amusing. Delicious too. As Galen filled her in on the news from Stoney Ridge, she found herself feeling weepy again. She knew what it had taken for him to give up a day of work just to sit here with her. He was not a man who sat and kept vigil.

She wasn't sure what the end of the day would bring, but she decided that from now on, she would savor sweet moments, like this one, as much as she could. Like one-bite doughnuts.

Galen and Rose had gone for a walk outside to get some fresh air. Delia stayed in the waiting area, flipping through an old copy of *People* magazine. They had invited her to walk with them but she said no. It was an ideal opportunity to give them time alone. There was precious little of that in their lives.

Delia had a sense about matchmaking and she could just see that there was more to Galen and Rose's relationship than friendship. She didn't think they realized it yet—certainly not Rose—but Delia could see it clearly. Galen and Rose spoke the same language, thought the same thoughts. True, he was younger than Rose, but in all the important ways, he seemed older.

As they drove in this morning, she had expected it to be a silent drive, but Galen was surprisingly talkative. Granted, she peppered him with questions, but he didn't freeze up like she thought he would. He answered her questions about his horse training business, Naomi's headaches, his other sisters and brothers who had married and moved away. The very fact that he steered any and all conversation away from Rose only led Delia to believe that he was in love with her.

Time passed in an instant. The last thing Vera remembered, she was fighting back tears as her hair was getting shaved off. She had never had her hair cut. Not once in her entire long life. And this morning, it was all shaved off.

An instant later, she woke up in a recovery room, feeling like a hen caught in the middle of a killing neck twist. What had happened? Her head was bandaged in gauze like a foreigner's head wraps. She saw such a thing once on a bus trip she took to Sarasota, Florida, to visit her cousin. What was the word for it? And underneath the gauze that was wrapped around her head were staples and glue. Staples!

There was one bright spot she hadn't expected: brain surgery was relatively painless. The nurse explained that even though there were many nerves in the brain, they were nerves that thought, not nerves that felt. "You'll be off those pain meds by tomorrow," she told Vera. "And I think you'll like the effects of the steroids the doctor will give you to control swelling. They'll make you happy and hungry. You might even like our hospital food."

Vera opened one eye to peer at the tray she had brought. "Doubt it," she mumbled. "That would take more than drugs." Who ate blue Jell-O? Before she left this hospital for home, she might try to get into the hospital kitchen and show the cook a thing or two about how the Amish managed to cook for big crowds.

Then that fine-looking doctor came in and asked her to count backward from one hundred. She couldn't. Each moment of silence that passed caused Vera's fears to grow. She had never been good at arithmetic. He asked her what day it was and who the president of the United States was right now. How should she know? She never voted. Rose did, but she never did.

Tears started to fill her eyes. The doctor's hand clasped hers and squeezed. "Right now there's tissue swollen from the surgery," he explained. "As the swelling goes down, everything will improve. It's too soon to worry, but I'm not expecting significant implications from the surgery."

It was never too soon to worry, Vera thought bitterly. How infuriating to have this invasive, frightening surgery, only to have it do nothing for her! She was in worse shape than she was before she had it. She should have never agreed to it.

The doctor wrote down a few things on her chart and told her he would be back later in the day to check on her. Then he sailed out of the room and left her alone with beeping machines.

A turban. *A turban.* That's what the gauze on her head felt like.

She remembered!

After the surgery, Rose was allowed into Vera's intensive care room for ten minutes. No longer. Vera looked peaked and drawn, but there was some fire in her too. "Get me out of here," she whispered to Rose.

"Not quite yet. As soon as Dr. Stoltz says you can go home."

Amazingly, that could be as soon as a few days, he had said, when he came into the waiting room to tell Rose that the surgery had been successful. He had walked through those swinging doors in his blue scrubs, a big grin on his face, and stopped abruptly. In the waiting room was not just Rose, but seven Amish people from Stoney Ridge, a crowd, peering at him with concerned faces under their black hats and bonnets. "Everything went very well, better than expected," Dr. Stoltz told the group, sounding satisfied. "We won't know more until she wakes up. I'm hopeful for a complete recovery as the swelling recedes, but, of course, I'm not the ultimate healer."

"I believe that position is already taken," said a woman's voice from the back of the Amish crowd. It came from Fern Lapp.

Fern had organized a Mennonite driver to take a few church members into Philadelphia and stay with Rose during the surgery. At the sound of her voice, Dr. Stoltz's dark eyebrows shot up and his entire countenance changed. That serious, extremely confident man suddenly seemed like a small boy who'd met up with a stern librarian with an overdue book in his hand.

But then, Fern Lapp—thin as a butter knife, wiry and active—had that effect on nearly everyone, with one exception: Vera. Those two women tried to outdo each other in everything: quilting, cooking, baking, gardening.

Fern offered to stay the night at the hospital so Rose could return home and rest. The driver was waiting in the parking lot for Galen and the others. "I'll stay the night so you can go on home," Fern said, after Dr. Stoltz made a hasty exit. "You look terrible. Awful. Like something the cat dragged in."

Rose hadn't slept a wink—partly because of that awful padded bench, but mostly because Vera kept hollering out things through the night she wanted Rose to know about . . . just in case. In case she died, she meant.

"Write this down: The farm goes to Tobe. I promised him!"

"Yes, Vera."

"Make sure Bethany gets *A Young Woman's Guide to Virtue*. She loves that book."

"Yes, Vera."

"My mother gave me that book. It was her book. Did I ever tell you that?"

"Yes, Vera. Try to sleep now."

But of course, Vera didn't want to sleep. As far as she was concerned, it might be the last night of her life on earth. Why spend it sleeping? she told Rose. Finally, Rose turned on the light and read the Bible aloud to her. Psalm 23, then 139. Vera quieted at those ancient words of comfort. Soon, she was snoring loud enough to rattle the windows. Rose closed the Bible, turned off the light, and tried to sleep.

After such a long night, the thought of Rose's own bed sounded heavenly, but she knew Vera needed her. "Thank you, Fern, but I'll stay."

Later, trying to get comfortable on the awful chairs in the waiting room for the ICU floor, she regretted that decision. Tomorrow night, if Vera continued to improve, she would take Delia up on her offer to stay at her house for the remaining nights until Vera was released. She spread a gray blanket over her that a nurse had brought out. Its color mirrored the reflective mood Rose was in. She thought of the kind and considerate friends who had waited with her all day in the hospital. Of Fern Lapp, who said she would take a meal over to Eagle Hill for tonight's supper. Of Delia Stoltz, who was staying at her own home tonight and promised to check in first thing in the morning. Of Hank Lapp, who kept everyone entertained with the box of dominoes he had brought with him.

Her mind traveled to Dean. His chief focus, especially in the last few years of his life, had been on making more and more money, but did money bring any greater happiness than friendship? She thought not.

Then she thought of Galen. He had given up a day of work to stay by her side, and she knew what that meant to him. And she had ended up hurting him.

Before Fern and the others had arrived, she and Galen had gone outside to get some fresh air. They stopped at a bench, blanketed in sunshine, and sat down. Out of the blue came the question, "Rose, have you given some thought about letting me court you?"

She had been dreading this conversation. "I've thought about it. I've thought about it plenty." The smile she gave him came a little shakily. "Can't things just go on between us the way they've been going? As good friends?"

"You don't know what you're asking of me. You might as well tell the grain to stay green. The way we are now might be fine for you, but not for me. I want more, Rose."

"I'm not right for you, Galen."

"What you really mean is . . . I'm not right for you."

She raised her head. Those piercing green eyes were looking down at her under the brim of his black hat, searching her face, trying to see into her heart. "Yes," she said softly. She felt him stiffen beside her and look away. It pained her to say those words to him—nearly as much as she knew it pained him to hear them, but it was the truth.

Slowly he turned back to her. His face was flat and empty, but a muscle ticked in his cheek and she could see the pulse beating in his neck, fast and hard. "I'll go see if there's any word about Vera." He walked to the door that led to the hospital waiting room, half turned at the door, then swung back. "The hard truth is that I'm not the one who's too stubborn and independent and unbending. You are. You won't let anyone help you. You don't mind having people rely on you, but you don't want to need anyone. If that's not pride, I don't know what is."

He waited, but there was nothing more she had to say to him, or at least she hadn't within her the words he wanted to hear. The silence hung between them, waiting for someone to act—but then they heard someone call Galen's name. They turned and saw a group of Amish church friends, climbing out of a Mennonite taxi at the curbside, who had come to help stand vigil. Galen walked over to meet them.

Pride? *Pride?* He thought she was prideful?! Rose was stung.

It was unfortunate that Bethany's first day of work at the Sisters' House happened to fall on the day Mammi Vera ended up having surgery. In a way, though, it helped Bethany to keep her mind from fretting about her grandmother. She couldn't do any good by just walking the walls of the hospital, anyway.

Early that morning, Bethany was met at the door of the Sisters' House by Ada. She led Bethany into the living room and told her to start from one corner and go from there. "Use your own judgment about what to keep or what to get rid of."

"Are you sure?" Bethany asked. "I don't really know what you might need." Not that there was anything worth salvaging, in her mind. Maybe a box of fabric for quilt scraps. A ball of yarn. Everything else? *Out!*

"Maybe you're right," Ada said. "We do use everything, sooner or later. I just hate that feeling of when you throw something out and—" *snap!* she clicked her knobby fingers— "next thing you know, you're looking high and low for it."

Bethany looked around the room. "I need three boxes," she

told Ada. "One for things you want to keep, one for things you want to donate, one for things to discard."

Twenty minutes later, Ada returned with four boxes. "I thought it might be wise if we leave one for things we can't decide about. Just in case."

All right, Bethany told her, and soon regretted it. One sister after another would mosey in and start weeding through the Donate and Discard pile and quietly move things into the Keep and Undecided boxes. By lunchtime, they had undone all the morning work Bethany had done.

Okay, this wasn't working. She decided to take a break and eat her lunch on the front porch. It was a pleasant day and she couldn't work with the sisters in the same room. Since there were five of them, they acted like slippery barn cats, oozing their way in and out of the living room, making off with something from the discard pile. When she finished her lunch, she went back inside and found Ada bent over the Undecided box, rooting through black sweaters. So many sweaters! All black.

"Maybe I'll just go tidy up the kitchen," Bethany said. Stick to the dishes, she decided.

Ada was thrilled by that suggestion which, Bethany knew, was because she worked too fast and made her nervous. Too many treasures ended up in the wrong boxes.

By day's end, Bethany was exhausted. She stopped by the phone shanty to check messages—hoping there might be word about Mammi Vera from Rose. And maybe a word from Jake.

She tried her very best not to call Jake every single day. She knew, from reading chapter 13 in *A Young Woman's Guide to Virtue*, that she should restrain herself. But each day, she found a reason or two to slip around the hard and fast rules of the book. Today, she wanted to talk to him about her grandmother's surgery, about losing her job at the Bar & Grill and taking the job at the Sisters' House. She hoped he might feel disappointed that she had committed to a new job, even if it was part time and very casual. She hoped he had plans for the two of them. But, like always, he didn't pick up. Before she thought twice, she left a message that she needed to talk to him and hung up.

As she was closing the door to the shanty, the phone rang. She lunged for the receiver. "Hello?"

"Bethany! Did you find the books?"

Not even a howdy. "No."

"You said you needed to talk to me. I thought it was about the books."

"I do need to talk to you, but I haven't found them yet."

"Are you looking?"

"Of course I'm looking! I've gone through the entire house, top to bottom. Mim mentioned that a lot of Mammi Vera's junk was hauled out to the hayloft, so I'll start there soon." She shuddered to think of spending hours in the dusty hayloft. She hated mice with their beady little eyes and long skinny tails. Hated them. "I do have other obligations, I hope you know." Like, a job with five certifiably crazy old ladies.

His voice softened. "I wish I could help. I'm sorry to leave this job to you."

"So . . . why can't you help?"

"Bethany—I told you. If your family were to see me, if Rose were to know about Tobe's problem, it puts her in a terrible spot." He let out a sigh. "Besides, I'm miles and miles away, looking for work."

The discouragement in his voice made her feel a tweak of

guilt. It didn't seem right to talk to him about her new job at the Sisters' House when he had lost his job and couldn't get hired anywhere else—all because of her father.

"Honey, what did you need me for, then?"

She loved it when he called her honey. "I . . . just wanted to hear your voice."

"That's sweet. I sure am missing you. As soon as you can find those books, I will hightail it back to Stoney Ridge. Once we get Tobe cleared . . . then . . ."

She held her breath. *Then what?*

". . . everything else will come together."

She let out her breath.

"I need to get going. Bye for now, honey."

For a long while, she stared at the receiver before she set it back in the cradle. She loved it when he called her honey. Loved it!

21

In every human heart, Rose thought, even the most forbidding, there was a place that could be touched. The difficulty was finding it; there were people who carefully concealed that place. Sometimes, though, their guard slipped for a moment or two, and the way to a heart lay open. She saw such a moment today. She thought of such things as miracles, though she knew Bishop Elmo would disagree. But to Rose, unexpected moments of healing and happiness pointed people to God. Wasn't that a miracle?

That moment came when she saw Charles and Delia Stoltz talking to each other in the hospital corridor. Standing close, listening carefully to each other. They didn't strike Rose as a couple who were heading to divorce court. They looked like they were finding their way back to each other.

Other unexpected miracles occurred today too. When Dr. Stoltz pronounced Vera ready to go home—four days after the surgery. Rose thought it might be a little premature, but it seemed the hospital staff was particularly eager to have Vera released—she was *that* bossy and critical.

Delia drove Rose and Vera back to Eagle Hill. They arrived

home to find the table set for dinner, the animals fed and tucked away for the night, the house tidied up, and a beautiful dinner waiting to be served. That felt like a miracle to Rose.

Rose tucked Vera straight into bed, promising her plenty of time for catch-up talks with the family in the days ahead. She tried to keep everyone quiet, but Vera said not to bother—that the sounds of family at the dinner table filled her with happiness. Soon, the house was a jumble of noise and confusion and joy. Another miracle!

Delia and Jimmy Fisher joined the family for supper. Rose sent Luke and Sammy over to invite Galen and Naomi and was disappointed when they declined. She wanted things to be as they were. Why couldn't Galen understand that life wasn't as simple for her as he made it out to be?

She was prideful, he told her. *Her!* That from a man who kept himself apart from others. Who only took on an apprentice because the deacon insisted. Well, if that's how Galen wanted things to be between them—all stiff and stern—that was fine with her. Just fine.

During the meal, Rose looked around the table with overflowing gratitude. It had always done her heart good to watch people eat the food from her kitchen, especially her own family and friends. To some, it might seem like such an ordinary thing. To her, it felt like a healing balm. All would be well.

Miracle number five.

Whenever a chore around the farm needed tending to, Luke and Sammy quietly slipped out of sight. Today, Saturday morning, Bethany had enough of their disappearances. She was tired of feeding chickens and sheep and a goat. She marched down to the roadside where they were trying to sell their junk. "You two get up to that barn and take care of your animals."

"Can't!" Luke said. "Saturday morning is our peak selling time."

"Who would buy your junk?" Bethany said, annoyed with their flimsy excuses.

"Tons of folks. We've been making a boatload of money." Sammy nodded solemnly. "A boatload."

"What do you two have that anybody would ever want?"

"It's all in the selling," Luke said. "Mim was right. If we call something an antique, it sells."

Bethany's eyes grazed over the cardboard table with disgust: old amber bottles, rabbit feet, rusty lanterns, blue jay feathers, a baseball cap the boys had found on the roadside that cars had run over a few times, jigsaw puzzles with missing pieces, some black books, galvanized milk pails, . . . wait a minute. Black books? Two black books with red bindings. Heart racing, she grabbed them and leafed through them. Pages and pages of names, dates, numbers. Tobe's books! "Where'd you find these?"

"In the bottom of a box in the hayloft," Sammy said. "Why?"

She hugged the books to her body. "Hallelujah and never you mind!"

The next day was bright and sunny, already warm by midmorning. Mim was watering the strawberry patch with a makeshift watering can that Luke had rigged up: a plastic jug of Tide laundry detergent with holes poked in the cap.

Nearby, two bluejays were having an argument. Mim wished Luke would come along with his handcarved slingshot to silence them, but he and Sammy were down by the road, trying to sell their junk. Her mother came out of the kitchen and stood at the edge of the garden. She watched quietly for a long time as Mim watered the rows of green little plants with delicate white flowers.

"Won't be long until we can make strawberry jam."

"I don't think it will be much of a crop," Mim said. "Not unless we get more rain."

"How does Mammi Vera seem to you?"

Mim gave that some thought as she refilled the Tide water bucket. When Mammi Vera had come into the house last night, she looked like she'd wrestled with a black bear and lost—her head was bandaged and she had dark circles under her eyes. But then she started complaining about how dirty the house was—it wasn't—and how noisy the boys were—they were—and Mim knew she would be fine. Her face got all soft and sweet when she saw Bethany. Her eyes shimmered with tears of joy—and then came the best part. No hiccups!

"She seems the same. A little better. But it might be too early to tell if she's fixed."

"How did the game of checkers go this morning?" The nurses at the hospital had told Vera to play a lot of board games and do puzzles. It was good exercise for the brain, they said. Luke, Sammy, and Mim set up a schedule to take turns playing games with her.

Mim straightened up. "Well, she cheated. But she always did cheat at checkers."

Her mother grinned. She walked over a few rows and cupped Mim's cheeks with her hands. "Mim, I do see you. I do hear you. I know this last year has been overwhelming at times, but I never want you to feel as if you're not important to me. You are."

Mim gave her mother a look that in half a minute went from anger to worry to sadness to resignation. "The letter. You read the letter." Bethany had kept everyone so busy getting ready for Mammi Vera's homecoming that Mim had completely forgotten to pick up yesterday's mail.

Her mother nodded. "I went through the mail last night before I went to bed."

Mim squinted her face. "How did you know it was from me?"

"How many typewriters have a letter *A* that is slightly crooked?"

Mim hung her head. She hadn't thought of letter *A*.

"I wondered if you might like to take some early walks with me this summer after school lets out? I'd like your company."

Her mother had never invited anyone on a morning walk, not even her father. Mim took off her glasses, polished them, and replaced them. "I suppose. I suppose I could do that."

Her mother smiled. "Let's plan on it, then."

Bethany felt bewildered, disoriented. She slammed the rolling pin down onto the ball of biscuit dough. She pushed hard and the dough flattened. She pulled and pushed the heavy wooden pin, pulled and pushed, rolling out the dough with such vigor that flour floated in a white cloud around her.

She stopped pushing the biscuit dough and stood in stillness a moment, bent over the table, her hands gripping the rolling pin. She straightened, dusted her hands off on her apron, and laughed at her silly nervousness. Wedding jitters. Every bride felt them. *A Young Woman's Guide to Virtue* said to expect them.

Bethany had called Jake to leave a message and tell him about the books and was surprised when he answered his phone. When she told him about the books, the phone went silent. Then he let out a huge sigh of relief. "Just in the nick of time. I'll be there tonight."

"What time? I have to be at a birthday party for a neighbor."

"Where's the party?"

"At Windmill Farm—just a few miles up the road from Eagle Hill."

"I'll be down at the end of Windmill Farm's driveway at 8 p.m. tonight. Be there with the books."

Now she was silent.

"Bethie?"

"What does that mean . . . just in the nick of time?"

"I've got a job opportunity in Somerset County. A good job. I've held off as long as I can. Because of you, because you found those books, I'll be able to help Tobe and get to that job."

"So will Tobe be coming home soon?"

"No doubt, honey. All because of you."

"What *about* me, Jake? You're just going to disappear again, aren't you?"

In the silence that followed, Bethany felt the air about her crackle and tremble, like the pause between lightning and thunder—something had to happen. She couldn't live this way any longer—waiting, waiting, waiting for Jake. If she was going to lose him in the end, better to face it now. "I'm no good at waiting."

In a raspy voice, almost choked up, Jake said, "Then come with me."

What?! She lurched to grab the counter so she didn't lose her balance. Weren't those the words she'd been longing to hear from him for over a year now? But now, faced with the reality of them . . . she wasn't sure if she was ready for them. "I don't know . . . I'm not sure I can leave my family . . ."

"Bethany, your family is doing fine. You told me so yourself. Everyone has adjusted. They don't need you now like they did. It's your time, honey." He paused again. "So . . . come with me."

She drew in a deep breath and then another. "You mean, as your wife?" she had asked. "Because that's the only way you'll ever have me, Jake Hertzler."

He had laughed then and asked her what kind of a low-down excuse of a man did she consider him to be? Then he said he needed to go, but he would be at the foot of Windmill Farm tonight at eight o'clock. And he told her he loved her.

He had never spoken of love to her before. As she hung up the phone on the cradle, she hugged herself with happiness. Jake loved her! He was coming to get her. They were going to be married and live happily ever after. She had dreamed of this day.

So why was her stomach twisting and turning?

If only Jake had asked her to marry him a year ago, before everything bad happened, then it all would have been so much easier. They could have had a proper church wedding, and her family would've embraced Jake as a son. Her father had already thought of him as a son.

She squeezed her eyes shut. That was then and this was now. Her father wasn't here any longer.

After moving to Stoney Ridge, Bethany had known that if she married Jake, it would come down to this: eloping. There were too many complications surrounding them—the messy problems of Schrock Investments, their different churches, her family. Her grandmother's heart was set on the grandchildren becoming Old Order Amish. Set like stone. She wasn't sure how many times her grandmother's heart could break and mend.

She took a deep cleansing breath, in and out. It would be fine, she reassured herself. Everything would be fine. Mammi Vera was well again. Tobe would be home soon. Like Jake said, it was her time now.

She laughed again, feeling light-headed all of a sudden. Everything would be fine.

Delia woke up feeling better than she had in a long time. She actually hummed as she went into the bathroom, turned on the faucet to get the hot water going, which, she had learned, could take several minutes, and started brushing her teeth.

As she rolled up the tube, trying to coax the last bit of toothpaste out, she thought about the conversations she'd been having with Charles. They had spent more time talking the past few days—about truly important things—than they had in years.

Just a few weeks ago Delia was so downhearted and depressed that she couldn't face the idea of even getting out of bed, and now, here she was humming to herself, cancer free, and ready to return home.

Home. Yes! She wanted to go home, she decided as she

spat a white stream into the sink and filled the cup with water to rinse her mouth. She reached behind the curtain to test the water. Almost hot enough. Another minute should do it.

Best of all, she thought, as she noticed the steam coming over the top of the plastic curtain, she was going home as a different person. Stronger, yet weaker. No—not weak. Humble. That's how she felt. She was a humble person learning to rely on a strong God. Somehow, that awareness made all the difference.

After she had dressed and started to pack, she spotted Rose on her way to the barn and hurried out to talk to her. "I hope this doesn't seem too sudden to you, but I'm ready to head back home."

Rose smiled. She understood. "Do you think your husband will be joining you?"

Delia looked thoughtful. "We're a ways from that. But I think we're heading in the right direction." She laughed. "I have Eagle Hill to thank for that."

"We can give the glory to God for bringing you here, right when we needed you. Imagine if your husband hadn't seen Vera that evening."

Delia nodded. "Did I ever tell you that Charles was raised Old Order Amish?"

Rose's head snapped to face Delia and her eyes went wide. "No, you never did. I think I would have remembered that particular piece of information."

"I'm ashamed to say that I have rarely asked him much about his upbringing. He never volunteered much about it and I wasn't all that interested. But now I am. And he's finally willing to talk about it."

Rose smiled. "Sounds like you're off to a fresh start."

"A fresh start. I like that. I hope you're right. Not just with my marriage. Also with my faith. Thank you for encouraging me, Rose. I hope to come back to Eagle Hill. Often."

Rose smiled. "You were our first guest. Our first blessed guest."

So true! Later, as Delia zipped up her suitcase and gave the guest flat one more lookover to make sure she hadn't forgotten anything, she rolled Rose's words around in her mind: a blessed guest.

She had come here on a whim and stayed for over a month! She took her suitcase out to her car and put it in the trunk. Her heart was suddenly too full for words as she let her gaze roam lovingly over the Inn at Eagle Hill: over the lofty barn and the large white clapboard house tucked against the hill. The creek that wove like a ribbon from the hill down to the road. The green pasture that held that silly goat and four sheep.

"Rose just told me. She said you're leaving today."

Delia turned to find Bethany watching her. "What you have here, Bethany, it's so special. So rare." Delia's gaze lingered on Bethany a moment and then shifted to the end of the driveway, where Sammy and Luke sat behind a cardboard table. "It's days like this that are worth the remembering. A day like this can stay with you, can settle down to live on in your soul forever."

"Maybe you should think about buying a farm."

Delia turned to her. "A farm? I didn't mean the land—though it is a beautiful property. I meant—" she lifted her palm and made a wide sweeping arc—"I meant your family. Your neighbors. Your church and community. Most people look for this their entire life and never find it. It's so . . . special. Never, ever let it go."

Her words fell into an empty silence.

When Delia spun around to look at Bethany, she was surprised to see the girl's eyes had filled with tears. Delia took a step toward Bethany, then another. She reached out her hand to touch her shoulder.

"Why, Bethany, whatever is wrong? Did I say something to upset you?"

Bethany covered her face with her hands, but just for a moment. "Don't mind me. I'm just having an emotional day." Her voice was shaky as she backed up a few steps. "I'm glad we met, Mrs. Stoltz." She turned and ran to the farmhouse.

Puzzled, Delia watched until she disappeared into the house. She felt as if she had gotten to know Bethany. Whenever Bethany had brought breakfast to the basement, she would linger for a chat. Delia had even taught her how to make tea the right way—real English steeped tea. But the girl sounded as if she thought they'd never see each other again.

She saw Galen lead a horse from the paddock to the barn and walked over to say goodbye to him. She found him in his workshop, starting to repair a harness. "I've come to say goodbye."

He stopped unbuckling the harness and gave his hat brim a tug. "Godspeed to you."

She hesitated, wanting to say more. In the hospital, she couldn't help but notice the way Galen and Rose interacted. There were times when Rose let her eyes linger on his face in a way that made Delia wonder if her feelings for Galen were quite as platonic as she claimed. Delia had asked her once if she thought she would ever love again, and Rose had seemed surprised by the question. "I never thought of it," she had told her. Delia understood why, but never was a very long time. Rose was a lovely young woman and Galen was a very special, very kind, very patient man. The type of man who would deserve someone like Rose.

Delia weighed her thoughts back and forth as Galen grew increasingly uncomfortable. He wanted to get back to work. Finally, Delia decided to just say what was on her mind. "I hope you don't mind if I speak in a forthright manner."

Galen's eyebrows lifted.

"I hope you will rouse yourself and propose to Rose. Soon."

Galen's eyes went wide with astonishment.

"You must not be a sissy about this."

He cleared his throat. "A sissy?"

"Galen, you love Rose. You know it. I know it. Rose is the one who doesn't know it. There. I've said what I've come to say."

His gaze drifted around the workshop, alighting everywhere but on her. "It's not quite that easy. I've tried. She's said no."

"You'll have to keep on trying."

"She doesn't see me that way. I'm just a friend to her. A neighbor."

"You can change that. She deserves someone like you."

He looked very unsure. "I don't know . . . what else to do."

"Well, for starters, did you happen to know that she wants a porch swing?"

Delia found Mim waiting patiently by her car with a wriggling puppy in her arms. "Why, Mim, what's this?"

"Mom said you're leaving today." She held the puppy out

to Delia. "I brought you something. You don't have to keep it if you don't want to."

Delia took a step toward her. The puppy was yellow, with long ears, curly hair, and a small, black button nose.

"Oh Mim! He's adorable." She took the puppy from Mim's arms and cradled it in her own. The puppy looked up at her with big brown, liquid eyes that seemed to beg for a home.

"Puppies are nothing but trouble," Mim warned. "That's a fact. I'll take him if you don't want him."

Delia smiled up at Mim. "What kind of dog is he?"

"A male, one of Chase's puppies. Apparently Chase had paid a call to a certain female yellow lab over at Windmill Farm. Fern Lapp's dog. She's named Daisy. Chase is quite taken with Daisy. He has good taste—she's a pretty girl. This puppy is definitely not purebred, so if that matters—"

"If he's part of Chase, it doesn't matter to me at all."

Mim reached over and scratched the puppy's ears. "I picked him out myself. He seemed like the calmest and smartest of the litter. He hasn't had his shots yet."

"My son can take care of that."

Mim went to the house and brought back dog food, a water bowl, and a towel for a bed. "This will take care of you for a while."

"I've never had a dog," Delia said, grinning as the little puppy sniffed around the car.

"Never? I can't remember ever not having a dog. Seems like everyone needs a good dog."

"I already love him. Thank you, Mim."

"You'll have to choose a name for him."

The puppy wandered around the yard, sniffing, running,

stopping, then bolted after a butterfly. "Maybe I'll name him *Miracula fieri hic* and call him Micky for short. To remember the miracle of being here."

Mim's face lit with a smile. She gazed at the puppy. "Hope you'll still feel that way after you've had him for a few days."

22

~~~~~~~~~~~~~~ ◆ ~~~~~~~~~~~~~~

Mim, Luke, and Sammy arrived at Hank Lapp's birthday party at Windmill Farm just as a softball game got under way on the front lawn. Galen dropped them off so they could join their friends, then he went to fetch the sisters at the Sisters' House. Bethany had walked over earlier, to help set up for the party, she said, and Mim was glad she had left the house because her sister was in a weird mood today. Teary one minute, snapping at Luke and Sammy in the next minute, humming with happiness the next.

Mim happened to notice that Danny Riehl was at bat, so she hurried to the team her brothers were on. She and Sammy were sent to the outfield. Luke was sent to cover first base. Jimmy Fisher was pitching. Hank Lapp was umpire. He was always the umpire. He said it was because his arthritis was acting up, but Galen said it was mainly because he had the loudest voice of anyone. Jimmy lobbed a ball to Danny and he hit it sailing, sailing, sailing, right to Sammy. The ball dropped out of his mitt and Luke let out a large groan. Then Sammy overthrew it to Luke when he should have thrown it to second base. By the time Luke retrieved the ball from the BBQ pit, Danny had made a home run. Luke glared at Sammy. That boy Luke, Mim decided, was getting too high and mighty.

But then Mim watched Sammy miss every ball that came his way, even ones where he didn't have to move an inch. Unexpected tears stung her eyes. He needed a father.

When it was time for dinner, Mim helped the women serve the food out on the picnic benches. She was filling glasses with iced tea when she spotted Galen King seated next to Jimmy Fisher. She reached around Galen for his glass and took her time filling it. "You should, you know," she whispered as she set his glass next to him, "teach Sammy how to catch a fly ball."

Surprised, Galen looked up. Before he could speak, she was gone.

One hour to go. Jake had said he would pick Bethany up at eight at the end of the driveway—just as it grew dark. She was feeling feverish inside, all shaky and sweat-sticky and cold. And she kept forgetting to breathe. *I must do this. I must.* If she didn't go with him tonight, she would lose Jake forever.

At seven thirty, she walked nervously around the yard, taking in the sight of her brothers and her sister, forcing it to her memory. How tall would her brothers be the next time she saw them? What about Mim? She was just on the threshold of becoming a woman.

Before she left for the party tonight, she had tucked a letter under each person's pillow, telling them she loved them and always would. Her grandmother was sleeping when she had to go, which was a relief. She knew she would burst into tears if she tried to say goodbye face-to-face. She slipped in and kissed her bandaged forehead.

She watched the five ancient sisters from the Sisters' House, sitting in lawn chairs on the grass, like little sparrows on a telephone pole. She had only worked for them one week, but she was growing fond of their quirky ways. She had left a letter for them under Rose's pillow, explaining that something important had come up. She hoped Jimmy Fisher would find someone special to work for them.

She saw Jimmy serve a volleyball—what was it about the sight of him that made her start to grin, even when he wasn't trying to be funny? There was just something about him . . .

I must do this. I must.

Fighting tears, she slipped quietly down the driveway, retrieving the ledgers she'd hidden behind a fence post. She tucked them under her apron and waited for Jake.

While she waited in the dark, a panic gripped her chest so tightly that she thought her heart had stopped beating.

Jimmy saw Bethany head toward the road and he tossed the volleyball to Sammy, who missed it. That boy needed a little work. He swooped up the volleyball, delivered it into Sammy's hands, tapped him on the head, and hurried after Bethany. What was she doing, heading down that way in the dark? She had seemed a little strange tonight—quiet and sad and nervous—and he thought she might be feeling poorly. He saw her about halfway down the driveway, arms crossed against her middle like she had a stomachache.

"Bethany?"

She spun around, her hands flew to her face. Her eyes looked wild.

"What's wrong? Are you sick?"

"I can't do it! I can't go. I can't leave them. I thought I could but I can't."

"Can't leave who?"

"I thought I loved him. And I do! I thought I did. But not enough. Not enough to leave my family. Not like this, anyway."

"What the Sam Hill are you talking about?"

"Jake Hertzler. He's coming for me. He wants me to run off with him. I said I'd go, but I can't. I can't leave my family. How will I tell him? He'll be devastated." She looked up, eyes shimmering with tears. "Will you stay here with me? Will you help me? Jake can be very persuasive. I don't trust myself to not cave in."

"Of course."

"Please, Jimmy. I need you to stay nearby because I'm not tough at all. I act like I am, but I'm not. Not really."

He had already known that about her. He wrapped his arm around her shoulders, bumping hips with her, clumsy and yet tender. He stood there for a moment, holding her, and it was like he didn't want the moment to ever end.

Then they saw the beam of two headlights in the distance and Bethany froze. A truck pulling a horse trailer stopped at the end of the driveway. The window rolled down. "Let's go, honey!"

Bethany took a sharp breath. "Promise you'll stay right here, Jimmy."

"You can count on me."

Bethany walked down to the truck and spoke through the

open window. He could hear their mumbling voices, then Jake Hertzler's voice grew louder. And louder. He was spitting mad, Jimmy could tell that, even in the dark. Jake started hollering at Bethany, saying ugly things and calling her unrepeatable names.

Wait a minute. Wait just a minute. Jimmy knew that voice.

Hank Lapp's party guests were starting to make noises about heading home, but he wouldn't let anyone leave without a final surprise. He wanted Jimmy Fisher to put on a fireworks show, but no one could find him. A short while ago, Mim had seen Jimmy head away from the gathering on the front yard and down the long driveway. She ran to tell Hank Lapp and the two of them walked over to see if they could find Jimmy.

They were about halfway down the driveway when they spotted Jimmy Fisher behind a tree, standing in utter stillness. Jimmy motioned to them with his arm, holding a finger up to his lips. Hank Lapp made a lot of noise, even walking. Jimmy pointed down the hill. It was getting dark, but Mim could hear Bethany arguing with someone in a truck on the road. "Mim, get Galen. Be quick about it. Don't let anyone know. Hank—stay with me. And for heaven's sake, man, be quiet."

She'd never heard that tone in Jimmy's voice. It didn't have the teasing sound that was never far away. It was . . . it was the sound of a grown man. Something was terribly wrong. She flew up the hill so fast that her hair was flying every which way out from under her prayer cap and she was panting hard from all that running. She found Galen over by the barbecue, spreading the red hot coals with a stick so they'd cool down. "Come with me!" She grabbed Galen's elbow, dragging him back down the hillside to meet Jimmy. Along the way, he kept asking what was wrong and all she could say was, "Jimmy needs you."

By the time they reached Jimmy, Hank Lapp was nowhere in sight. "Galen," Jimmy whispered. "I think the fellow Bethany is talking to down there is the horse trader who's been scamming me."

Mim strained her ears. "Why, that's Jake Hertzler!"

"Also known as Jonah Hershberger," Jimmy said. "Horse swindler. First-rate con-artist."

"Why is Bethany crying?" Mim said.

"She's saying goodbye to him."

Jake had just grabbed something from Bethany's hands and was shouting at her. "He's not liking it." Mim started to feel frightened.

Galen's gaze went from Mim to Jimmy, then down to the end of the road. "Well, Jimmy, have you got a plan?"

"Always." Jimmy turned to Mim. "You stay put. If anything happens, you run to Amos and get help." Then he nodded his head to Galen. "Let's go."

Mim watched as the two men walked down to the end of the driveway, cucumber calm. Jimmy approached Bethany as Galen slid around to the driver's side. Mim took a few steps down the hill, scared, worried about Bethany, but not wanting to miss what was being said. Where did Hank Lapp go, anyway?

Jimmy put his hands on Bethany's shoulders and moved her away from the truck, then leaned against the window edge. "Well, well, Jonah Hershberger. We meet again."

"Jonah?" Bethany said. "What are you talking about, Jimmy? Are you crazy?"

"Jonah Hershberger. The fellow who keeps selling me the same horse."

"What?" Bethany said. "Jake is the horse trader?"

Jake pulled back from the open window. "Bethany," he said, nearly growling, "for the last time, get in the truck."

"She's not going anywhere," Galen said from the other side of the truck.

Jake's head whipped around, then back to Bethany.

"We've got a little business to discuss," Galen said. "You owe my partner here a sizable amount of money. Plus a horse."

With that, Jake flipped the ignition, revved the engine, and stepped on the gas. The truck sped off down the dark road and into the night.

But the trailer remained. Hank Lapp stood in front of the horse trailer. The trailer was slightly hitched up, the unplugged electrical cords dangled. "IS THAT WHAT YOU WANTED ME TO DO, BOY?"

Jimmy grinned. "It was, Hank. It was, indeed."

23

Hank Lapp's birthday party would become the talk of the town for days afterward. The story would become bigger and more dramatic with every telling—all but one piece of it. Jimmy Fisher would omit the part that Bethany was planning to run off with Jake. No one would know. He would tell no one.

But Rose figured it out that night.

While the party was going on, Rose had found Bethany's goodbye letter on her nightstand as she came upstairs to look for a book to read. She read it through, twice, heart pounding. There was a second letter addressed to the sisters at the Sisters' House.

Rose wished she could run through the privet and ask Galen his opinion, but she couldn't. Mainly, because he was at the party, but even if he weren't, there was a strain between them. She had come outside when he arrived to pick up the children and he hadn't even come down from his buggy. He wore the pain she had given him in his eyes.

It hurt so much that she was the one to look away.

On a hunch, she had gone to Mim and the boys' bedroom and found letters left on their pillows. Then she tiptoed into Vera's room and grabbed the letter on the nightstand, grateful Vera hadn't seen it yet. If Bethany did leave with Jake tonight, she didn't want Mim or Vera or the boys to read her goodbye letters before going to bed. Morning would come soon enough. Such news could wait.

She thought about what Galen would say if she were to tell him she found the letters Bethany had left, informing everyone she was leaving home. What would he say if she were to tell him she wanted to stop Bethany from making the biggest mistake of her life? She could practically hear Galen's deep voice: "What good would it do to try and stop her if she wants to go? Bethany has her own life to lead, including making her own mistakes." And then he would remind her, "God is faithful, even when we are not."

Galen was right, of course. Just like he was right about Rose being unbending and stubborn. It *was* a hard truth, but it was the truth. In a way, it was prideful to be unwilling to ask for or receive help. It was prideful to think she could handle everything on her own. She blew out a puff of air. How she missed him. She missed her friend.

So Rose sat at the kitchen table with a cup of tea and her well-loved Bible and prayed like she had never prayed before. She prayed for a miracle to intervene in Bethany's life. She prayed for something unexpected to occur. She prayed for Bethany's well-being, and her future. She prayed for heaven's protection over her beautiful, impulsive stepdaughter.

An hour later, when Galen's buggy pulled into the driveway, Rose nearly flew outside. She let out a gasp of silent thanks when Bethany tumbled out of the buggy and hurried past her into the house. "We had a little excitement tonight," Galen said. "I'll let Mim and the boys tell you all about it."

As he drove away, Mim and Luke and Sammy took turns talking over each other to tell Rose the news: Jimmy's horse swindler was their very own Jake Hertzler! Rose listened carefully, asked a few questions, and pieced together the story until she had a pretty good idea what had happened. When she saw Bethany had come downstairs, Rose sent the children up to bed. Bethany stood with her back against the wall, pale and sad, hugging her elbows tight against her body the way she did when she was a little girl.

Rose handed her the letters. "Are you looking for these?"

Slowly, Bethany reached out and took the letters from her. Then she tore them into pieces and threw them in the garbage can under the sink. She balled her hands into fists, her voice shaking. "I'm such a fool."

Rose crossed the room and looked into Bethany's face, so young, so beautiful, so filled with incomprehensible misery. She reached out and gently unfurled her tight fists. "Only if you don't become wiser through this."

A few tears trickled out of the corners of Bethany's eyes, and she wiped them away with her sleeve. "Rose, how could he have left like that?"

Rose shrugged. "Jake had everybody fooled. Myself included."

"Not Jake." She shook her head and the tears splattered. "Dad. How could he leave us like he did, just let his family go? I couldn't do that! I tried and I couldn't." She squeezed her eyes tightly shut, trying to hold back the tears. But they came faster and faster, until she couldn't stop their coming. "Tobe is the lucky one. He took the easy way out."

"There is no easy way out of this." Rose pulled her into her arms as she started to sob—deep heaving sobs, finally subsiding into a few shudders. "Go on, now. Get your cry out," Rose said, rubbing her back in small circles. Sadness had a way of piling up inside a person until there was nothing for it but to let it all out. "Cry it all out."

On Monday afternoon, after she finished readying the basement with fresh linens for the next guest who was due to arrive any minute, Rose called Allen Turner of the Securities and Exchange Commission. She told him that Jake Hertzler had turned up and left with the company books. They had been hidden on the farm all this time. All this time! "He's been horse trading around the county, using another name: Jonah Hershberger," Rose said. "He said he had a job opportunity in Somerset County, but I don't know if that was true."

Allen Turner was silent for a long moment. "He's probably halfway to Canada or Mexico by now. But then again, he's pretty bold. Could be he's sticking around, like a bad penny. In the meantime, we're still looking for your stepson."

"Jake said Tobe had been staying with his mother, but I don't know where she's living. I don't know anything about her except her maiden name: Mary Miller."

"Mary Miller?" He groaned. "Could there be a more common name among the Amish?"

She said goodbye, hung up the phone, and walked over to Galen's. She found him in front of his barn, tossing a softball back and forth with Sammy, back and forth. He looked up at her and smiled when he saw her. There was something about the smile that touched her; as if he had been hoping she would come by.

"Is something wrong, Rose? Is Vera all right?"

"Vera's fine. It's me—I'd like to ask you something."

"Sammy," he said. "Go take that hay out to the horses in the far pasture. Scatter it around this time. Don't just leave it in a clump."

Sammy threw the ball back to Galen, but it went sailing over his head. He hollered out an apology as he ran to the wheelbarrow filled with hay and started to push it down the dirt path to the pasture. Galen picked up the ball and walked to Rose. "If he could just remember to plant his feet when he aims at something, he might stand a chance as an outfielder."

"Could I see this horse that Jimmy paid for a few times over?"

"Of course. He's in the barn in a double stall."

She followed behind Galen. The barn held a mixture of sweet and pungent smells, summer hay and the sour tang of manure, the ripening sunlight pouring through the open door. She took in a deep breath, feeling almost dizzy.

Galen continued down the aisle and stopped at a stall. He turned and gave a puzzled look at Rose, still by the door.

She walked to the stall and peered in at the stallion. She gasped when she saw its flaxen mane. "That might be the most beautiful horse I've ever seen."

"That he is. He's a fine stud. Jimmy actually knew what he was talking about."

"Jimmy said you're going to stable him here."

"For now. We have to break his Houdini habit. Keeping him in such a big stall will help."

She chanced a glance at him. "Did you really call Jimmy Fisher your partner?"

Galen groaned. He moved a pitchfork out of the way and opened the top half of the Dutch door of the stall. "He's crowing about it all over town, I suppose."

"He is. Seems pretty pleased about it."

Lodestar stuck his head over the stall door. Galen reached out to stroke the horse's nose.

Rose looked at Galen's hands—beautiful, capable hands. Scarred, strong, deft. Hands that had the power to control a hot-blooded horse but the gentleness to caress its velvet nose. Hands she trusted.

"Would it be such an impossible thing for an independent fellow like you? Having a partner?"

His gaze met hers over the horse's head.

"Makes a lot of sense, you know. The Bible teaches us that 'two are better off than one, because together they can work more effectively. If one of them falls down, the other can help him up. Two people can resist an attack that would defeat one person alone. A rope made of three cords is hard to break.'"

He had yet to take his eyes off her. He didn't seem to be breathing. "Are we still talking about horses?"

She stroked the horse's blond forelock. "Why haven't you ever married?"

"I've never met anyone I wanted to marry. Not until you came along."

Her throat was hot and tight, full of the things she wanted to say. "Galen, I'm carrying a very big burden. I feel such deep shame over all that happened with Dean and his company. I need to pay people back for the money he lost. I can't ask you to share that burden. That's why I've kept you at a distance. That's why I keep pushing you away. Maybe you're right. Maybe it's pride. Stubbornness. I need to learn to ask for help. Help is a gift."

There was quiet—complete quiet.

And on and on the silence went, not a word out of Galen, not a sound. He stared at her for what seemed like an endless amount of time. A stain of color spread across his sharp cheekbones. "I would move heaven and earth for you."

"I know. I know you would." She laid the back of her hand against his cheek. "The problem, you see, is I've also been too stubborn to realize how much I care for you."

Galen's gaze traveled gently over her face, in that loving way he had of looking at her, and stopped at her lips. And then he dropped the pitchfork and it clattered to the concrete floor in the quiet of the barn. He reached around Lodestar's big head and grabbed Rose up in his arms. He swirled her around and around in a big circle and set her down again, then bent over and cupped her face in his hands. He leaned closer and brushed his mouth across hers, almost reverently. He started to pull away, but she reached up and wrapped her arms around his neck, holding him until he reached down to kiss her.

The next day, Mim found a note tucked inside of her desk when she arrived at school. "Super Moon. Tonight. 8 PM. Same place. DR"

She bit on her lip to keep from smiling. She would not look at Danny Riehl. She would not, would not, would not.

She looked.

She saw his eyes flit her way for a second and her stomach did a little flip-flop. After finding such a note, how could a girl ever concentrate on her schoolwork?

That evening, she met Danny on the hill behind the schoolhouse right at eight o'clock sharp. Danny wasn't even peering through the telescope. "You really don't need a telescope to see the night sky—just a dark night and your eyes." His head was tilted back, looking with awe at the full moon, the color of rich cream, so beautiful and round and low on the horizon. "It's called a perigee moon. Perigee means that it's at its closest point to the earth. An apogee moon is when it is farthest away."

Perigee. Apogee. Two new words for Mim to collect.

"The perigee moon occurs once a year. The orbit of the moon brings it about sixteen thousand miles closer to the earth. NASA said this super moon appears 14 percent bigger and 30 percent brighter than other full moons." He pushed his glasses up on the bridge of his nose. "I read those facts in a magazine for future astronauts."

Mim had always been fond of the moon. To her it was a more interesting thing to observe than the sun, which did the same thing every day. The moon changed, it moved around the sky; it waxed and waned. She had read that the moon moved the seas, but she hadn't been able to get her head around that. How could a moon move an ocean?

On a night when the moon rose, shining so brightly, like tonight, it seemed so close that she could almost climb a tree and step right on it. Even on nights when the moon was just a little white thumbnail, she tended to lose her worries when she gazed at it. Sometimes, she would sit by her window and imagine sitting on that hook, peering around the universe, untroubled about all that was happening on the little blue and green earth. She wondered how Danny would react if she shared those thoughts with him. Would he laugh at her?

He might be shocked. He might expect her to stick to facts. So she said, "Is this what they call a blue moon?"

"No. That happens when a full moon appears twice in one month. A blue moon only occurs about once every three years." He stepped toward the telescope, peered into it, and twisted some dials. "The size of the moon is about the same size as the continent of Africa. Some people think it's flat, but it has valleys and craters and basins and mountains on it."

She would have to remember to tell Sammy these moon facts.

They took turns looking at the moon through the telescope, then stood side by side, heads craned back, to study the moon without any device. It was . . . glorious. Resplendent. Majestic.

"We're not moving away after all," Danny said quietly. "My mother said no."

Mim froze. Her heart sang with happiness. Goose bumps danced all over her arms. Her toes wanted to tap.

She cut a sideways glance at Danny at the same moment that he looked at her. They smiled, then they both looked away.

Later tonight, she thought she might have to write again to Lonesome and tell her that "Yes, true love can definitely make everything better."

Rose's plan this morning was to walk to her favorite spot and watch the sun rise. Her plans changed when she saw how hard the rain was coming down. She steeped a cup of tea, à la Delia Stoltz's style, and took the mug outside to sit in the new porch swing. Chase followed along and curled up by her feet. The scent of summer was in the air, a whisper of promise. She loved this time of year, when the earth seemed to be warming up from within. She took a deep breath. A handful of memories were tied to the scent of the rain, damp grass, and mist. Good memories. The kind that filled you with peace and happiness and satisfaction.

She could think of Dean now without the crushing burden of grief. Remember the good times and smile, grateful for the life they'd shared. She was thankful for the incredible gift of her children. She'd loved her husband, faults and all, and his death had badly shaken her world and her sense of self.

Lately, the only thing she'd been able to count on was that things change. But they had made it through the worst. Vera was under a doctor's care and her condition was stable. Bethany had turned an important corner into adulthood. Mim and the boys had their ups and downs, but they were adjusting. And she always had a hope that Tobe would return.

And then there was yesterday's news: at Galen's urging, she had gone to the bishop to let him know she was trying to pay back investors. She surprised the bishop so, his face flushed red above his gray beard. "Rose, Rose," he said in his kind voice. "Why would you think you were all alone in this? That was a burden God never meant for you."

He told her a group of Amish and Mennonites had formed a committee to handle the settlement of claims outside the court process. They would use donations from Amish and Mennonite communities nationwide to reimburse those investors, the Plain people, who wouldn't be using the court process.

Those people—all those sad, sad letters—they would be paid back. She still couldn't believe it! She simply couldn't believe it.

She told the bishop about Tobe's involvement, about the elusive Jake Hertzler. At first, she wondered if knowing about Tobe might change the committee's mind about reimbursing people. But no, Bishop Elmo said that revelation had no bearing on their decision.

"The Lord doesn't ask us to judge how or why needs occur," Bishop Elmo told her, his spiky gray eyebrows drawing together. "He only asks us to take care of those in need. We all have need, Rose. Each one of us."

On the way home from the bishop's house, she was a little sorry that he had wanted that phrase removed—"*Miracula fieri hic*"—from the bottom of the Inn at Eagle Hill sign. Miracles did occur, every day. Maybe they weren't the kinds of miracles that could be scrutinized for scientific proof, but how could you ever test for a change of a heart? Or a healing of an emotional wound? Or the power of forgiveness? Miracles meant that God was at work.

Her thoughts drifted to the letter she had from Delia yesterday. She said that her son, Will, might be moving to Lancaster County in the fall to head up a new Wild Bird Rescue Center. "He has had some wonderful offers from veterinary clinics but thinks he will be turning them down," she wrote. "I think it might have something to do with that lady vet he met at your farm." Then she added that Charles had agreed to go to marriage counseling with her. "Things can get good again," she had written and underlined it twice.

Yes, they can, Rose thought to herself. Corners could be turned. The pendulum would swing. Everything could change. As it would again, and again, and again.

She smiled, running a hand along the smooth arm of the white porch swing that Galen had made for her as a surprise.

He called it their courting swing. Dear, kind, faithful Galen. She knew that he hadn't been good to her because he expected anything in return but because he was who he was—a man with a genuine desire to help fix what was broken. He was good at that.

She felt a hard band let loose around her ribs and took in a long breath. This place, Eagle Hill, was her home. Soon, the cares of the day would creep in. She would need to rouse the boys and get the day started. There were new guests in the basement and she liked to bake her blueberry cornbread for first-time guests. Blessed guests.

But first, she'd just sit here, listen to the rain, and be thankful. Be thankful for the new day.

Rose's Blueberry Cornbread

2 large eggs
1 cup buttermilk
¼ cup butter, melted
⅔ cup all-purpose flour
1⅓ cup cornmeal
¼ cup sugar
1½ teaspoons baking powder
½ teaspoon salt
1 cup fresh or frozen blueberries, rinsed

In a bowl, beat eggs, buttermilk, and butter to blend. In another bowl, mix flour, cornmeal, sugar, baking powder, and salt.

Stir flour mixture into egg mixture just until evenly moistened. Gently stir in berries. Spread level in a buttered 8-inch square pan.

Bake in a 375 degree oven until a wooden skewer inserted into the center comes out clean, 25 to 35 minutes, depending on your oven. Let cool 10 minutes, then cut into 9 squares.

Discussion Questions

1. This story begins and ends at moments when Rose Schrock meets the sunrise. The rising of the sun contains all sorts of symbolism. What does it mean to Rose?

2. How were concerns for family different for each of the characters? Rose Schrock? Her mother-in-law, Vera Schrock? Delia Stoltz? Even Galen King, Rose's neighbor?

3. Several kind people end up playing significant roles in the Schrocks' life. Who is your favorite and why?

4. Delia Stoltz tells her husband, Charles, that a sincere apology, even if the committed wrong was accidental, helps the victim get on with his or her life. Do you agree with her? Why does Delia believe that an apology holds that much power?

5. Vera Schrock believes that her family has finally returned to the right church. Rose has a different point of view—she feels that she can worship God in any church. What are your thoughts?

6. Bethany has to learn a hard lesson: Jake Hertzler wasn't the person she thought he was. Name someone in your

life who has surprised you as you've gotten to know him or her—in a good way or a bad way. What has that experience taught you?

7. The reader never learns the truth of how or why Dean Schrock died. What do you think—was it an accident? Or did Dean take his own life?

8. In this first in the series, that uncertainty over Dean's death lingered over many characters' heads: Rose, Tobe, even Vera. What is the significance of living with un-answered questions?

9. One theme in this story is that God works through all things for good (Rom. 8:28). When have you seen his hand in your life, where something bad turned into something good?

Author Note

This novel is entirely a work of fiction, and all the main characters are products of my imagination. However, the part about Schrock Investments was inspired by a true story. In the news recently was a story about a Plain man who ran an investment company that went bankrupt. Amish and Mennonite communities took up a donation to reimburse the Plain investors for their losses, because they would not, unlike the other investors, make claims with the Securities and Exchange Commission to be reimbursed out of liquidated assets. Such claims would be contrary to their beliefs about not judging another or taking an individual to court. I found that piece of the news story to be fascinating, and that was why I wove it into this story. Any other similarities are coincidental and not intentional.

Acknowledgments

With each new book, my appreciation for the Revell team continues to grow. It's quite astonishing to realize the care they take to get a book right—its cover, scenes and characters, grammar—and then the marketing and promotion too. Each person goes above and beyond to get a book ready for the shelf and into the readers' hands. Special thanks to Andrea Doering (aka ACFW 2011 Editor of the Year); to Barb Barnes (Grammar Queen), Michele Misiak, Janelle Mahlmann, Robin Barnett, and Twila Bennett (Marketing & Publicity Geniuses), Cheryl Van Andel and Paula Gibson (Cover Artists Extraordinaire) for your keen eye with all the details. To Amy Lathrop, for being so much more than a publicist.

As always, my gratitude extends to Joyce Hart of The Hartline Literary Agency. The only agent who was willing to take me on! I hope I've made you glad for that fateful decision, Joyce. I know I couldn't be in better hands.

A smile to my family, who has a way of keeping a healthy

perspective about this writing gig—bumping into my chair as they pass by on the way to the washer and dryer, texting me with grocery lists during my radio show, using my computer to check their Facebook updates when they *know* they are not allowed to touch it. Sigh. Where would I be without all of you?! Without 3-D characters, that's where.

My heartfelt appreciation goes to my first readers, Lindsey Ciraulo, Wendrea How, and Nyna Dolby, for being such a huge help with that critical first draft (and second draft too!). A thank-you to Chip Conradi, who took time to give me excellent legal insights. He helped to make the downfall of Schrock Investments as credible as possible. And to my husband, Steve, for sharing his know-how in the world of accounting and investments over coffee at our favorite little coffee shop. Steve doesn't even like coffee.

A thank-you to Jeff Camp for answering questions about brain surgery. Jeff said he was particularly grateful for excellent care from the neurology staff at the University of California, San Francisco. A big hug to AJ Salch for answering equine questions with me. And one last thank-you to Lindsey Bell and Melinda Busch, my crackerjack Latin translators, for helping me with the phrase, *Miracula fieri hic*. Miracles are made here.

And to the Author of all miracles . . . how can I ever thank you enough? You've blessed me in ways I never imagined and never deserved. To God be the glory, amen.

Suzanne Woods Fisher is the author of the bestselling Lancaster County Secrets and Stoney Ridge Seasons series. *The Search* received a 2012 Carol Award and *The Waiting* was a finalist for the 2011 Christy Award. Suzanne's grandfather was raised in the Old Order German Baptist Brethren Church in Franklin County, Pennsylvania. Her interest in living a simple, faith-filled life began with her Dunkard cousins. Suzanne is also the author of the bestselling *Amish Peace: Simple Wisdom for a Complicated World* and *Amish Proverbs: Words of Wisdom from the Simple Life*, both finalists for the ECPA Book of the Year award, and *Amish Values for Your Family: What We Can Learn from the Simple Life*. She is the host of *Amish Wisdom*, a weekly radio program on toginet.com. She lives with her family and big yellow dogs in the San Francisco Bay Area.

Meet Suzanne online at

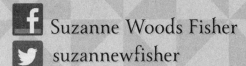 Suzanne Woods Fisher

suzannewfisher

www.SuzanneWoodsFisher.com

Suzanne is also the host of
Amish Wisdom,
a weekly radio program on **toginet.com**
and available to download at iTunes.com.

DON'T MISS THE STONEY RIDGE SEASONS SERIES!

Suzanne Woods Fisher — *The* KEEPER

Suzanne Woods Fisher — *The* HAVEN

Suzanne Woods Fisher — *The* LESSON

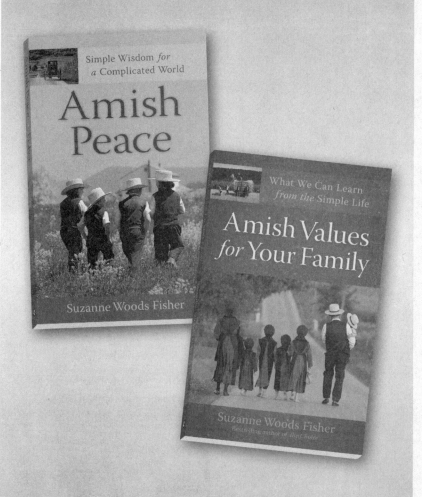

Every day is a *new adventure!*

Mary Ann Kinsinger
Suzanne Woods Fisher

Life with Lily
Book One

Mary Ann Kinsinger
Suzanne Woods Fisher

A New Home for Lily
Book Two

Mary Ann Kinsinger
Suzanne Woods Fisher

A Big Year for Lily
Book Three

For children ages 8–12

Mary Ann Kinsinger
Suzanne Woods Fisher

A Surprise for Lily
Book Four

For a child, every day is a thing of wonder. And for young Lily Lapp, every day is a new opportunity for blessings, laughter, family, and a touch of mischief.

AdventuresofLilyLapp.com

able Wherever Books Are Sold
lso Available in Ebook Format